Love Life

Stories by
Bobbie Ann Mason

PERENNIAL LIBRARY

Harper & Row, Publishers, New York
Grand Rapids, Philadelphia, St. Louis, San Francisco
London, Singapore, Sydney, Tokyo, Toronto

The stories in this collection first appeared in the following publications: "Love Life," "Midnight Magic," "Bumblebees," "Coyotes," "Memphis," and "Wish" in *The New Yorker;* "Hunktown," "Private Lies," and "Airwaves" in *Atlantic Monthly;* "Marita" and "Big Bertha Stories" in *Mother Jones;* "The Secret of the Pyramids" in the *Boston Globe Sunday Magazine;* "Piano Fingers" in *Southern Magazine;* "State Champions" in *Harper's;* "Sorghum" in the *Paris Review.*

Grateful acknowledgment is made to Willesden Music for the quotation from "Rebels Rule" by Brian Setzer.

A hardcover edition of this book was published in 1989 by Harper & Row, Publishers.

First PERENNIAL LIBRARY edition published 1990.

The Library of Congress has catalogued the hardcover edition as follows:

Mason, Bobbie Ann.
    Love life.

    I. Title.
PS3563.A7877L68   1989   813'.54   88-45535
ISBN 0-06-016042-X

ISBN 0-06-091668-0 (pbk.)
90 91 92 93 94 FG 10 9 8 7 6 5 4 3 2 1

For Roger Angell

Contents

*Love
Life*

Love Life

O pal lolls in her recliner, wearing the Coors cap her niece Jenny brought her from Colorado. She fumbles for the remote-control paddle and fires a button. Her swollen knuckles hurt. On TV, a boy is dancing in the street. Some other boys dressed in black are banging guitars and drums. This is her favorite program. It is always on, night or day. The show is songs, with accompanying stories. It's the music channel. Opal never cared for stories—she detests those soap operas her friends watch—but these fascinate her. The colors and the costumes change and flow with the music, erratically, the way her mind does these days. Now the TV is playing a song in which all the boys are long-haired cops chasing a dangerous woman in a tweed cap and a checked shirt. The woman's picture is in all their billfolds. They chase her through a cold-storage room filled with sides of beef. She hops on a motorcycle, and they set up a roadblock, but she jumps it with her motorcycle. Finally, she slips onto a train and glides away from them, waving a smiling goodbye.

On the table beside Opal is a Kleenex box, her glasses case, a glass of Coke with ice, and a cut-glass decanter of clear liquid that could be just water for the plants. Opal pours some of the liquid into the Coke and sips slowly. It tastes like peppermint candy, and it feels soothing. Her fingers tingle. She feels happy. Now that she is retired, she doesn't have to sneak into the teachers' lounge for a little swig from the jar in her pocketbook. She still dreams algebra problems, complicated quadratic equations with shifting values and no solutions. Now kids are using algebra to program computers. The kids in the TV stories remind her of her students at Hopewell High. Old age could have a grandeur about it, she thinks now as the music surges through her, if only it weren't so scary.

But she doesn't feel lonely, especially now that her sister Alice's girl, Jenny, has moved back here, to Kentucky. Jenny seems so confident, the way she sprawls on the couch, with that backpack she carries everywhere. Alice was always so delicate and feminine, but Jenny is enough like Opal to be her own daughter. She has Opal's light, thin hair, her large shoulders and big bones and long legs. Jenny even has a way of laughing that reminds Opal of her own laughter, the boisterous scoff she always saved for certain company but never allowed herself in school. Now and then Jenny lets loose one of those laughs and Opal is pleased. It occurs to her that Jenny, who is already past thirty, has left behind a trail of men, like that girl in the song. Jenny has lived with a couple of men, here and there. Opal can't keep track of all of the men Jenny has mentioned. They have names like John and Skip and Michael. She's not in a hurry to get married, she says. She says she is going to buy a house trailer and live in the woods like a hermit. She's full of ideas, and she exaggerates. She uses the words "gorgeous," "adorable," and "wonderful" interchangeably and persistently.

Last night, Jenny was here, with her latest boyfriend, Randy Newcomb. Opal remembers when he sat in the back row in her geometry class. He was an ordinary kid, not especially smart, and often late with his lessons. Now he has a real-estate agency and drives a Cadillac. Jenny kissed him in front of Opal and told him he was gorgeous. She said the placemats were gorgeous, too.

Jenny was asking to see those old quilts again. "Why do you hide away your nice things, Aunt Opal?" she said. Opal doesn't think they're that nice, and she doesn't want to have to look at them all the time. Opal showed Jenny and Randy Newcomb the double-wedding-ring quilt, the star quilt, and some of the crazy quilts, but she wouldn't show them the craziest one—the burial quilt, the one Jenny kept asking about. Did Jenny come back home just to hunt up that old rag? The thought makes Opal shudder.

The doorbell rings. Opal has to rearrange her comforter and magazines in order to get up. Her joints are stiff. She leaves the TV blaring a song she knows, with balloons and bombs in it.

At the door is Velma Shaw, who lives in the duplex next to Opal. She has just come home from her job at Shop World. "Have you gone out of your mind, Opal?" cries Velma. She has on a plum-colored print blouse and a plum skirt and a little green scarf with a gold pin holding it down. Velma shouts, "You can hear that racket clear across the street!"

"Rock and roll is never too loud," says Opal. This is a line from a song she has heard.

Opal releases one of her saved-up laughs, and Velma backs away. Velma is still trying to be sexy, in those little color-coordinated outfits she wears, but it is hopeless, Opal thinks with a smile. She closes the door and scoots back to her recliner.

Opal is Jenny's favorite aunt. Jenny likes the way Opal ties her hair in a ponytail with a ribbon. She wears muumuus and socks. She is tall and only a little thick in the middle. She told Jenny that middle-age spread was caused by the ribs expanding and that it doesn't matter what you eat. Opal kids around about "old Arthur"—her arthritis, visiting her on damp days.

Jenny has been in town six months. She works at the courthouse, typing records—marriages, divorces, deaths, drunk-driving convictions. Frequently, the same names are on more than one list. Before she returned to Kentucky, Jenny was waitressing in Denver, but she was growing restless again, and the idea of going home seized her. Her old rebellion against small-town conventions gave way to curiosity.

In the South, the shimmer of the heat seems to distort everything, like old glass with impurities in it. During her first two days there, she saw two people with artificial legs, a blind man, a man with hooks for hands, and a man without an arm. It seemed unreal. In a parking lot, a pit bull terrier in a Camaro attacked her from behind the closed window. He barked viciously, his nose stabbing the window. She stood in the parking lot, letting the pit bull attack, imagining herself in an arena, with a crowd watching. The South makes her nervous. Randy Newcomb told her she had just been away too long. "We're not as countrified down here now as people think," he said.

Jenny has been going with Randy for three months. The first night she went out with him, he took her to a fancy place that served shrimp flown in from New Orleans, and then to a little bar over in Hopkinsville. They went with Kathy Steers, a friend from work, and Kathy's husband, Bob. Kathy and Bob weren't getting along and they carped at each other all evening. In the bar, an attractive, cheerful woman sang requests for tips, and her companion, a blind man, played the guitar. When she sang, she looked straight at him, singing to him, smiling at him reassuringly. In the background, men played pool with their girlfriends, and Jenny noticed the sharp creases in the men's jeans and imagined the women ironing them. When she mentioned it, Kathy said she took Bob's jeans to the laundromat to use the machine there that puts knifelike creases in them. The men in the bar had two kinds of women with them: innocent-looking women with pastel skirts and careful hairdos, and hard-looking women without makeup, in T-shirts and jeans. Jenny imagined that each type could be either a girlfriend or a wife. She felt odd. She was neither type. The singer sang "Happy Birthday" to a popular regular named Will Ed, and after the set she danced with him, while the jukebox took over. She had a limp, as though one leg were shorter than the other. The leg was stiff under her jeans, and when the woman danced Jenny could see that the leg was not real.

"There, but for the grace of God, go I," Randy whispered to Jenny. He squeezed her hand, and his heavy turquoise ring dug into her knuckle.

"Those quilts would bring a good price at an estate auction," Randy says to Jenny as they leave her aunt's one evening and head for his real-estate office. They are in his burgundy Cadillac. "One of those star quilts used to bring twenty-five dollars. Now it might run three hundred."

"My aunt doesn't think they're worth anything. She hides all her nice stuff, like she's ashamed of it. She's got beautiful dresser scarves and starched doilies she made years ago. But she's getting a little weird. All she does is watch MTV."

"I think she misses the kids," Randy says. Then he bursts out laughing. "She used to put the fear of God in all her students! I never will forget the time she told me to stop watching so much television and read some books. It was like an order from God Almighty. I didn't dare not do what she said. I read *Crime and Punishment*. I never would have read it if she hadn't shamed me into it. But I appreciated that. I don't even remember what *Crime and Punishment* was about, except there was an ax murderer in it."

"That was basically it," Jenny says. "He got caught. Crime and punishment—just like any old TV show."

Randy touches some controls on the dashboard and Waylon Jennings starts singing. The sound system is remarkable. Everything Randy owns is quality. He has been looking for some land for Jenny to buy—a couple of acres of woods—but so far nothing on his listings has met with his approval. He is concerned about zoning and power lines and frontage. All Jenny wants is a remote place where she can have a dog and grow some tomatoes. She knows that what she really needs is a better car, but she doesn't want to go anywhere.

Later, at Randy's office, Jenny studies the photos of houses on display, while he talks on the telephone to someone about dividing up a sixty-acre farm into farmettes. His photograph is on several certificates on the wall. He has a full, well-fed face in the pictures, but he is thinner now and looks better. He has a boyish, endearing smile, like Dennis Quaid, Jenny's favorite actor. She likes Randy's smile. It seems so innocent, as though he would do anything in the world for someone he cared about. He doesn't really want to sell her any land. He says he is afraid she will get raped if she lives alone in the woods.

"I'm impressed," she says when he slams down the telephone. She points to his new regional award for the fastest-growing agency of the year.

"Isn't that something? Three branch offices in a territory this size—I can't complain. There's a lot of turnover in real estate now. People are never satisfied. You know that? That's the truth about human nature." He laughs. "That's the secret of my success."

"It's been two years since Barbara divorced me," he says later, on the way to Jenny's apartment. "I can't say it hasn't been fun being free, but my kids are in college, and it's like starting over. I'm ready for a new life. The business has been so great, I couldn't really ask for more, but I've been thinking— Don't laugh, please, but what I was thinking was if you want to share it with me, I'll treat you good. I swear."

At a stoplight, he paws at her hand. On one corner is the Pepsi bottling plant, and across from it is the Broad Street House, a restaurant with an old-fashioned statue of a jockey out front. People are painting the black faces on those little statues white now, but this one has been painted bright green all over. Jenny can't keep from laughing at it.

"I wasn't laughing at you—honest!" she says apologetically. "That statue always cracks me up."

"You don't have to give me an answer now."

"I don't know what to say."

"I can get us a real good deal on a house," he says. "I can get any house I've got listed. I can even get us a farmette, if you want trees so bad. You won't have to spend your money on a piece of land."

"I'll have to think about it." Randy scares her. She likes him, but there is something strange about his energy and optimism. Everyone around her seems to be bursting at the seams, like that pit bull terrier.

"I'll let you think on it," he says, pulling up to her apartment. "Life has been good to me. Business is good, and my kids didn't turn out to be dope fiends. That's about all you can hope for in this day and time."

Jenny is having lunch with Kathy Steers at the Broad Street House. The iced tea is mixed with white grape juice. It took Jenny a long time to identify the flavor, and the Broad Street House won't admit it's grape juice. Their iced tea is supposed to have a mystique about it, probably because they can't sell drinks in this dry county. In the daylight, the statue out front is the color of the Jolly Green Giant.

People confide in Jenny, but Jenny doesn't always tell things back. It's an unfair exchange, though it often goes unnoticed. She is curious, eager to hear other people's stories, and she asks more questions than is appropriate. Kathy's life is a tangle of deceptions. Kathy stayed with her husband, Bob, because he had opened his own body shop and she didn't want him to start out a new business with a rocky marriage, but she acknowledges now it was a mistake.

"What about Jimmy and Willette?" Jenny asks. Jimmy and Willette are the other characters in Kathy's story.

"That mess went on for months. When you started work at the office, remember how nervous I was? I thought I was getting an ulcer." Kathy lights a cigarette and blows at the wall. "You see, I didn't know what Bob and Willette were up to, and they didn't know about me and Jimmy. That went on for two years before you came. And when it started to come apart—I mean, we had *hell*! I'd say things to Jimmy and then it would get back to Bob because Jimmy would tell Willette. It was an unreal circle. I was pregnant with Jason and you get real sensitive then. I thought Bob was screwing around on me, but it never dawned on me it was with Willette."

The fat waitress says, "Is everything all right?"

Kathy says, "No, but it's not your fault. Do you know what I'm going to do?" she asks Jenny.

"No, what?"

"I'm taking Jason and moving in with my sister. She has a sort of apartment upstairs. Bob can do what he wants to with the house. I've waited too long to do this, but it's time. My sister keeps the baby anyway, so why shouldn't I just live there?"

She puffs the cigarette again and levels her eyes at Jenny. "You know what I admire about you? You're so independent. You say what you think. When you started work at the office, I said to myself, 'I wish I could be like that.' I could tell you had been around. You've inspired me. That's how come I decided to move out."

Jenny plays with the lemon slice in the saucer holding her iced-tea glass. She picks a seed out of it. She can't bring herself to confide in Kathy about Randy Newcomb's offer. For some reason, she is embarrassed by it.

"I haven't spoken to Willette since September third," says Kathy.

Kathy keeps talking, and Jenny listens, suspicious of her interest in Kathy's problems. She notices how Kathy is enjoying herself. Kathy is looking forward to leaving her husband the same way she must have enjoyed her fling with Jimmy, the way she is enjoying not speaking to Willette.

"Let's go out and get drunk tonight," Kathy says cheerfully. "Let's celebrate my decision."

"I can't. I'm going to see my aunt this evening. I have to take her some booze. She gives me money to buy her vodka and peppermint schnapps, and she tells me not to stop at the same liquor store too often. She says she doesn't want me to get a reputation for drinking! I have to go all the way to Hopkinsville to get it."

"Your aunt tickles me. She's a pistol."

The waitress clears away the dishes and slaps down dessert menus. They order chocolate pecan pie, the day's special.

"You know the worst part of this whole deal?" Kathy says. "It's the years it takes to get smart. But I'm going to make up for lost time. You can bet on that. And there's not a thing Bob can do about it."

Opal's house has a veranda. Jenny thinks that verandas seem to imply a history of some sort—people in rocking chairs telling stories. But Opal doesn't tell any stories. It is exasperating, because Jenny wants to know about her aunt's past love life, but Opal won't reveal her secrets. They sit on the veranda and observe each other. They smile, and now and then roar with laughter over something ridiculous. In the bedroom, where she snoops after using the bathroom, Jenny notices the layers of old wallpaper in the closet, peeling back and spilling crumbs of gaudy ancient flower prints onto Opal's muumuus.

Downstairs, Opal asks, "Do you want some cake, Jenny?"

"Of course. I'm crazy about your cake, Aunt Opal."

"I didn't beat the egg whites long enough. Old Arthur's visiting again." Opal flexes her fingers and smiles. "That sounds like the curse. Girls used to say they had the curse. Or they had a visitor." She looks down at her knuckles shyly. "Nowadays, of course, they just say what they mean."

The cake is delicious—an old-fashioned lemon chiffon made from scratch. Jenny's cooking ranges from English-muffin mini-pizzas to brownie mixes. After gorging on the cake, Jenny blurts out, "Aunt Opal, aren't you sorry you never got married? Tell the truth, now."

Opal laughs. "I was talking to Ella Mae Smith the other day—she's a retired geography teacher?—and she said, 'I've got twelve great-great-grandchildren, and when we get together I say, "Law me, look what I started!" ' " Opal mimics Ella Mae Smith, giving her a mindless, chirpy tone of voice. "Why, I'd have to use quadratic equations to count up all the people that woman has caused," she goes on. "All with a streak of her petty narrow-mindedness in them. I don't call that a contribution to the world." Opal laughs and sips from her glass of schnapps. "What about you, Jenny? Are you ever going to get married?"

"Marriage is outdated. I don't know anybody who's married and happy."

Opal names three schoolteachers she has known who have been married for decades.

"But are they really happy?"

"Oh, foot, Jenny! What you're saying is why are *you* not married and why are *you* not happy. What's wrong with little Randy Newcomb? Isn't that funny? I always think of him as little Randy."

"Show me those quilts again, Aunt Opal."

"I'll show you the crazies but not the one you keep after me about."

"O.K., show me the crazies."

Upstairs, her aunt lays crazy quilts on the bed. They are bright-colored patches of soft velvet and plaids and prints stitched together with silky embroidery. Several pieces have initials embroidered on them. The haphazard shapes make Jenny imagine odd, twisted lives represented in these quilts.

She says, "Mom gave me a quilt once, but I didn't appreciate the value of it and I washed it until it fell apart."

"I'll give you one of these crazies when you stop moving around," Opal says. "You couldn't fit it in that backpack of yours." She polishes her glasses thoughtfully. "Do you know what those quilts mean to me?"

"No, what?"

"A lot of desperate old women ruining their eyes. Do you know what I think I'll do?"

"No, what?"

"I think I'll take up aerobic dancing. Or maybe I'll learn to ride a motorcycle. I try to be modern."

"You're funny, Aunt Opal. You're hilarious."

"Am I gorgeous, too?"

"Adorable," says Jenny.

After her niece leaves, Opal hums a tune and dances a stiff little jig. She nestles among her books and punches her remote-control paddle. Years ago, she was allowed to paddle students who misbehaved. She used a wooden paddle from a butter churn, with holes drilled in it. The holes made a satisfying sting. On TV, a 1950s convertible is out of gas. This is one of her favorites. It has an adorable couple in it. The girl is wearing bobby socks and saddle oxfords, and the boy has on a basketball jacket. They look the way children looked before the hippie element took over. But the boy begins growing cat whiskers and big cat ears, and then his face gets furry and leathery, while the girl screams bloody murder. Opal sips some peppermint and watches his face change. The red and gold of his basketball jacket are the Hopewell school colors. He chases the girl. Now he has grown long claws.

The boy is dancing energetically with a bunch of ghouls who have escaped from their coffins. Then Vincent Price starts talking in the background. The girl is very frightened. The ghouls are so old and ugly. That's how kids see us, Opal thinks. She loves this story. She even loves the credits—scary music by Elmer Bernstein. This is a story with a meaning. It suggests all the feelings of terror and horror that must be hidden inside young people. And inside, deep down, there really are monsters. An old person waits, a nearly dead body that can still dance.

Opal pours another drink. She feels relaxed, her joints loose like a dancer's now.

Jenny is so nosy. Her questions are so blunt. Did Opal ever have a crush on a student? Only once or twice. She was in her twenties then, and it seemed scandalous. Nothing happened— just daydreams. When she was thirty, she had another attachment to a boy, and it seemed all right then, but it was worse again at thirty-five, when another pretty boy stayed after class to talk. After that, she kept her distance.

But Opal is not wholly without experience. There have been men, over the years, though nothing like the casual affairs Jenny has had. Opal remembers a certain motel room in Nashville. She was only forty. The man drove a gray Chrysler Imperial. When she was telling about him to a friend, who was sworn to secrecy, she called him "Imperial," in a joking way. She went with him because she knew he would take her somewhere, in such a fine car, and they would sleep together. She always remembered how clean and empty the room was, how devoid of history and association. In the mirror, she saw a scared woman with a pasty face and a shrimpy little man who needed a shave. In the morning he went out somewhere and brought back coffee and orange juice. They had bought some doughnuts at the new doughnut shop in town before they left. While he was out, she made up the bed and put her things in her bag, to make it as neat as if she had never been there. She was fully dressed when he returned, with her garter belt and stockings on, and when they finished the doughnuts she cleaned up all the paper and the cups and wiped the crumbs from the table by the bed. He said, "Come with me and I'll take you to Idaho." "Why Idaho?" she wanted to know, but his answer was vague. Idaho sounded cold, and she didn't want to tell him how she disliked his scratchy whiskers and the hard, powdery doughnuts. It seemed unkind of her, but if he had been nicer-looking, without such a demanding dark beard, she might have gone with him to Idaho in that shining Imperial. She hadn't even given him a chance, she thought later. She had been so scared. If anyone from school had seen her at that motel, she could have lost her job. "I need a woman," he had said. "A woman like you."

On a hot Saturday afternoon, with rain threatening, Jenny sits under a tent on a folding chair while Randy auctions off four hundred acres of woods on Lake Barkley. He had a road bull-dozed into the property, and he divided it up into lots. The lakefront lots are going for as much as two thousand an acre, and the others are bringing up to a thousand. Randy has several assistants with him, and there is even a concession stand, offering hot dogs and cold drinks.

In the middle of the auction, they wait for a thundershower to pass. Sitting in her folding chair under a canopy reminds Jenny of graveside services. As soon as the rain slacks up, the auction continues. In his cowboy hat and blue blazer, Randy struts around with a microphone as proudly as a banty rooster. With his folksy chatter, he knows exactly how to work the crowd. "Y'all get yourselves a cold drink and relax now and just imagine the fishing you'll do in this dreamland. This land is good for vacation, second home, investment—heck, you can just park here in your camper and live. It's going to be paradise when that marina gets built on the lake there and we get some lots cleared."

The four-hundred-acre tract looks like a wilderness. Jenny loves the way the sun splashes on the water after the rain, and the way it comes through the trees, hitting the flickering leaves like lights on a disco ball. A marina here seems farfetched. She could pitch a tent here until she could afford to buy a used trailer. She could swim at dawn, the way she did on a camping trip out West, long ago. All of a sudden, she finds herself bidding on a lot.

The bidding passes four hundred, and she sails on, bidding against a man from Missouri who tells the people around him that he's looking for a place to retire.

"Sold to the young lady with the backpack," Randy says when she bids six hundred. He gives her a crestfallen look, and she feels embarrassed.

As she waits for Randy to wind up his business after the auction, Jenny locates her acre from the map of the plots of land. It is along a gravel road and marked off with stakes tied with hot-pink survey tape. It is a small section of the woods—her block on the quilt, she thinks. These are her trees. The vines and underbrush are thick and spotted with raindrops. She notices a windfall leaning on a maple, like a lover dying in its arms. Maples are strong, she thinks, but she feels like getting an ax and chopping that windfall down, to save the maple. In the distance, the whining of a speedboat cuts into the day.

They meet afterward at Randy's van, his mobile real-estate office, with a little shingled roof raised in the center to look rustic. It looks like an outhouse on wheels. A painted message on the side says, "REALITY IS REAL ESTATE." As Randy plows through the mud on the new road, Jenny apologizes. Buying the lot was like laughing at the statue at the wrong moment—something he would take the wrong way, an insult to his attentions.

"I can't reach you," he says. "You say you want to live out in the wilderness and grow your own vegetables, but you act like you're somewhere in outer space. You can't grow vegetables in outer space. You can't even grow them in the woods unless you clear some ground."

"I'm looking for a place to land."

"What do I have to do to get through to you?"

"I don't know. I need more time."

He turns onto the highway, patterned with muddy tire tracks from the cars at the auction. "I said I'd wait, so I guess I'll have to," he says, flashing his Dennis Quaid smile. "You take as long as you want to, then. I learned my lesson with Barbara. You've got to be understanding with the women. That's the key to a successful relationship." Frowning, he slams his hand on the steering wheel. "That's what they tell me, anyhow."

Jenny is having coffee with Opal. She arrived unexpectedly. It's very early. She looks as though she has been up all night.

"Please show me your quilts," Jenny says. "I don't mean your crazy quilts. I want to see that special quilt. Mom said it had the family tree."

Opal spills coffee in her saucer. "What is wrong with young people today?" she asks.

"I want to know why it's called a burial quilt," Jenny says. "Are you planning to be buried in it?"

Opal wishes she had a shot of peppermint in her coffee. It sounds like a delicious idea. She starts toward the den with the coffee cup rattling in its saucer, and she splatters drops on the rug. Never mind it now, she thinks, turning back.

"It's just a family history," she says.

"Why's it called a burial quilt?" Jenny asks.

Jenny's face is pale. She has blue pouches under her eyes and blue eye shadow on her eyelids.

"See that closet in the hall?" Opal says. "Get a chair and we'll get the quilt down."

Jenny stands on a kitchen chair and removes the quilt from beneath several others. It's wrapped in blue plastic and Jenny hugs it closely as she steps down with it.

They spread it out on the couch, and the blue plastic floats off somewhere. Jenny looks like someone in love as she gazes at the quilt. "It's gorgeous," she murmurs. "How beautiful."

"Shoot!" says Opal. "It's ugly as homemade sin."

Jenny runs her fingers over the rough textures of the quilt. The quilt is dark and somber. The backing is a heavy gray gabardine, and the nine-inch-square blocks are pieced of smaller blocks of varying shades of gray and brown and black. They are wools, apparently made from men's winter suits. On each block is an appliquéd off-white tombstone—a comical shape, like Casper the ghost. Each tombstone has a name and date on it.

Jenny recognizes some of the names. Myrtle Williams. Voris Williams. Thelma Lee Freeman. The oldest gravestone is "Eulalee Freeman 1857–1900." The shape of the quilt is irregular, a rectangle with a clumsy foot sticking out from one corner. The quilt is knotted with yarn, and the edging is open, for more blocks to be added.

"Eulalee's daughter started it," says Opal. "But that thing has been carried through this family like a plague. Did you ever see such horrible old dark colors? I pieced on it some when I was younger, but it was too depressing. I think some of the kinfolks must have died without a square, so there may be several to catch up on."

"I'll do it," says Jenny. "I could learn to quilt."

"Traditionally, the quilt stops when the family name stops," Opal says. "And since my parents didn't have a boy, that was the end of the Freeman line on this particular branch of the tree. So the last old maids finish the quilt." She lets out a wild cackle. "Theoretically, a quilt like this could keep going till doomsday."

"Do you care if I have this quilt?" asks Jenny.

"What would you do with it? It's too ugly to put on a bed and too morbid to work on."

"I think it's kind of neat," says Jenny. She strokes the rough tweed. Already it is starting to decay, and it has moth holes. Jenny feels tears start to drip down her face.

"Don't you go putting my name on that thing," her aunt says.

Jenny has taken the quilt to her apartment. She explained that she is going to study the family tree, or that she is going to finish the quilt. If she's smart, Opal thinks, she will let Randy Newcomb auction it off. The way Jenny took it, cramming it into the blue plastic, was like snatching something that was free. Opal feels relieved, as though she has pushed the burden of that ratty old quilt onto her niece. All those miserable, cranky women, straining their eyes, stitching on those dark scraps of material.

For a long time, Jenny wouldn't tell why she was crying, and when she started to tell, Opal was uncomfortable, afraid she'd be required to tell something comparable of her own, but as she listened she found herself caught up in Jenny's story. Jenny said it was a man. That was always the case, Opal thought. It was five years earlier. A man Jenny knew in a place by the sea. Opal imagined seagulls, pretty sand. There were no palm trees. It was up North. The young man worked with Jenny in a restaurant with glass walls facing the ocean. They waited on tables and collected enough tips to take a trip together near the end of the summer. Jenny made it sound like an idyllic time, waiting on tables by the sea. She started crying again when she told about the trip, but the trip sounded nice. Opal listened hungrily, imagining the young man, thinking that he would have had handsome, smooth cheeks, and hair that fell attractively over his forehead. He would have had good manners, being a waiter. Jenny and the man, whose name was Jim, flew to Denver, Colorado, and they rented a car and drove around out West. They visited the Grand Canyon and Yellowstone and other places Opal had heard about. They grilled salmon on the beach, on another ocean. They camped out in the redwoods, trees so big they hid the sky. Jenny described all these scenes, and the man sounded like a good man. His brother had died in Vietnam and he felt guilty that he had been the one spared, because his brother was a swimmer and could have gone to the Olympics. Jim wasn't athletic. He had a bad knee and hammertoes. He slept fitfully in the tent, and Jenny said soothing things to him, and she cared about him, but by the time they had curved northward and over to Yellowstone the trip was becoming unpleasant. The romance wore off. She loved him, but she couldn't deal with his needs. One of the last nights they spent together, it rained all night long. He told her not to touch the tent material, because somehow the pressure of a finger on the nylon would make it start to leak at that spot. Lying there in the rain, Jenny couldn't resist touching a spot where water was collecting in a little sag in the top of the tent. The drip started then, and it grew worse, until they got so wet they had to get in the car. Not long afterward, when they ran short of money, they parted. Jenny got a job in Denver. She never saw him again.

Opal listened eagerly to the details about grilling the fish together, about the zip-together sleeping bags and setting up the tent and washing themselves in the cold stream. But when Jenny brought the story up to the present, Opal was not prepared. She felt she had been dunked in the cold water and left gasping. Jenny said she had heard a couple of times through a mutual friend that Jim had spent some time in Mexico. And then, she said, this week she had begun thinking about him, because of all the trees at the lake, and she had an overwhelming desire to see him again. She had been unfair, she knew now. She telephoned the friend, who had worked with them in the restaurant by the sea. He hadn't known where to locate her, he said, and so he couldn't tell her that Jim had been killed in Colorado over a year ago. His four-wheel-drive had plunged off a mountain curve.

"I feel some trick has been played on me. It seems so unreal." Jenny tugged at the old quilt, and her eyes darkened. "I was in Colorado, and I didn't even know he was there. If I still knew him, I would know how to mourn, but now I don't know how. And it was over a year ago. So I don't know what to feel."

"Don't look back, hon," Opal said, hugging her niece closely. But she was shaking, and Jenny shook with her.

Opal makes herself a snack, thinking it will pick up her strength. She is very tired. On the tray, she places an apple and a paring knife and some milk and cookies. She touches the remote-control button, and the picture blossoms. She was wise to buy a large TV, the one listed as the best in the consumer magazine. The color needs a little adjustment, though. She eases up the volume and starts peeling the apple. She has a little bump on one knuckle. In the old days, people would take the family Bible and bust a cyst like that with it. Just slam it hard.

On the screen, a Scoutmaster is telling a story to some Boy Scouts around a campfire. The campfire is only a fireplace, with electric logs. Opal loses track of time, and the songs flow together. A woman is lying on her stomach on a car hood in a desert full of gas pumps. TV sets crash. Smoke emerges from an eyeball. A page of sky turns like a page in a book. Then, at a desk in a classroom, a cocky blond kid with a pack of cigarettes rolled in the sleeve of his T-shirt is singing about a sexy girl with a tattoo on her back who is sitting on a commode and smoking a cigarette. In the classroom, all the kids are gyrating and snapping their fingers to wild music. The teacher at the blackboard with her white hair in a bun looks disapproving, but the kids in the class don't know what's on her mind. The teacher is thinking about how, when the bell rings, she will hit the road to Nashville.

Midnight Magic

Steve leaves the supermarket and hits the sunlight. Blinking, he stands there a moment, then glances at his feet. He has on running shoes, but he was sure he had put on boots. He touches his face. He hasn't shaved. His car, illegally parked in the space for the handicapped, is deep blue and wicked. The rear has "Midnight Magic" painted on it in large pink curlicue letters with orange-and-red tails. Rays of color, fractured rainbows, spread out over the flanks. He picked the design from a thick book the custom painters had. The car's rear end is hiked up like a female cat in heat. Prowling in his car at night, he could be Dracula.

Sitting behind the wheel, he eats the chocolate-covered doughnuts he just bought and drinks from a carton of chocolate milk. The taste of the milk is off. They do something weird to chocolate milk now. His father used to drive a milk truck, before he got arrested for stealing a shipment of bowling shoes he found stacked up behind a shoe store. He had always told Steve to cover his tracks and accentuate the positive.

It is Sunday. Steve is a wreck, still half drunk. Last night, just after he and Karen quarreled and she retreated to his bathroom to sulk, the telephone rang. It was Steve's brother, Bud, wanting to know if Steve had seen Bud's dog, Big Red. Bud had been out hunting with Big Red and his two beagles, and Big Red had strayed. Steve hadn't seen the stupid dog. Where would he have seen him—strolling down Main Street? Bud lived several miles out in the country. Steve was annoyed with him for calling late on a Saturday night. He still hadn't forgiven Bud for the time he shot a skunk and left it in Steve's garbage can. Steve popped another beer and watched some junk on television until Karen emerged from the bathroom and started gathering up her things.

"Why don't you get some decent dishes?" she said, pointing to the splotched paper plates littering the kitchen counter.

"Paper plates are simpler," he said. "Money can't buy happiness, but it can buy paper plates." He pulled her down on the couch and tousled her hair, then held her arms down, tickling her.

"Quit it!" she squealed, but he was sure she didn't mean it. He was just playing.

"You're like that old cat Mama used to have," she said, wrenching herself away from him. "He always got rough when you played with him, and then he'd start drumming with his hind legs. Cats do that when they want to rip out a rabbit's guts."

Steve will be glad when his friends Doran and Nancy get home. Whenever Doran wrestled Nancy down onto the couch at Steve's apartment and tickled her, she loved it. Doran and Nancy got married last week and went to Disney World, and Steve has promised to pick them up at the airport down in Nashville later today. Doran met Nancy only six weeks ago—at the Bluebird Cocktail Lounge and Restaurant, over in Paducah. Doran was with Steve and Karen, celebrating Karen's twenty-third birthday. Nancy and another waitress brought Karen's birthday cake to the table and sang "Happy Birthday." The cake was sizzling with lighted sparklers. Nancy wore clinging sports tights—hot pink, with black slashes across the calves—and a long aqua sweatshirt that reached just below her ass. Doran fell in love—suddenly and passionately. Steve knew Doran had never stayed with one girl long enough to get a deep relationship going, and suddenly he was in love. Steve was surprised and envious.

Nancy has a cute giggle, a note of encouragement in response to anything Doran says. Her hips are slender, her legs long and well proportioned. She wears contact lenses tinted blue. But she is not really any more attractive than Karen, who has blond hair and natural blue eyes. And Nancy doesn't know anything about cars. Karen has a working knowledge of crankshafts and fuel pumps. When her car stalls, she knows it's probably because the distributor cap is wet. Steve wishes he and Karen could cut up like Nancy and Doran. Nancy and Doran love "The New Newlywed Game." They make fun of it, trying to guess things they should know about each other if they were on that show. If Nancy learned that grilled steak was Doran's favorite food, she'd say, "Now, I'm going to remember that! That's the kind of thing you have to know on the 'Newlyweds.' "

During those weeks of watching Doran and Nancy in love, Steve felt empty inside, doomed. When Karen was angry at him last night, it was as if a voice from another time had spoken through her and told him his fate. Karen believes in things like that. She is always telling him what Sardo says in the Sunday-night meetings she goes to at the converted dance hall, next to the bowling alley. Sardo is a thousand-year-old American Indian inhabiting the body of a teenage girl in Paducah. Until Karen started going to those meetings, she and Steve had been solid together—not deliriously in love, like Doran and Nancy, but reasonably happy. Now Steve feels confused and transparent, as though Karen has eyes that see right through him.

In his apartment, on the second floor of a big old house with a large landlady (gland problem), he searches for his laundry. Karen must have hidden his clothes. If he's lucky, she has taken them home with her to wash. The clipping about Nancy's wedding flutters from the stereo. He is saving it for her. "The bride wore a full-length off-white dress with leg-of-mutton sleeves, dotted with seed pearls." There's a misprint in the story: "The bridgeroom, Doran Palmer, is employed at Johnson Sheet Metal Co." Steve smiles. Doran will get a kick out of that. Before he and Nancy left for Florida, Doran told Steve he felt as though he had won a sweepstakes. "She really makes me feel like somebody," Doran said. "Isn't that all anybody wants in the world—just to feel like somebody?"

Steve's clothes are under his bed, along with some dust fluffs.

From the television screen a shiny-haired guy in a dark-blue suit yells at him about salvation. There is an 800-number telephone listing at the bottom of the screen. All Steve has to do is send money. "You send *me* some money and I'll work on *your* soul," Steve tells the guy. He flips through all the stations on cable, but nothing good is on. He picks up the telephone to call Karen, then replaces it. He has to think of what to say. He cracks his knuckles. She hates that.

Steve stuffs all his laundry into one big bag, grabs his keys, and slams out of his place. As usual, the bag slung over his shoulder makes him think of Santa Claus. At the laundromat he packs everything into one machine. He pours powder in and rams in the quarters, pretending he's playing a slot machine. The laundromat is crowded. It's surprising how many people skip church nowadays. But it's good that there are fewer hypocrites, he decides. Catholic priests are dying from AIDS, and here in town half the Baptists are alcoholics. A pretty woman in purple jeans is reading a book. He considers approaching her, then decides not to. She might be too smart for him. He leaves his clothes churning and cruises past McDonald's and Hardee's to see if there's anyone he knows. Should he go over to Karen's? While he thinks about it, he pulls into the Amoco station and gasses up. Steve's friend Pete squirts blue fluid on Steve's windshield—a personal service not usually provided at the self-serve island. Pete leans into Steve's car and tugs the lavender garter dangling from the rearview mirror. "Hey, Steve, looks like you got lucky."

"Yeah." It was Nancy's, from the wedding. It was supposed to be blue, but she got lavender because it was on sale. Doran told Nancy that her blue-tinted contact lenses would do for "something blue." Nancy threw the garter to Steve—the same way she tossed her bridal bouquet to her girlfriends. He thought that catching her garter meant he was next in line for something. Something good—he doesn't know what. Maybe Karen could ask Sardo, but whatever Sardo said, Steve wouldn't believe it. Sardo is a first-class fake.

Steve has been banging on the pump, trying to get his gas cap to jump off the top. When it does, he catches it neatly: infield-fly rule. The gas nozzle clicks and he finishes the fill-up.

"Well, Steve, don't you go falling asleep on the job," Pete says as Steve guns the engine.

That's an old joke. Steve works at the mattress factory. The factory is long and low and windowless, and bales of fiberfill hug the walls. Steve steers giant scissors across soft, patterned fabric fastened on stretchers. After he crams the stuffing into the frame, Janetta and Lynn do the finishing work. The guys at the plant tease those girls all day. Janetta and Lynn play along, saying, "Do you want to get in my bed?" Or, "Let's spend lunch hour in the bed room." The new mattresses are displayed beneath glaring fluorescent lights—not the sexiest place to get anything going. But Steve likes the new-bed smell there. He likes the smell of anything new. The girls are nice, but they're not serious. Lynn is engaged, and she's three years older than Steve.

At the laundromat he transfers the soggy, cold load into a dryer and flips each dime on the back of his hand before inserting it. Two heads, two tails. He slides a dollar bill into the change machine and watches George Washington's face disappear and turn into dimes. He laughs, imagining George Washington coming back in the twentieth century and trying to make sense out of laundromats, Midnight Magic, and crazy women. The woman in the purple pants is still there, reading her book. He drives off, screeching loudly out of his parking spot.

Karen's apartment is above a dry cleaner's, next to a vacant lot. It's a lonesome part of town, near the overhead bridge that leads out of town. The parking lot has four cars in it, including her red Escort. An exterior wooden stairway with several broken steps leads to her apartment. There's a rapist in town, and he has struck twice in Karen's neighborhood. Now she sleeps with a knife beside her bed and a shotgun beneath it.

"Are you still mad at me?" he asks when she opens the door. She just woke up and her hair is shooting off in several directions.

"Yeah." She lets him in and returns to her bed.

"What did I do?" He sits down on the edge of the bed.

She doesn't answer that. She says, "When I came in last night I was too nervous to sleep, so I painted that wall." She points to the bedroom wall, now a pale green. The other walls are pink. The colors are like the candy mints at Nancy and Doran's wedding. "The landlord said if I paint everything he'll take it off the rent," Karen says.

"He ought to put bars on the windows," Steve says. Lined-up Coke bottles stand guard on the windowsills, along with spider plants that dangle their creepy arms all the way to the floor.

"If that rapist comes in through the window I'll be ready for him," she says. "I'll blast him to kingdom come. I mean it, too. I'll kill that sucker *dead*." She scrunches up her pillow and hugs it. "I need some coffee."

"Want me to go get you some? I can get some at McDonald's when I go get my clothes out of the dryer."

"I'll just turn on the coffeepot," she says, swinging out of bed. She's wearing a red football shirt with the number 46 on the front. Steve thumps his fist on the mattress. It's a poor mattress. He doesn't like sleeping with her here. He wanted her to stay with him last night.

Karen flip-flops into the kitchen and runs water into her coffeepot. She measures coffee into a filter paper and sets it in the cone above the pot, then pours the water into the top compartment of the coffee maker. He envies her. He can't even make a pot of coffee. He should do more for her—maybe get her a new mattress, at cost. Her apartment is small, decorated with things she made in a crafts club.

"You ought to move," he says.

She laughs. "Hey! I'm trying to lure the guy here. I want that five-thousand-dollar reward!"

"You could move in with me." He's never said anything like that before, and he's shocked at himself.

She disappears into her bedroom and returns in a few minutes wearing jeans and a sweatshirt. The dripping coffee smells like burning leaves, with acorns. Steve likes the smell, but he doesn't really like coffee. When he was little, the smell of his mother's percolator in the morning was intoxicating, but when he got old enough to drink it he couldn't believe how bitter it was.

"Did you find your clothes?" Karen asks after she has poured two mugs of coffee and dosed them with milk and sugar.

"Yeah, I had to haul 'em out from under the bed. Some fluffy little animals had made their nests in them." He reaches over and draws her near him.

"What kind of animals?" she says, softening.

"Little kittens and bunnies," he says into her hair.

She breathes into his neck. "I wish I knew what to do about you," she murmurs.

"Trust me."

"I don't know," she says, pulling away from him.

He starts playing with the can opener, opening and closing the handles.

"Don't do that," she says. "It makes me nervous. I didn't get enough sleep. I'm not going to get a good night's sleep till they catch that guy."

"Why don't you ask Sardo who that rapist is? Old Sardo's such a know-it-all."

"Oh, shut up. You never take anything seriously."

"I *am* serious. I asked you to move in with me."

She drinks from her coffee mug, and her face livens up. She says, "I've got a lot to do today. I'm going to write letters to my sister and my nephews in Tallahassee. And I want to alter that new outfit I bought and clean my apartment and finish painting the bedroom." She sighs. "I'll never get all that done."

As she talks, he has been playing air guitar, like an accompanying tune. He turns to box playfully at her. "Go to Nashville with me today to get Doran and Nancy," he says.

"No, I've got too much to do before tonight's meeting. It's about recognizing your inner strength." She stares at him, in mingled exasperation and what he hopes is a hint of love. "I have to get my head together. Leave me alone today—O.K.?"

Jittery on Karen's coffee but feeling optimistic, he drives back to the laundromat. He spends half his life chasing after his clothes.

Traffic is heavy; families are heading home from church for fried chicken and the Cardinals game. People getting out of church must feel great, he thinks. He has heard that religion is a sex substitute. Karen told him Sardo is both sexes. "Double your pleasure, double your fun" was Steve's reply. Karen said, "Sardo says the answers are in yourself, not in God." On TV, the evangelists say the answers are in God. When people bottom out, they often get born again and discover Jesus. That's exactly what happened to Steve's father. He sends Steve pathetic letters filled with Bible quotations. His father used to live for what he could get away with, but now he casually dumps his shit in Christ's lap. Steve hopes he never gets that low. He'd rather trust himself. He's not sure he could trust anybody, especially Sardo—even if Sardo's message is to trust yourself. He's afraid Karen is getting brainwashed. He has heard that the girl who claims to be Sardo is now driving a Porsche.

At the laundromat, he finds his clothes piled up on top of the dryer, which is whirring with someone else's clothes. His laundry is still damp and he has to wait till another dryer is free. Fuming, he sits in the car and listens to the radio, knowing that his impatience is pointless, because when his laundry is finished, all he'll probably do is drive around and listen to the radio. "Keep it where you got it," says the DJ. "Ninety-four-five FM."

Through the window, he sees the woman in purple pants remove her laundry from the dryer he had used. He slouches out of Midnight Magic and enters the laundromat. Her laundry, in a purple laundry basket, includes purple T-shirts and socks and panties.

"Looks like you're into purple," he says to her as he wads his damp clothes into the vacated dryer.

"It's my favorite color, is all," she says, giving him a cool look. She grabs the panties in her laundry just as he reaches for them. She's quick.

"Do you want to hear a great joke?" he asks.

"What?"

"Why did Reagan bomb Libya?"

"I don't know. Why?"

"To impress Jodie Foster."

"Who's Jodie Foster?" she asks.

"You're kidding!" When Doran told Nancy that joke she got the giggles.

The woman folds a filmy nightgown into thirds, then expertly twines together a pair of purple socks. No children's T-shirts, no men's clothes in her pile.

"I just had some coffee and it makes me shake," he says, holding out his hand in front of her face. He makes his hand tremble.

"You oughtn't to drink coffee, then," she says.

"You really know how to hurt a guy," he says to her. "When you say something like that, it's like closing a door."

She doesn't answer. She hip-hugs her laundry basket and leaves.

The red light at the intersection of Walnut and Center streets is taking about three hours, and there's not a car in sight, so Steve scoots through. He drives back to Karen's apartment building and pulls in beside her Escort, trying to decide what to do. The small parking lot is wedged between Karen's building and the service entrance of a luncheonette. After business hours the place is deserted. Karen's windows look out on the roof of the luncheonette. At night the parking lot is badly lighted. He hates himself for letting her drive home alone last night, but he was too drunk to drive and she refused to let him. Last night, he suddenly remembers, he pretended to be the rapist. That was why she was so furious with him. But she didn't say anything about it today. Maybe he terrified her so much she was afraid to bring it up. "Don't do that again!" she cried when she broke free of his clutches last night. "But wouldn't it be a relief to know it was only me?" he asked. That was where tickling her on the couch had led. He couldn't stop himself. But it was just a game. She should have known that.

If he were the neighborhood rapist scouting out her apartment, he would hide in the dark doorway of the delivery entrance of the dry cleaner's downstairs, and when she came in at night, pointing the way with the key, he'd grab her tight around her waist. His weapon, hidden in his jacket, would press into her back. Catching her outside would be easier than coming through the window, smashing bottles to the floor and then being attacked by those spider plants of hers. Steve shudders. The rapist would simply twist her knife out of her hand and use it on her. He would grab her shotgun away from her, as easily as Steve pinned her on the bed last night.

Steve eases into reverse and creeps out of the parking lot. At a stop sign a pickup pulls around him, beeping. It's Bud.

"I found Big Red!" Bud yells. "He turned up at the back door this morning, starved." Big Red wobbles in the truck bed, his tongue hanging out like a handkerchief from a pocket.

"I knew he'd come back," Steve calls over.

"You didn't know that! Irish setters take a notion to run like hell and they get lost."

"Tell Big Red to settle down," says Steve. "Tell him some bedtime stories. Feed him some hog fat."

"Are you O.K., Steve?"

"Yeah, why?"

"You look like death warmed over." A car behind them blows. "Take it easy," says Bud.

Steve takes home a Big Mac and a double order of fries and eats in his kitchen, with a beer. The Cardinals game is just beginning. He feels at loose ends. Sometimes he has sudden feelings of desperation he can't explain—as if he has to get rid of something in his system. Like racing the engine to burn impurities out of his fuel line. He realizes a word has been tumbling through his mind all morning. Navratilova. The syllables spill out musically, to the tune of "Hearts on Fire," by Bryan Adams. Navratilova—her big arms like a man's. He imagines Nancy coming over—in her leg-of-lamb sleeves, her hot-pink tights. She's always in a good mood. He's sure she would be an immaculate housekeeper. Everything would be clean and pretty and safe, but she wouldn't mention how she slaved over it. Steve has noticed that most people feel sorry for themselves for having to do what they have actually maneuvered themselves into doing. His dad complaining about the food in jail. Bud moaning about his lost dog. Karen painting her wall. Or having to get her chores done so she won't be late to her meeting. When she had to get new tires, she fussed about the cost for weeks. He realizes he and Karen can never be like Doran and Nancy. There has to be some chemistry between two people, something inexplicable. Why is he involved with someone who follows the bizarre teachings of a teenager who says she's a reincarnated Indian? In a moment, he realizes how illogical his thoughts are. He wants something miraculous, but he can't believe in it. His head buzzes.

He finishes eating and surveys the damage. His place is straight out of Beirut. The waste can overflows with TV-dinner boxes and paper plates. In the oven, he finds a pizza box from last Sunday. Two leftover slices are growing little garden plots of gray mold. He locates a garbage bag and starts to clear out his kitchen. He's aware he's cleaning it up for Karen to move in; otherwise he wouldn't bother until it got really bad. If she moves in, she can have the alcove by the bedroom for her crafts table. He pops another beer. The Cards game is away, in a domed stadium. He can never really tell from TV what it would feel like to be inside such a huge place. He can't imagine how a whole ball field, with fake grass, can be under one roof. Playing baseball there seems as crazy as going fishing indoors. He picks up an earring beside the couch.

Then the telephone rings. It's Doran. "Steve, you crazy idiot! Where in Jesus' name are you?"

"I'm right here. Where are you?"

"Well, take a wild guess."

"I don't know. Having a beer with Mickey Mouse?"

"Nancy and me are at the Nashville airport, and guess who was supposed to meet us."

"Oh, no! I thought it was tonight."

"One o'clock, Flight 432."

"I wrote it down somewhere. I thought it was seven o'clock."

"Well, we're here, and what are we going to do about it?"

"I guess I'll have to come down and get you."

"Well, hurry. Nancy's real tired. She had insomnia last night."

"Are you still in love?" Steve blurts out. He's playing with Karen's earring, a silver loop within a loop.

Doran laughs strangely. "Oh, we'll tell you all about it. This has been a honeymoon for the record books."

"Go watch the ball game in the bar. And hang on, Doran. I'll be there in two and a half hours flat."

"Don't burn up the road—but hurry."

Steve puts the rest of the six-pack in a cooler and takes off. He heads out to the parkway that leads to I-24 and down to Nashville. He can't understand Doran's tone. He spoke as though he'd discovered something troubling about Nancy. Steve is miles out of town before he remembers he didn't pick up his laundry. He wishes Karen were along. She likes to go for Sunday drives in his car. He considers turning around, giving her a call at a gas station. He can't decide. On the radio a wild pitch distracts him and he realizes he's already too far along to turn around. The beer is soothing his headache.

Steve passes the Lake Barkley exits and zooms around a truck on a hill. The highway is easy and open, no traffic. As he drives, the muddle in his mind seems to be smoothing out, like something in a blender. Early in the summer he and Karen spent a Saturday over here at the Land Between the Lakes. At one of the tourist spots they saw an albino deer in a pen. Later, as they cruised down the Trace, the highway that runs the length of the wilderness, Karen said the deer was spooky. "It was like something all bleached out. It wasn't all *there*. It was embarrassing, like not having a tan in the summer."

"Maybe we ought to get Ted Turner to come here and colorize it," Steve said. "Like he's doing those movies."

Karen laughed. He used to be able to cheer her up like that before she got tangled up with Sardo. Before Sardo—B.S. Maybe he should become a cult-buster and rescue her. He has no idea how much money Sardo is costing her. She keeps that a secret.

Before long, he crosses the Tennessee line. Tennessee, the Volunteer State. For several miles, he tries to think of something that rhymes with Tennessee, then loses his train of thought. Suddenly he spots something lying ahead on the bank by the shoulder. It is large—perhaps a dead deer. As he approaches, he tries to guess what it is. He likes the way eyes can play tricks—how a giant bullfrog can turn out to be a cedar tree or a traffic sign. He realizes it's a man, lying several yards off the shoulder. He wonders if it's just a traveler who has stopped to take a nap, but there is no car nearby. Steve slows down to fifty. It is clearly a man, about twenty feet from the shoulder, near a bush. The man is lying face down, in an unnatural position, straight and flat—the position of a dead man. He's wearing a plaid shirt and blue running shoes and faded jeans. Lying out there in the open, he seems discarded, like a bag of trash.

Steve glides past the nearby exit, figuring that someone has probably already called the police. With beer in the car and on his breath, Steve doesn't want to fool with the police. They would want to know his license number, probably even bring him in for questions. If he stopped, he might leave footprints, flecks of paint from Midnight Magic. For all he knows, the mud flaps could have flung mud from Steve's driveway straight toward the body as he passed. But he's letting his imagination run away with him. He tries to laugh at this habit of his. He gulps some beer and tunes the ball game in over another station. It was fading away. Karen says to trust yourself, your instincts—know yourself.

"You don't need a thousand-year-old Indian to tell you that," he told her a few days ago. "I could have told you that for free."

The Clarksville exit is coming up. "Last Train to Clarksville" runs through his mind. The man lying out there in broad daylight bothers him. It reminds him of the time he fell asleep at lunch hour in the mattress room, and when he woke up he felt like a patient awakening after surgery. Everyone was standing around him in a circle, probing him with their eyes. Without really planning it, he curves onto the exit ramp. He slows down, turns left, then right. He pulls up to the side of a gas station, in front of the telephone booth. He leaves the motor running and feels in his pocket for a quarter. He flips the quarter, thinking heads. It's tails. There are emergency numbers on the telephone. The emergency numbers are free. He pockets the quarter and dials. A recorded voice asks him to hold.

In a moment, a woman's voice answers. Steve answers in a tone higher than normal. "I was driving south on I-24? And I want to report that I saw a man laying on the side of the road. I don't know if he was dead or just resting."

"Where are you, sir?"

"Now? Oh, I'm at a gas station."

"Location of gas station?"

"Hell, I don't know. The Clarksville exit."

"North or south?"

"South. I said south."

"What's the telephone number you're speaking from?"

He spreads his free hand on the glass wall of the telephone booth and gazes through his fingers at pie-slice sections of scenery. Up on the interstate, the traffic proceeds nonchalantly, as indifferent as worms working the soil. The woman's voice is asking something else over the phone. "Sir?" she says. "Are you there, sir?" His head buzzes from the beer. On his knuckle is a blood blister he doesn't know where he got.

Steve studies his car through the door of the phone booth. It's idling, jerkily, like a panting dog. It speeds up, then kicks down. His muffler has been growing throatier, making an impressive drag-race rumble. It's the power of Midnight Magic, the sound of his heart.

Hunktown

Joann noticed that her daughter Patty had started parting her hair on the left, so that it fell over the right side of her forehead, hiding the scar from her recent car accident.

"That scar doesn't show, Mom," said Patty, when she caught Joann looking. Patty had the baby on her hip, and her little girl, Kristi, was on the floor, fooling with the cat.

"Where's Cody?" Patty asked.

"Gone to Nashville. He got tired of waiting for that big shot he met in Paducah to follow up on his word, so he's gone down with Will Ed and them to make a record album on his own." Joann's husband, Cody Swann, was going to make a record album. She could hardly believe it. Cody had always wanted to make a record album.

"Is it one of those deals where you pay the studio?" Patty asked suspiciously.

"He pays five hundred dollars for the studio, and then he gets ten percent after they sell the first thousand."

"That's a rip-off," said Patty. "Don't he know that? I saw that on 'Sixty Minutes.' "

"Well, he got tired of waiting to be discovered. You know how he is."

The baby, Rodney, started to cry, and Patty stuck a pacifier in his mouth. She said, "The thing is, will they distribute the record? Them companies get rich making records for every little two-bit

33

band that can hitchhike to Nashville. And then they don't distribute the records."

"Cody says he can sell them to all his fans around here."

"He could sell them at the store," Patty said. She worked at a discount chain store.

"He took off this morning in that van with the muffler dragging. He had it wired up underneath and tied with a rope to the door handle on the passenger side."

"That sounds just like Cody. For God's sake, Kristi, what are you doing to that cat?"

Kristi had the cat upside down between her knees. "I'm counting her milkers. She's got four milkers."

"That's a tomcat, hon," said Joann gently.

Joann was taking her daughter shopping. Patty, who had gotten a ride to Joann's, was depending on her mother for transportation until the insurance money came through on her car. She had totaled it when she ran into a blue Buick, driven by an old woman on her way to a white sale in town. Patty's head had smashed against the steering wheel, and her face had been so bruised that for a while it resembled a ripe persimmon blackened by frost.

With the children in the back seat, Joann drove Patty around town on her errands. Patty didn't fasten her seat belt. She had had two wrecks before she was eighteen, but this latest accident was not her fault. Cody said Patty's middle name was Trouble. In high school, she became pregnant and had to get married, but a hay bale fell on her and caused a miscarriage. After that, she had two babies, but then she got divorced. Patty had a habit of flirting with Cody and teasing her mother for marrying such a good-looking man. Cody had grown up in a section of town known as Hunktown because so many handsome guys used to live there. That part of town—a couple of streets between Kroger's and the high school—was still known as Hunktown. The public housing project and the new health clinic were there now. Recently, a revival of pride in Hunktown had developed, as though it had been designated a historic area, and Cody had a Hunktown T-shirt. He wore cowboy outfits, and he hung his hats in a row on the scalloped trim of the china cabinet that Joann had antiqued.

Joann had known Cody since high school, but they had married only three years ago. After eighteen years of marriage to Joe Murphy, Joann found herself without a man—one of those women whose husbands suddenly leave them for someone younger. Last year, Phil Donahue had a show on that theme, and Joann remembered Phil saying something ironic like "It looks like you've got to keep tap-dancing in your negligee or the son of a gun is going to leave you." Joann was too indignant to sit around and feel sorry for herself. After filing for divorce, she got a new hairdo and new clothes and went out on weekends with some women. One night, she went to a place across the county line that sold liquor. Cody Swann was there, playing a fancy red electric guitar and singing about fickle women and trucks and heartache. At intermission, they reminisced about high school. Cody was divorced, and he had two grown children. Joann had two teenagers still living at home, and Patty had already left. In retrospect, Joann realized how impulsive their marriage had been, but she had been happy with Cody until he got laid off from his job, four months ago. He'd worked at the Crosbee plant, which manufactured electrical parts. Now he was drinking too much, but he assured Joann he couldn't possibly become an alcoholic on beer. Their situation was awkward, because she had a good job at the post office, and she knew he didn't like to depend on her. He had thrown himself into rehearsing for his album with his friends Will Ed and L.J. and Jimmy. "What we really need is a studio," Cody kept saying impatiently. They had been playing at county fairs and civic events around western Kentucky off and on for years. Every year, Cody played at the International Banana Festival, in Fulton, and recently he had played for the Wal-Mart grand opening and got a free toaster.

"Being out of work makes you lose your self-respect," Cody had told Joann matter-of-factly. "But I ain't going to let that happen to me. I've been fooling around too much. It's time to get serious about my singing."

"I don't want you to get your hopes up too much and then get disappointed," Joann said.

"Can't you imagine me with a television series? You could be on it with me. We'd play like we were Porter Wagoner and Dolly Parton. You could wear a big wig and balloons in your blouse."

"I can just see me—Miss Astor, in my plow shoes!" Joann said, squealing with laughter at the idea, playing along with Cody's dream.

"Do you care if we drive out to that truck patch and pick a few turnip greens before I take you home?" Joann asked Patty. "It's on the way."

"You're the driver. Beggars can't be choosers." Patty rummaged around on the floor under the bucket seat and found Rodney's pacifier, peppered with tobacco and dirt. She wiped it on her jeans and jammed it into the baby's mouth.

On the CB, a woman suddenly said, "Hey, Tomcat, you lost something back here. Come in, Tomcat. Over." A spurt of static followed. The woman said, "Tomcat, it looks like a big old sack of feed. You better get in reverse."

"She's trying to get something started with those cute guys in that green pickup we passed," Patty said.

"Everybody's on the make," Joann said uneasily. She knew what that was like.

At the truck patch, Patty stood there awkwardly in her high heels, like a scarecrow planted in the dirt.

"Let me show you how to pick turnip greens," Joann said. "Gather them like this. Just break them off partway down the stem, and clutch them in your hand till you get a big wad. Then pack them down in the sack."

"They're fuzzy, and they sting my hands. Is this a turnip green or a weed?" Patty held up a leaf.

"That's mustard. Go ahead and pick it. Mustard's good." Joann flicked the greens off expertly. "Don't get down into the stalk," she said. "And they wilt down when they're cooked, so pack them real good."

Kristi was looking for bugs, and Rodney was asleep in the car. Joann bent over, grabbing the greens. Some of the turnips were large enough to pull, their bulbs showing above ground like lavender pomanders. The okra plants in a row next to the turnip patch were as tall as corn, with yellow blossoms like roses. Where the blossoms had shriveled, the new okras thrust their points skyward. Joann felt the bright dizziness of the Indian-summer day, and she remembered many times when nothing had seemed important except picking turnip greens. She and Cody had lived on her parents' farm since her father died, two years before, but they had let it go. Cody wasn't a farmer. The field where her father used to grow turnips was wild now, spotted with burdock and thistles, and Cody was away in Nashville, seeking fame.

At a shed on the edge of the patch, Joann paid for the turnip greens and bought half a bushel of sweet potatoes from a black man in overalls, who was selling them from the back end of a pickup truck. The man measured the sweet potatoes in a half-bushel basket, then transferred them to grocery sacks. When he packed the sweet potatoes in the basket, he placed them so that their curves fit into one another, filling up the spaces. The man's carefulness was like Cody's when he was taping, recording a song over and over again. But Cody had tilled the garden last week in such a hurry that it looked as though cows had trampled the ground.

The man was saying, "When you get home with these, lay them in a basket and don't stir them. The sweet will settle in them, but if you disturb them, it will go away. Use them off the top. Don't root around in them."

"I'll put them in the basement," Joann said, as he set the sacks into her trunk. She said to Patty, who was concentrating on a hangnail, "Sweet potatoes are hard to keep. They mold on you."

That evening, Joann discovered one of Cody's tapes that she had not heard before. On the tape, he sang "There Stands the Glass," a Webb Pierce song that made her cry, the way Cody sang it so convincingly. When Cody sang "The Wild Side of Life" on the tape, Joann recalled Kitty Wells's answer to that song. "It wasn't God who made honky-tonk angels," Kitty Wells had insisted, blaming unfaithful men for every woman's heartbreak. Joann admired the way Kitty Wells sang the song so matter-of-factly, transcending her pain. A man wrote that song, Cody had told her. Joann wondered if he was being unfaithful in Nashville. She regarded the idea in a detached way, the way she would look at a cabbage at Kroger's.

Now Cody was singing an unfamiliar song. Joann rewound the tape and listened.

> *I was born in a place they call Hunktown,*
> *Good-lookin's my middle name—*

The song startled her. He had been talking about writing his own material, and he had started throwing around terms like "backup vocals" and "sound mixing." In this song, he sang along with himself to get a multiple-voice effect. The song was a lonesome tune about being a misfit. It sounded strangely insincere.

When Cody returned from Nashville, his voice bubbled along enthusiastically, like a toilet tank that ran until the handle was jiggled. He had been drinking. Joann had missed him, but she realized she hadn't missed his hat. It was the one with the pheasant feathers. He hung it on the china cabinet again. Cody was happy. In Nashville, he had eaten surf-and-turf, toured the Ryman Auditorium, and met a guy who had once been a sideman for Ernest Tubb.

"And here's the best part," said Cody, smacking Joann on the lips again. She got a taste of his mint-flavored snuff. "We got a job playing at a little bar in Nashville on weekends. It just came out of the blue. Jimmy can't do it, because his daddy's real bad off, but Will Ed and L.J. and me could go. Their wives already said they could."

"What makes you think I'll let you?" she said, teasing.

"You're going with me."

"But I've got too much to do." She set his boots on a carpet sample near the door to the porch. Cold air was coming through the crack around the facing. Cody had pieced part of the facing with a broken yardstick when he installed the door, but he had neglected to finish the job.

Cody said, "It's just a little bar with a little stage and this great guy that runs it. He's got a motel next to it and we can stay free. Hey, we can live it up in Nashville! We can watch Home Box Office and everything.''

"How can I go? Late beans are coming in, and all them tomatoes."

"This is my big chance! Don't you think I sing good?"

"You're as good as anybody on the 'Grand Ole Opry.' "

"Well, there you go," he said confidently.

"Patty says those studio deals are rip-offs. She saw it on 'Sixty Minutes.' "

"I don't care. The most I can lose is five hundred dollars. And at least I'll have a record album. I'm going to frame the cover and put it in the den."

In bed, they lay curled together, like sweet potatoes. Joann listened to Cody describe how they had made the album, laying down separate tracks and mixing the sound. Each little operation was done separately. They didn't just go into a studio and sing a song, Joann realized. They patched together layers of sound. She didn't mention the new song she had heard. She had put the tape back where she had found it. Now another of Cody's tapes was playing—"I'd Rather Die Young," a love song that seemed to have pointless suffering in it. Softly, Cody sang along with his taped voice. This was called a backup vocal, Joann reminded herself, trying to be very careful, taking one step at a time. Still, the idea of his singing with himself made her think of something self-indulgent and private, like masturbation. But country music was always like that, so personal.

"I'm glad you're home," she said, reaching for him.

"The muffler fell off about halfway home," Cody said, with a sudden hoot of laughter that made the covers quiver. "But we didn't get caught. I don't know why, though. It's as loud as a hundred amplifiers."

"Hold still," Joann said. "You're just like a wiggle-worm in hot ashes."

Cody was trying on his new outfit for the show, and Joann had

the sewing machine out, to alter the pants. The pants resembled
suede and had fringe.

"They feel tight in the crotch," Cody said. "But they didn't
have the next size."

"Are you going to tell me what you paid for them?"

"I didn't pay for them. I charged them at Penney's."

Joann turned the hem up and jerked it forward so that it fell
against his boot. "Is that too short?" she asked.

"Just a little longer."

Joann pulled the hem down about a quarter inch and pinned it.
"Turn around," she said.

The pants were tan with dark-brown stitching. The vest was
embroidered with butterflies. Cody turned around and around,
examining himself in the long mirror.

"You look wonderful," she said.

He said, "We may get deeper in debt before it's over with, but
one thing I've learned: You can't live with regret. You have to get
on with your life. I know it's a big risk I'm taking, but I don't want
to go around feeling sorry for myself because I've wasted so
much time. And if I fail, at least I will have tried."

He sat on the bed and pulled his boots and then his pants off.
The pants were too tight, but the seams were narrow, and there
was no way Joann could let them out.

"You'll have to do something about that beer gut," she said.

The Bluebird Lounge looked as innocent as someone's kitchen: all
new inside, with a country decor—old lanterns, gingham curtains, and a wagon wheel on the ceiling. It seemed odd to Joann
that Cody had said he didn't want to live with regret, because his
theme was country memories. He opened with "Walking the
Floor Over You," then eased into "Your Cheatin' Heart," "The
Wild Side of Life," and "I'd Rather Die Young." He didn't sing
the new song she had heard on the tape, and she decided that he
must be embarrassed by it. She liked his new Marty Robbins
medley, a tribute to the late singer, though she had always detested the song "El Paso." In the pleasant atmosphere of the bar,

Cody's voice sounded professional, more real there, somehow, than at home. Joann felt proud. She laughed when Will Ed and L.J. goofed around onstage, tripping over their electric cords and repeating things they had heard on "Hee Haw." L.J. had been kidding Joann, saying, "You better come to Nashville with us to keep the girls from falling all over Cody." Now Joann noticed the women, in twos and threes, sitting close to the stage, and she remembered the time she went across the county line and heard Cody sing. He still looked boyish, and he didn't have a single gray hair. She had cut his bangs too short, she realized now.

"They're really good," the cocktail waitress, Debbie, a slim, pretty woman in an embroidered cowboy shirt, said to Joann. "Most of the bands they get in here are so bad they really bum me out, but these guys are good."

"Cody just cut an album," Joann said proudly.

Debbie was friendly, and Joann felt comfortable with her, even though Debbie was only a little older than Patty. By the second night, Joann and Debbie were confiding in each other and trading notes on their hair. Joann's permanent was growing out strangely, and she was afraid getting a new permanent so soon would damage her hair, but Debbie got a permanent every three months and her hair stayed soft and manageable. In the rest room, Debbie fluffed her hair with her fingers and said, looking into the mirror, "I reckon I better put on some lipstick to keep the mortician away."

During the intermission, Debbie brought Joann a free Tequila Sunrise at her corner table. Cody was drinking beer at the bar with some musicians he had met.

"You've got a good-looking guy," Debbie said.

"He knows it, too," said Joann.

"He'd be blind if he didn't. It must be hard to be married to a guy like that."

"It wasn't so hard till he lost his job and got this notion that he has to get on the 'Grand Ole Opry.' "

"Well, he just might do it. He's good." Debbie told her about a man who had been in the bar once. He turned out to be a talent scout from a record company. "I wish I could remember his name," she said.

"I wish Cody would sing his Elvis songs," Joann said. "He can curl his lip exactly like Elvis, but he says he respects the memory of Elvis too much to do an Elvis act like everybody's doing. It would be exploitation."

"Cody sure is full of sad, lonesome songs," Debbie said. "You can tell he's a guy who's been through a lot. I always study people's faces. I'm fascinated by human nature."

"He went through a bad divorce," Joann said. "But right now he's acting like a kid."

"Men are such little boys," Debbie said knowingly.

Joann saw Cody talking with the men. Their behavior was easygoing, full of laughter. Women were so intense together. Joann could feel Cody's jubilation all the way across the room. It showed in the energetic way he sang the mournful music of all the old hillbilly singers.

Debbie said, "Making music must make you feel free. If I could make music, I'd feel that life was one big jam session."

Coming home on Sunday was disorienting. The cat looked impatient with them. The weather was changing, and the flowers were dying. Joann had meant to take the potted plants into the basement for the winter. There had been a cold snap, but not a killing frost. The garden was still producing, languidly, after a spurt of growth during the last spell of warm weather. After work, during the week, Joann gathered in lima beans and squash and dozens of new green tomatoes. She picked handfuls of dried Kentucky Wonder pole beans to save for seed. Burrs clung to the cuffs of her jeans. Her father used to fight the burdock, knowing that one plant could soon take over a field.

Cody stayed indoors, listening to tapes and playing his guitar. He collected his unemployment check, but when someone called about a job opening, he didn't go. As she worked in the garden, Joann tried to take out her anger on the dying plants that she pulled from the soil. She felt she had to hurry. Fall weather always filled her with a sense of urgency.

Patty stopped by in her new Lynx. She had come out ahead on the insurance deal. Cody paraded around the car, admiring it, stroking the fenders.

"When's your album coming out, Cody?" Patty asked.

"Any day now."

"I asked at the store if they could get it, but they said it would have to be nationally distributed for them to carry it."

"Do you want a mess of lima beans, Patty?" Joann asked. "There's not enough for a canning, so I'll let you have them."

"No, this bunch won't eat any beans but jelly beans." Patty turned to Cody, who was peering under the hood of her car. "I told all the girls at work about your album, Cody. We can't wait to hear it. What's on it?"

"It's a surprise," he said, looking up. "They swore I'd have it by Christmas. The assistant manager of the studio said he thought it was going to be big. He told that to the Oak Ridge Boys and he was right."

"Wow," said Patty.

When Cody patted the pinch of snuff under his lip, she said, "I think snuff's kind of sexy."

Joann hauled the baby out of the car seat and bounced him playfully on her shoulder. "Who's precious?" she asked the baby.

In the van on the way to Nashville that Friday, they sang gospel songs, changing the words crazily. "Swing Low, Sweet Chariot" became "Sweet 'n Low, Mr. Coffee pot, perking for to hurry my heart." Cody drove, and Joann sat in the back, where she could manage the food. She passed out beer and the sandwiches she had made before work that morning. She had been looking forward to the weekend, hoping to talk things over with Debbie.

Will Ed sat in the back with Joann, complaining about his wife, who was taking an interior-decorating course by correspondence. "She could come with us, but instead she wants to stay home and rearrange the furniture. I'm afraid to go home in the dark. I don't know where to walk." He added with a laugh, "And I don't know *who* I might stumble over."

"Joyce wouldn't cheat on you," said Joann.

"What do you think all these songs we sing are about?" he asked.

At that moment, Cody was humming "Pop a Top," a song about a wandering wife. He reached back for another beer, and Joann pulled the tab off for him. Cody set the can between his legs and said, "Poor Joann here's afraid we're going to get corrupted. She thinks I ought to be home spreading manure and milking cows."

"Don't 'poor Joann' me. I can take care of myself."

Cody laughed. "If men weren't tied down by women, what do you reckon they'd do with themselves? If they didn't have kids, a house, installments to pay?"

"Men want to marry and have a home just as much as women do, or they wouldn't do it," Joann said.

"Tell him, Joann," said L.J.

"Listen to this," said Will Ed. "I asked Joyce what was for supper? And she says, '*I'm* having a hamburger. What are *you* going to have?' I mean you can't say a word now without 'em jumping on you."

"Y'all shut up," said Joann. "Let's sing another song. Let's sing 'The Old Rugged Cross.' "

"The old rugged cross" turned into "an old Chevrolet," a forlorn image, it seemed to Joann, like something of quality lost in the past. She imagined a handsome 1957 Chevrolet, its fins slashed by silver arrows, standing splendidly on top of a mountain.

"This is better than showing up at the plant with a lunch box!" Cody cried. "Ain't it, boys?" He blasted the horn twice at the empty highway and broke into joyous song.

At the Bluebird, Joann drank the Tequila Sunrises Debbie brought her. The drink was pretty, with an orange slice—a rising sun—on the rim of the glass. Between customers, Debbie sat with Joann and they talked about life. Debbie knew a lot about human nature, though Joann wasn't sure Debbie was right about Cody being a man who suffered. "If he's suffering, it's because I'm bringing in the paycheck," she said. "But instead of looking for work, he's singing songs."

"He's going through the change," Debbie said. "Men go through it, too. He's afraid he's missed out on life. I've seen a lot of guys like that."

"I don't understand what's happening to people, the way they can't hold together anymore," Joann said. "My daughter's divorced, and I think it's just now hitting me that I got divorced too. In my first marriage, I got shafted—eighteen years with a man, working my fingers to the bone, raising three kids—but I didn't make a federal case out of it. I was lucky Cody came along. Cody says don't live with regret, but it's awful hard to look forward when there's so little you can depend on."

Debbie jumped up to get a draft beer for a man who signaled her. When she returned, she suddenly confessed to Joann, "I had my tubes tied—but I was such an idiot! And now I've met this new guy, and he doesn't know. I think I'm serious about him, but I haven't got the heart to tell him what I did."

"When did you have it done?" Joann cried, horrified.

"Last spring." She lit a cigarette and exhaled smoke furiously. "You know why I got my tubes tied? Because I hate to be categorized. My ex-husband thought I had to have supper on the table at six on the dot, when he came home. I was working too, and I got home about five-thirty. I had to do all the shopping and cleaning and cooking. I hate it when people *assume* things like that—that I'm the one to make supper because I've got reproductive organs."

"I never thought of it that way exactly."

"I was going to add kids to those responsibilities? Like hell." Debbie punched holes in a cocktail napkin with her ballpoint pen. The napkin had jokes printed on it, and she punched out the jokes. "It's the little things," she said. "I don't care about equal pay as much as I care about people judging me by the way I keep house. It's nobody's damn business how I keep house."

Joann had never heard of anything like what Debbie had done.

She hadn't known a woman would go that far to make a point to a man. Later, Debbie said, "You don't know what problems are till you go through tubal litigation." Joann had a feeling that that was the wrong term, but she didn't want to mention it.

"I hate to see you so upset," Joann said. "What can I do?"

"Tell them to stop playing those lovesick songs. All these country songs are so stupid. They tell you to stand by your man, but then they say he's just going to use you somehow."

Joann thought she understood how Debbie felt about telling her new boyfriend what she had done. It seemed like a dreadful secret. Debbie had had her tubes tied rather than tell her husband in plain English to treat her better. The country songs were open and confessional, but in reality people kept things to themselves. The songs were an invasion of privacy. Debbie must have felt something like that about her housekeeping and her husband's demands. Debbie should have sung a song about it, instead of getting herself butchered, Joann thought. But maybe Debbie couldn't sing. Joann was getting drunk.

The next afternoon, at the motel, Cody said to Joann, "They want us to play five nights a week at the bar. They've guaranteed me six months." He was smiling and slamming things around happily. He had just brought in some Cokes and Big Macs. "Will Ed and L.J. have to stay home and work, but I can get some backup men from here, easy. We could get a little apartment down here and put the house up for sale."

"I don't want to sell Daddy's place." Joann's stomach was churning.

"Well, we ain't doing nothing with it."

"They say they're going to hire again at the plant in the spring," Joann said.

"To hell with the plant. I gave 'em nineteen years and six months of my life and they cut me off without a pension. Screw *them*."

Joann placed the Big Macs and Cokes on a tray. She and Cody sat on one of the two beds to eat. She nibbled at her hamburger. "You're telling me to quit my job," she said.

"You could find something in Nashville."

"And be a cocktail waitress like Debbie? No, thanks. That's a rough life. I like my job and I'm lucky to have it."

On TV, a preacher was blabbing about reservations for heaven. Cody got up and flipped the dial, testing all the channels. "Just look how many TV channels we could get if we lived down here," he said.

"Don't do it, Joann," Debbie said flatly that evening.

"Cody and I haven't been together that long," Joann said. "Sometimes I feel I don't even know him. We're still in that stage where I ought to be giving him encouragement, the way you should do when you're starting out with somebody." She added, sarcastically, "Stand by your man."

"We're always caught in one cliché or another," Debbie said. "But you've got to think about yourself, Joann."

"I should give him more of a chance. He's got his heart set on this, and I'm being so contrary."

"But look what he's asking you to do, girl! Look what-all you've worked for. You've got your daddy's homeplace and that good job. You don't want to lose all that."

"We wouldn't come out ahead, after we pay off the mortgage. Maybe he wants to move to Nashville because there's ninety-nine TV stations to choose from. Well, the cable's coming down our road next year, and we'll have ten channels. That's enough television for anybody. They're bidding on the franchise now."

"I never watch television," Debbie said. "I can't stand watching stuff that's straight out of my own life."

At home, Cody was restless, full of nervous energy. He repaired some fences, as if getting the place ready to sell, but Joann hadn't agreed to anything. In the den one evening, after "Dynasty" had ended, Cody turned the sound down and said, "Let's talk, Jo." She waited while he opened a beer. He had been drinking beer after beer, methodically. "I've been thinking a lot about the way things are going, and I feel bad about how I used to treat my first wife, Charlene. I'm afraid I'm doing you the same way."

"You don't treat me bad," Joann said.

"I've taken advantage of you, letting you pay all the bills. I know I should get a job, but damn it, there's got to be more to life than punching a time clock. I think I always expected a lot more out of life than most people. I used to be a real hell-raiser. I thought I could get away with anything because people always gave me things. All my life, people gave me things."

"What things?" Joann was sitting on the couch, and Cody was in the easy chair. The only light came from the television.

"In grade school, I'd get more valentines than anybody, and the valentines would have candy in them, little hearts with messages like 'Be Mine' and 'Cutie' and things like that. When I graduated from high school, all the storekeepers in town gave me stuff and took me in their back rooms and gave me whiskey. I had my first drink in the pharmacy in the back of the Rexall. I just breezed through life, letting people give me things, and it didn't dawn on me for a long time that people wanted something back. They expected something from me and I never gave it to them. I didn't live up to their expectations. Somehow, I want to give something back."

"People always admired you, Cody. You're so good-natured. Isn't that giving something?"

Cody belched loudly and laughed. "When I was about twelve, a man gave me five dollars to jack him off in the alley behind the old A and P."

"Did you do it?"

"Yep. And I didn't think a thing about it. I just did it. Five bucks was five bucks."

"Well, what do you owe *him*?" Joann said sharply.

"Nothing, I reckon, but the point is, I did a lot of stuff that wasn't right. Charlene was always thumping the Bible and hauling me off to church. I couldn't live with that. I treated her like dirt, the way I cheated on her. I always wanted what was free and available. It was what I was used to. I had a chance once, about fifteen years ago, to play in a little bar in Nashville, but the kids were little, and Charlene didn't want me to go. I've regretted that to this day. Don't you see why this chance means so much to me?

I'm trying to *give* something of myself, instead of always taking. Just go along with me, Joann. Take this one risk with me."

"What can I say when you put it that way?"

"A person has to follow his dream."

"That sounds like some Elvis song," she said, sounding unexpectedly sarcastic. She was thinking of Elvis's last few years, when he got fat and corrupted. She rearranged some pillows on the couch. The weather news was on TV. The radar was showing rain in their area. Slowly, her eyes on the flashing lines of the radar map, she said, "What you want to do is be in the spotlight so people can adore you. That's the same thing as taking what's free."

"That's not true. Maybe you think it's easy to be in the spotlight. But it's not. Look what happened to Elvis."

"You're not Elvis. And selling the place is too extreme. Things can't be all one way or the other. There has to be some of both. That's what life is, when it's any good." Joann felt drained, as though she had just had to figure out all of life, like doing a complicated math problem in her head.

Cody turned the TV off, and the light vanished. In the dark, he said, "I cheated on Charlene, but I never cheated on you."

"I never said you did."

"But you expect it," he said.

Patty came over to ask Joann to keep the kids that weekend. She had a new boyfriend, who was taking her to St. Louis.

"If I can take 'em to Nashville," Joann told Patty. "I have to go along to keep the girls away from Cody." She looked meaningfully at Cody.

It was meant to be a casual, teasing remark, she thought, but it didn't come out that way. Cody glared at her, looking hurt.

"The kids will be in the way," he said. "You can't take them to the Bluebird Lounge."

"We'll stay in the motel room," Joann said. "I wanted to watch *On Golden Pond* on HBO anyway. Nashville has so much more to offer. Remember?"

She realized that taking the children to Nashville was a bad idea, but she felt she had to go with Cody. She didn't know what might happen. She hoped that having the kids along would make her and Cody feel they had a family to be responsible for. Besides, Patty was neglecting the kids. Joann had kept them three nights in a row last week while Patty went out with her new boyfriend.

In the van on the way down, Rodney cried because he was teething, and L.J. gave him a piece of rawhide to chew on. Kristi played with a bucket of plastic toys. Will Ed practiced the middle eight of a new song they had learned. It seemed pointless to Joann, since Cody planned to dump Will Ed and L.J. from his act. Will Ed played the passage over and over on his guitar, until Kristi screamed, "Shut up!" Cody said little. L.J. was driving, because Joann didn't want Cody to drive and drink beer, with the children along.

Daylight saving time had ended, and the dark came early. The bright lights at the edge of Nashville reminded Joann of how soon Christmas was.

She liked being alone in the motel room with the kids. It made her think of when she'd had small children and her first husband had worked a night shift. She had always tried to be quiet around sleeping children, but nowadays children had more tolerance for noise. The TV didn't bother them. She sat in bed, propped against pillows. The children were asleep. In the large mirror facing the bed, she could see herself, watching TV, with the sleeping bundles beside her. Joann felt expectant, as if some easy answers were waiting for her—from the movie, from the innocence of the children.

Suddenly Kristi sat straight up and shouted, "Where's Mommy?"

"Hush, Kristi! Mommy's gone to St. Louis. We'll see her Sunday."

Kristi hurled herself out of bed and ran around the room. She looked in the closet and in the bathroom. Then she began to shriek. Joann grabbed her and whispered, "Shush, you'll wake up your little brother!"

Kristi wiggled away from her and looked under the bed, but the bed was boxed in—a brilliant construction, Joann thought, so far as cleaning was concerned. Kristi bumped into a chair and fell down. She began bawling. Rodney stirred, and then he started to cry. Joann huddled both children in the center of the bed and began singing to them. She couldn't think of anything to sing except the Kitty Wells song about honky-tonk angels. The song was an absurd one to sing to kids, but she sang it anyway. It was her life. She sang it like an innocent bystander, angry that that was the way women were, that they looked on approvingly while some man went out and either did something big or made a fool of himself trying.

When Cody came in later, she had fallen asleep with the children. She woke up and glanced at the travel alarm. It was three. The TV was still on. Cody was missing the Burt Reynolds movie he had wanted to watch. He stumbled into the bathroom and then fell into the other bed with all his clothes on.

"I was rehearsing with those new guys," he said. "And then we went out to eat something." Joann heard his boots fall to the floor, and he said, "I called home around ten-thirty, between shows, to wish Mama a happy birthday, and she told me Daddy's in the Memphis hospital."

"Oh, what's wrong?" Joann sat up and pulled her pillow behind her. Cody's father, who was almost seventy-five, had always bragged about never being sick.

"It's cancer. He had some tests done. They never told me anything." Cody flung his shirt to the foot of the bed. "Lung cancer comes on sudden. They're going to operate next week."

"I was *so* afraid of that," Joann said. "The way he smoked."

Cody turned to face her across the aisle between the two beds. He reached over and searched for her hand. "I'll have to go to Memphis tomorrow night after the show. Mama's going down tomorrow."

Rodney squirmed beside Joann, and she pulled the covers around his shoulders. Then she crept into bed with Cody and lay close to him while he went on talking in a tone of disbelief about his father. "It makes me mad that I forgot it was Mama's birthday. I thought of it during the first show, when I was singing 'Blue Eyes Crying in the Rain.' I don't know how come me to think of it then."

"Do you want me to go to Memphis with you?"

"No. That's all right. You have to get the kids home. I'll take the bus and then come back here for the show Tuesday." Cody drew her near him. "Were you going to come back here with me?"

"I've been thinking about that. I don't want to quit my job or sell Daddy's place. That would be crazy."

"Sometimes it's good to act a little crazy."

"No. We have to reason things out, so we don't ruin anything between us." She was half-whispering, trying not to wake the children, and her voice trembled as though she were having a chill. "I think you should come down here by yourself first and see how it works out."

"What if my album's a big hit and we make a million dollars?" His eyes were on the TV. Burt Reynolds was speeding down an interstate.

"That would be different."

"Would you move to Nashville if I got on the 'Grand Ole Opry'?"

"Yes."

"Is that a promise?"

"Yes."

On Monday, Cody was still in Memphis. The operation was the next day, and Joann took off from work early in order to go down to be with Cody and his parents. She was ready to leave the house when the delivery truck brought the shipment of record albums. The driver brought two boxes, marked "1 of 3" and "2 of 3."

"I'll bring the third box tomorrow," the driver said. "We're not allowed to bring three at once."

"Why's that?" Joann asked, shivering in the open doorway to the porch.

"They want to keep us moving."

"Well, I don't understand that one bit."

Joann shoved the boxes across the threshold and closed the door. With a butcher knife, she ripped open one of the boxes and slipped out a record album. On the cover was a photograph of Cody and Will Ed and L.J. and Jimmy, sitting on a bench. Above them, the title of the album was a red-and-blue neon sign: "HUNKTOWN." Cody and his friends were all wearing Hunktown T-shirts, cowboy boots, and cowboy hats. They had a casual, slouchy look, like the group called Alabama. It was a terrible picture. Looking at her husband, Joann thought no one would say he was really handsome. She held the cover up to the glass door to get a better light on his face. He looked old. His expression seemed serious and unforgiving, as though he expected the world to be ready for him, as though this were his revenge, not his gift. That face was now on a thousand albums.

But the picture was not really Cody at all, she thought. It was only his wild side, not the part she loved. Seeing it was something like identifying a dead body: it was so unfamiliar that death was somehow acceptable. She had to laugh. Cody had meant the album to be a surprise, but he would be surprised to see how he looked.

Joann heard a noise outside. She touched her nose to the door glass and left a smudge. On the porch, the impatiens in a hanging basket had died in the recent freeze. She had forgotten to bring the plant inside. Now she watched it sway and twist in a little whirl of wind.

Marita

I was named after two aunts, Mary and Rita. Sometimes I think Marita is a ridiculous name, but sometimes I realize it's pretty. Mom thought it sounded Spanish. Once, she dressed me up like a Spanish fan dancer for a costume party. Then my date threw up in my lap. I had to rake the vomit out with my fan. Mom had gone all over town looking for that fan. She said, "You can't flirt without a fan." Mom should know—she's a champion. She flirts with the guys I go out with, even when she calls them "twerps" and "numb-chucks" behind their backs. She turns on all her charms to awe them, to make them think they're not good enough for me. I felt so dumb in that Spanish-dancer costume. It wasn't me. She thinks she knows me and that she can help me work on my personality. She's short and I'm tall, but we have the same full lips, deep-set eyes, thick eyebrows. People mistake us for sisters. It's embarrassing, because she's the beautiful one. My feet are too big and I'm short-waisted.

It's the same old same old, as my grandmother is fond of saying, though I doubt she's referring to our particular story—our cliché, the one where the mother lives her life through her daughter. Clichés! I hate them. Mom wanted me to have choices. She's scared I'll marry too young and get trapped in a kitchen without ever having a chance to see a Broadway show or go backpacking. I don't really blame her, after what she went through with her two husbands—neither of whom was my father. One was crazy, the other a brute. She never really loved either one, and she's a romantic fool about my father only because he's dead.

At night I watch her creaming her face before her lighted makeup mirror, rubbing slowly with little concentric movements, like the whorls of fingerprints. She looks so innocent, as though nothing bad ever happened to her.

Sue Ellen felt rushed. She was applying her makeup at the kitchen table. The two cats sat on the table, agreeably sharing a placemat and eyeing the milk pitcher. Coupons Sue Ellen had been sorting into her coupon wallet were still stacked in piles on the table. She was furious with her daughter. Marita was dawdling, not even dressed, late for work. Since she had unexpectedly come home from college and started working at the off-price mall, Marita had been sleeping late, her snooze alarm popping on at intervals and the cats jumping on her bed. She had dropped out of college—her first semester—shortly after the tuition was no longer refundable. Sue Ellen was both angry and disappointed. Marita's explanation: "I missed you, Mom."

Sue Ellen had begun to enjoy living alone. Late at night, her habit was to crawl in bed with her magazines and some cream sherry and the talk shows. It was her private time, when she didn't have to smile. She couldn't be a hostess around the clock. She could watch those people on TV, desperate about their images ("How am I doing?"), and laugh at them—the fools. Jobs that required smiles were among the most stressful, she had read. Sometimes she felt she had been a hostess in the way she raised her daughter, always dealing with her diplomatically and pleasantly. She was tired of that.

"It's nine-fifteen," she said to Marita, who was still in her nightgown. "Are you going to wear the blue jacket with the shoulder pads?" Carefully, Sue Ellen smudged her eyeliner with a sponge-tipped wand. The face in the mirror was hard, not really her.

Marita was lazily flipping through the mail. "Listen to this, Mom," she said. "The names in this catalogue are like tongue twisters." She spoke carefully: "Homespun Donegal Tweed Sweaters. That's hard to say!"

"I could say that, if I had time." Sue Ellen dabbed again at her eyeliner. She had to stop being so snappy.

"Try this one: Lambswool Camel-Hair Cardigan."

"Lambswool Camel-Hair Cardigan. Lambswool Camel-Hair Cardigan," Sue Ellen said fast. "Hey, I'm pretty good at this!"

"I love this one: Whip Stitch Tassel Flat." Marita laughed and Sue Ellen got tickled at her. "Georgia Fatwood!" Marita cried, tears popping out of her eyes. "Trak Bushwacker Skis," she said. "Shorty Tackle Pack Vest. This is killing me." Marita's face streamed with tears. "I love funny words," she said.

Marita looked twelve, a giggling little girl. Sue Ellen wished she could stay here all day and laugh with her. She wanted to hold Marita close and hug her. She wanted to read her mind, so she could revise it and stick in some things Marita needed to think about.

"Hurry, hon," Sue Ellen said, twisting open her lipstick brush. "I'll drop you off and I'll meet you at one and we'll go to Wendy's for lunch, O.K.?"

"I can't stand the Paycheck Discount. I have to stand up all day, and I'm sure it's not good for my feet. I'm too flatfooted."

"But nobody's looking at your feet."

"I've decided I want to work somewhere where I can serve a useful purpose."

Sue Ellen's eye-shadow case flew across the table, scattering chunks of color and causing the cats to jump down from the table together, like a trained act. "You find fault with everything you try," she said as calmly as she could. Coupons fluttered to the floor. Sue Ellen snatched up a fifty-cent coupon for Sara Lee croissants that she meant to buy today.

"I can't help it," said Marita. "I'm bored."

"Bored," said Sue Ellen, nodding.

In late August, they had gone to Penney's and excitedly picked out pink sheets with white piping and a print comforter with matching curtains for Marita's dorm room. But Marita's new roommate brought a clashing plaid bedspread. Marita said the girl smelled.

College was not what I expected. I was always studious in high school, and I made good grades, but in college nothing important seemed quite real. Only the unimportant things stood out, like glaring imperfections. When I was a sophomore in high school, I wanted to be an artist, and Mom encouraged that because she used to like to draw. Now she's too tired to do anything creative. She just drinks wine and watches TV when she comes home from the restaurant where she works. She stays up late, watching "Nightline" and David Letterman. I think she exhausted the supply of men around here. Too many cowboys, she said one night. Now she stays home because of AIDS. I used to hear her tiptoeing in late at night. She used to drink hard liquor, but now she's into health. She says beer and wine are healthful. That was one thing wrong with college—the way the kids drank and got silly.

At the university I signed up for English, French, art appreciation, history, and chemistry. They made me take the science course, but it turned out to be the most interesting subject. I had planned to study French and become an interpreter, but the teacher was gay and the way he lisped *Parlez-vous français* was revolting. I blame him for ruining my career. If I'd had a good teacher, I might not have gotten into the trouble I am in.

And my roommate was another problem. She was from some little place in the mountains where they are ignorant and don't know how to act. At five o'clock she and her fan club of fellow nerds would head for the cafeteria, bobbing their heads and quacking like a cluster of ducks headed for water. The clash between her red-plaid bedspread and the pink cabbage roses on my comforter made my flesh crawl. She wasn't someone I could talk to. Her name was Louann Long, but she was about five feet tall and everybody called her "Shorty." Shorty Long.

Mom keeps asking me what happened at college.

I went out with fraternity boys. Sometimes we went to a bar

where they weren't picky about IDs. Mostly we hung out at the malls until they closed, then went out driving and ended up at someone's apartment, in the dark. By then, I might have forgotten who I was with, or what for. There were nights when we'd drive and drive—past the horse farms, around the belt line, out into Scott County, through the bumpy little hills that at night seemed like dark curves of ocean waves. I felt we were tossing in a storm, riding the waves. We would glide into port, some gas station near a railroad track. We'd hit the filthy rest room, the Coke machine, and then we'd be gone again.

When I first started getting sick in the mornings, I thought it was because of Shorty Long—her dirty sheets, her plaid bedspread. The air in the dorm was polluted. I kept cutting my nine o'clock. I'd go to the botanical gardens behind the art center and breathe deeply. The flowers were dying. Beside the floral clock was an enormous bed of white flowers with bright-blue leaves. Every day I'd see the blue leaves and notice, half-consciously, how strange they were. After about a week it dawned on me that someone had carefully spray-painted the leaves blue. Blue and white are the school colors. Go, Wildcats.

I always told Mom everything, but I can't tell her what happened because I don't really know. I don't know who he was—it was one of two interchangeable guys, guys I don't know or care to know. It doesn't matter. It was one of those hot nights in late September. I didn't think it could happen to me. I know what she'll say. She was so careful, teaching me everything so I wouldn't be like forty percent of the girls in my high-school class—the highest percentage in the state. So I tell her college wasn't for me. I tell her this until I can decide what to do. I'm so sleepy. All I can do is sleep. At the Paycheck, I got so sleepy, but I didn't dare drink coffee to stay awake. They say coffee is dangerous. One of the cashiers told Janet in Housewares she thought I was on drugs because I had been away to college.

"Would you like pancakes for breakfast?" Sue Ellen asked Marita on Sunday. Marita had quit her job and had been lounging around the house most of the time. She hadn't gone out, even though a couple of guys from her high-school class had called.

Marita shuddered. "You know I don't like pancakes—not since that time the cat threw up that hairball on my pancakes."

"That was a good five years ago."

"It's not something you'd forget."

"Let's have a nice leisurely Sunday morning together," urged Sue Ellen cheerfully. "Let's have a brunch, the way they do in fine restaurants." The restaurant where she worked had Happy Hour but it was closed on Sundays. Once, a man she met at Happy Hour invited her to an elegant Sunday brunch on the *Delta Queen* riverboat. The brunch included tiny crab claws and a champagne fountain flowing into a seashell-shaped bowl. Giddily, she imagined herself as Venus, washing up on shore, guided by little sea creatures.

"How about French toast?" she asked her daughter.

"O.K. French toast." Marita fluttered the pages of the front section of the Sunday newspaper. She had been carefully following the news lately and was upset about the stock market. Last week it was science-fiction novels. Before that, she was studying religions. It was good to be exposed to a lot of ideas, Sue Ellen told herself.

"I'll make a big pot of coffee and we'll just sit around and relax," she said.

"I don't want any coffee."

"Oh?" Sue Ellen filled the coffeepot half-full, poured the water into the coffeemaker, snapped the filter in place. She stole a glance at Marita. They had the same honey-beige complexion and could wear each other's foundation. Marita had naturally thick eyelashes, which she accented with dark mascara and frosty silver shadow, blended with a lighter matte beige to make her eyes appear larger. Sue Ellen had started putting makeup on Marita when she was only ten, to see what she would look like grown. Marita's father never knew about her. He was killed in a car wreck in Muscle Shoals, Alabama, where he had gone to work at the missile plant. Sue Ellen never forgave herself for writing him a "Dear John" letter a month before he died. The fact that his name was actually John seemed to make it worse. She sometimes imagined that if she hadn't written that letter, the series of minor events leading to his being in that car at that moment might have been different.

"I know what's going on," she said to Marita when the French toast was ready.

"Did you know that Moses and Aristotle were both stutterers?" said Marita, looking up from the newspaper.

"Fascinating. Did you hear what I said?"

"Do you know what I want to do?" Marita pointed to an ad in the paper. "I want to go to beauty school. I could earn a living. I'd be good at it, you know I would," she said excitedly. "You've taught me the basics anyway. It says here in this ad they need people at the Head Shack, and they'll guarantee you a job when you get a license."

Sue Ellen slapped French toast onto one of her good plates and set it in front of Marita. She said, "Forget about beauty school, hon. I want you to get an abortion and go back to college in January."

Marita scooted her chair away from the table, as if she were retreating into the corner. "How did you know?"

"It's obvious."

"It's only a couple of months," said Marita, looking down at herself. "You can't see."

"But I know you. You're so much like me, I recognized the signs."

"I'm going to keep it."

"No, you're not."

"I don't want anybody sticking a vacuum cleaner up me."

"I taught you how to be careful."

"I knew you'd say that!" Marita screamed.

"If you have it, do you know who will end up taking care of that baby? *I* will. Because you'll lose interest, the way you do with every single thing you start. You change your mind so often it's like switching channels with a remote-control paddle." Sue Ellen instantly regretted her words. They came tumbling out, like tangled necklaces in her jewelry box. She said quietly, as she stabbed the table with the syrup bottle, "Are you going to eat that French toast or not?"

"It looks like squirrel barf."

On Friday night I went out with a guy who works at the mall. He's a sales manager of some kind. I could tell he was ashamed to be with me because of what I was wearing. Around here, if you don't wear coordinated pastel polyester, people look at you funny. He got a wrong impression of me from the clothes I was forced to wear at the Paycheck Discount. When we went out I wore a calf-length print skirt and boots, with a denim vest and a wide scarf. Mom said I looked great. She was glad for me to get out, circulate a little. This guy, Tom, suggested that I wait in the car when he stopped at the mall to buy a battery. I knew he didn't want to be seen with me. I sat there and thought about Mom's judgment. Mom ripping out those perfume sample cards that come in magazines and hiding them in her panty drawer. Mom stuffing bubble wrap in her bra for her hostess job. What does she expect out of life?

Now I don't go anywhere. I stay at home and read magazines and newspapers and do my nails and listen to Pink Floyd and Cyndi Lauper and some other records a guy I know sent me. He keeps asking me out, to concerts in Nashville and Memphis. He's twenty-three years old and has a résumé that says "Ten years experience as a sound engineer." Imagine calling yourself a sound engineer at age thirteen. He was probably making secret tapes under his parents' bed.

My body keeps sending signals, little flutters and tugs from places I didn't know were there. I'm conscious of every cell. I can concentrate on a certain point, say the top of my knee, and make it warm, just by thinking. In the *Courier-Journal*, I noticed a list of the hot lines and support groups, all related to people's bodies. Alcohol, asthma, allergies, pregnancy counseling, crime victims, epilepsy, hyperactive children, rape, poison, Tourette's syndrome, spinal cord injuries. The body is a prison. Imagine having a twisted spine and a nervous tic, with your face jerking out of control. And then you get raped! And you end up an alcoholic, and finally it's all too much and you grab the poison to end it all. But you can still call the hot line. Someone is always there.

When Mom leaves for work, the cats romp through the house and slide on the scatter rugs. Mud Puddle stalks Spooky from behind a fold in the rug. Spooky pretends not to notice until a second before the ambush, then Mud Puddle stops in mid-pounce and starts licking his shoulder in an unconcerned way. Mud Puddle is black and Spooky is white. I wish my life could be that clear. My body feels heavy, and I'm slow. My mind is slow. The cats curl up together on the bed and I curl up with them, and we sleep through whole sides of records. Sometimes I wake up scared. Today Mud Puddle woke up out of a dead sleep and went shooting backwards across the room. He must have had the same nightmare I did.

Sue Ellen insisted on taking Marita to Dr. Posek—to make sure everything was all right, she told her. Irregular things could happen. Sue Ellen trusted Dr. Posek. He had removed the mole from her back when it kept getting irritated by her bra. And he had performed even more intimate surgery on her—something embarrassing that no one else knew about. When she was engaged to Marita's father, John Cross, she had something wrong with her and she couldn't enjoy making love with him. She pretended with him because she wanted to love him, but there was something missing. Sex was like visiting the gynecologist. It was years later that Dr. Posek discovered her deformity—a hooded clitoris, a thick piece of skin that deadened all sensation. Dr. Posek snipped it off, using only a local anesthetic, and after that Sue Ellen went crazy with desire. It was like a raw nerve exposed. She married twice, but still there was a disparity between sex and love—it seemed that she chose the best sexual partners, but the worst human beings, to marry. And in her imagination she always revised those cold love scenes with John.

"What did he say?" Sue Ellen asked when Marita emerged from Dr. Posek's office.

"He poked me all over. His fingers were fat and thick, like greasy sausages. It was awful. It hurt."

On the way home, they stopped at the Mini-Mart for bread and cat food. Right in the canned-goods aisle, Marita said, "I think you're right, Mom. I think I should get an abortion."

In astonishment, Sue Ellen dropped the package of English muffins she was carrying. "What did Dr. Posek say?"

Marita shrugged. "He just said, 'Come on, Marita, let's pull that baby out of you. It's not going to do you any good.' "

"That's all?"

"Yeah. But he made a lot of sense. It sounded right."

"God damn!" cried Sue Ellen. "I beat my head against a wall trying to talk some sense into you, and all some man has to say is 'jump' and you say 'how high.' "

"Hush, Mom," said Marita. "Everybody's looking."

On the way to the clinic in Louisville, a four-hour drive, Marita seemed in a good mood, sure of her decision. They laughed and sang along with the radio for a while, just as they had done only a few months before when Sue Ellen drove Marita to college.

Sue Ellen felt relieved. She wanted to get this over with as simply as possible and not think about it. The night before, staring at the TV, she kept imagining what it would be like if Marita had insisted on having the baby. The talk-show guests were talking about their movies, their dogs, their children, their vacation homes, and in the haze of cream sherry she imagined the same sounds, the same rhythms of language, as if they were discussing abortion instead. It made her mad the way David Letterman humiliated them. The whole definition of host, and hostess, had changed, she thought—probably about the same time airlines no longer had just "hostesses" but attendants of both sexes. Now the meaning of hospitality seemed perverted and confused. David Letterman was the opposite of a host, someone who didn't make you feel welcome yet made you feel grateful you were on his show. She had a nightmare, in which David Letterman made her recite a long restaurant menu to Marita, forcing her daughter to choose on the spot. Sue Ellen kept trying to fight David Letterman, but because it was television, she had to go through with it or lose face. It was an oddly complicated set of contradictions, she thought, on waking.

The parkway sliced through small hills, exposing layered slabs of rock. Water ran down the rock walls, making little waterfalls in some places. Marita had a change purse handy for tolls. They stopped at the Beaver Dam plaza to go to the bathroom and get Cokes. Marita said she felt bloated. Sue Ellen had brought along health-food snacks. She brought Mummy Food, a dried-fruit snack that was a recipe of Edgar Cayce's, the Hopkinsville mystic. But both of them were too nervous to eat.

Marita said, "I read that if you have a lot of heartburns, the baby will have a lot of hair. I had heartburns last night."

"It's not really a baby yet," Sue Ellen said.

In the parking lot behind the clinic, she thought about saying to Marita, "I know I've rushed you into this, and you can think about it again. It's your choice, honey."

And she imagined Marita saying, "It's O.K., Mom. But thanks for giving me the choice."

But that exchange would be like a scene from a soap opera. It wouldn't go that way in reality. Sue Ellen didn't dare offer Marita an out. What Marita might really say was, "This is what you wished you could have done eighteen years ago."

The clinic was a small brick building between a Sunoco station and an interior-decorating business. The waiting room had framed seascapes on the wall and a window surveying the parking lot. Surprisingly, there was no Muzak. They sat on hard vinyl chairs in a corner, next to a nervous girl in cowboy boots. Across from them, a teenage couple, dressed alike in jeans and denim jackets, whispered angrily to each other. Marita leafed through copies of *Time* and *People*. She chewed gum. Sue Ellen had brought a racy novel to take her mind off what was happening. The book was called *The Red Zero*, which Marita pointed out was appropriate.

Looking up from her magazine, Marita said, "Mom, it says here the stuff in Elvis's bedroom at Graceland is just like he left it. Even his jockstrap is on the floor where he left it."

"That's just like a man," said Sue Ellen. "God, they're all alike. I'm glad I don't have one to pick up after."

"You don't mean that for one minute," said Marita, cracking her gum and turning the page.

Sue Ellen studied the people: a country couple with hardened hands and windburned complexions, with their young daughter sitting between them; a middle-aged woman in a pale-aqua smock like food-service workers wear; the denim-covered teenagers who apparently hated each other.

A fat woman emerged from the interior of the clinic and announced, "Thank God it was a 'east infection! I thought it might be the herpes or the AIDS."

The woman waiting for her replied, "I was real careful going to the bathroom. I put down three layers of paper."

"I'm scared," Marita said to Sue Ellen quietly. She was sitting with her hands tucked under her thighs. Her magazine had fallen to the floor.

Just then Marita's name was called, and she looked at Sue Ellen questioningly.

"I'm coming in with you," said Sue Ellen, closing her book.

Everything is still blurry, and I feel cozy and warm under the cabbage roses. All the way home I slept in the back seat. It was no big deal. The Catholics don't believe in abortion, but it's like what they do all the time—they sin and then go to confession. It's like taking back a nasty remark you couldn't resist saying. The operation was easy. Mom says I should have a baby someday when the circumstances are right: meaning a good-looking man with money. She said she would have ended up taking care of the baby and she's too old to go through that again. But that's not true. I see Mud Puddle and Spooky playing together on the rug, so innocently, and they make me cry. Mom's at work and this secret world goes on here when she's away. We're like the Borrowers in those children's books I used to read to my cousins.

We're tiny and quiet, living in the cabbage roses. Now I don't
need to go to beauty school. That was just an idea I had, a way to
support a child, but now I don't have any reason to go to beauty
school, to help others with their appearance. And I've remembered that I'm sensitive to permanent-wave solutions. I told Mom
I'd go back to college. When she left this afternoon, she gave me
my medication. She was smiling proudly.

Late last night, she had a little party for me. It was like a
birthday. She brought you-peel-'em shrimp and peppermint ice
cream from the restaurant. I was asleep when she came in, but
she woke me up for the impromptu party. And she gave me a
present—a new nightgown with a shirred yoke and lace trim and
a matching peignoir. She called it a Penny War, to make me
laugh. The present was wrapped in pink flamingo paper with a
miniature pink flamingo made with real feathers tied in the
center. It was a sweet gift, and it cheered me up. I'm lost in pink,
lying under my pink cabbage roses, my pink Penny War hanging
in the closet. Spooky's pink pads knead my chest. I lie there
half-awake, with the TV on, thinking of names: Shannon, Mi-
chelle, Krystal, Traci, Sonny Boy, Lonzo, Woody, Bert, Algie,
Gala, Drake, Violet, Wink, Wolf. On TV, scientists have discovered a parasitic worm in the brain of a mummy. The scientists are
reconstructing the mummy's face. It reminds me of learning to
give facials in beauty school.

In junior year in Home Ec, we had to make flour babies and
carry them everywhere. They were something like Cabbage
Patch dolls—flour-filled stretch knit—and they weighed about
ten pounds, so they felt like babies. We had to take them everywhere all day in school. We couldn't leave them in our lockers
when we went to lunch. In class, the flour babies had to sit on our
desks or in our laps. It was a reminder that a baby was a constant
presence. They don't have sex education in this dumb state, so
this was supposed to teach us the responsibility of having a
baby—something that you couldn't just toss away. I think the
whole idea backfired. Some of the girls really wanted to get
pregnant so the flour babies would come to life. They loved on
their dolls and talked creepy baby talk. The first one I made had

warty ears and a big nose and a blue birthmark on its cheek. I snagged it on my earrings and the flour leaked out, and Mrs. Stevens required me to make another flour baby. I made a prettier one, with red yarn hair and button eyes, and people autographed it, like a cast. Some of the kids got attached to their flour babies, and they'd bring diaper bags to school with them. They'd change their diapers in the middle of class.

Some of the mothers wrote letters to the newspaper. One of them stands out in my memory: "I'm against the use of Flour Babies in the schools on the ground that it makes a mockery of the family. These teenagers are not children and they should not be playing dolls. I have seen some of the horrible things some of the students are doing to the Flour Babies and I can only say it is sick." Mom and I got a laugh out of that letter. She fastened it to the refrigerator and it stayed there till it yellowed and curled. Most people thought it was unnecessary for the boys to have to wag around the flour babies too, but they had to for the course, and after that the requirement was dropped for the boys. At the end of the course, some of us had a baby-basher against the outside wall of the gym. A few of the girls cried then, but I didn't. I ran away from the gym, tracking flour down the sidewalk, out into the soccer field where I ran free—like a young dog after a flying Frisbee, like someone in love.

The Secret
of the Pyramids

Barbara drives slowly from her apartment through the downtown loop to the west side of town. The morning traffic swirls around her, like chocolate in a marble cake. It is already eighty-three degrees, and her cotton skirt is wrinkling beneath her. She hardly slept last night. Her eyes burn.

The marquee at the mall says:

HOT-AIR BALLOONS 5 P.M.

PANTY RIOT, 3 FOR $5 AT GREEN'S

At the store, Glenda has already made the coffee. The employees' lounge is in a corner of the stockroom. Glenda works in Housewares, Barbara in Children's Wear. "Oh, Barbara, I'm such a fool!" Glenda says, greeting her with exaggerated intimacy. "I let Jim borrow fifty dollars, and I know I'll never see it again. Why do I keep doing things like that?"

Barbara pours coffee into a throwaway cup. Glenda's coffee is always strong enough to walk. Barbara stirs in powdered creamer with the spoon Glenda used. "Did you get your air conditioner fixed?" asks Barbara, laying the spoon on the paper towel spread on a yellow plastic tray.

"Hell, no! I thought I was having heat stroke in the middle of the night. The landlord sent two jacklegs over to fix it last Tuesday, and they blew the thing up and haven't been back since." Glenda digs a nail file out of her purse and saws at her nails while Barbara stares at the morning newspaper, which is lying face down on the table. Cautiously, she turns the paper over. On the front page, below the fold, is the headline, spread across three columns:

CITY BUSINESS LEADER KILLED IN HEAD-ON COLLISION

She cannot read the small print of the story because her eyes blur. Then Glenda says, "Oh, wasn't that awful about Bob Morganfield?"

"I know. I heard about it on the news last night."

"Why, I just saw him yesterday in front of his store! I can't believe it."

Barbara folds the newspaper and tucks it under her arm. She sips her coffee. "I have to go to the bathroom," she says.

In the stall, Barbara cries quietly into a wad of toilet paper while other employees come in. After a moment, she realizes they are discussing the accident. A squeaky voice she recognizes from Appliances says, "That's a big shame. I'm not surprised, though. Everybody knows he drank like a fish."

"But he was so nice. Everybody liked him."

"I got these shoes at his store this spring."

"I just love those. I wish I could wear spike heels."

Barbara hears the women drowning their cigarettes, then washing their hands. When they are gone, she emerges and retouches her eyeliner. She wonders if Bob's wife will have him cremated or if some mortician is at this moment slapping makeup on him.

Last night when the ten-o'clock news reported the wreck, she was ready for bed, her night cream on and her paperback novel open. The accident had just occurred, and the announcer seemed shocked. He stumbled over his words. It was at the dangerous curve on Forest Road near the intersection with the belt line, he said. Barbara sat in bed, stunned, long into the sports and weather.

Although she had occasionally seen Bob at the mall, she hadn't been with him since April 12, the night she told him she had to stop seeing him. She was surprised by his reaction. He said he had been thinking along the same lines. "I've considered it from all angles, and I've realized I can't afford a scandal." He spoke in such a businesslike way, she felt he probably fired employees at his shoe store in exactly the same tone. Angrily, she told him she could get along perfectly well without him. She said she was tired of hiding, like an illegal alien. Later, unbelievably, he started a rumor about her—that she had stolen a pair of shoes from his store. When the story got back to her boss, she almost lost her job. She knew Bob started the rumor because he couldn't bear to be rejected, and she yelled furiously at him on the telephone. She knew the words of their quarrel by heart. She thought she hated him, but hearing he was dead confused her. In death, debts are canceled, quarrels resolved. Everyone loves you when you're dead, she thought.

She dragged on shorts and a T-shirt and left the TV on. She got in her car. She didn't know where she was going. The street lights arced out of the darkness like long-necked ghosts. The belt line was spooky. Paducah's first mall, now called the "price-down mall," seemed forlorn, like an abandoned movie set. A squealing pickup ripped out of the parking lot beside a neon-lit bar. She turned onto Forest Road, slowing down on the curve. There was no clue that there had been an accident so recently. Barbara kept remembering the startled announcer, reading from the paper handed to him. The TV report might not have been true, she told herself. Thomas Dewey was elected president, but not really. Kitty Kallen, a singer from the fifties Barbara's mother had been fond of, was reported dead on the TV news once, but it wasn't so.

She parked on the shoulder beyond the curve and sat there as occasional cars, their brights on, passed. She realized the radio had been playing since she got in the car. The snatches of songs were like pieces of broken, discarded furniture. She got out and crossed Forest Road. On the other side was a scattering of glass.

In the headlights of an approaching car, the glass sparkled like the rhinestones Barbara had glued onto her denim jacket that afternoon.

Barbara rings up a six-pack of children's socks, six colors for $2.99. The store is having a red-tag sale, and she stays busy all morning. After arguing with each other about the size, an aged couple buys an Easter dress at half price for their great-granddaughter. "She'll grow into it," the woman assures the man. "Well, all right," he says reluctantly, plowing into his back pocket for his billfold. The woman says to Barbara, "I should have left him out in the car."

At one o'clock, Barbara goes out to get a taco salad for her boss, Sue Ann Goodman, but she gets nothing for herself. Back in the lounge, she drinks more bitter coffee. A stockboy who has been taking karate lessons playfully knocks a pair of *nunchakus* at her.

"Hey, who gave you them black eyes?" he asks.

"It's a new style," she says, taking her compact from her purse. Her makeup is running again.

At one-thirty, her friend Kay pokes her head into the lounge. "Are you O.K., Barb?"

Barbara nods. Kay is the only person who knows about Barbara's affair with Bob. Last night, Kay stayed up with Barbara until three. Barbara called her after leaving the accident site.

"Do you want to go to the funeral home this evening?" Kay asks.

"Oh, I better not."

"We'll just sign the register and pay our respects."

"If I show up, Denise will know it was me he was fooling around with." Barbara glances around cautiously to see if anyone might overhear.

Kay touches Barbara's arm. "But you have to work out your grief somehow, Barbara."

"Grief?" Barbara says. "Is that what it is? Yesterday I hated him, and today I feel—I don't know what. I feel awful. If only we hadn't parted on bad terms—"

Sue Ann rushes in then, brandishing an armload of jogging

outfits. Kay gives Barbara's hand a quick, affectionate pat. "I'll call you after work," she says.

Barbara has occasionally seen Bob's wife, Denise, at the store. One day in early May, after she broke up with Bob, Barbara waited on Denise, who was yanking at girls' jeans on a rack. Denise was already tanned from playing golf, her skin leathery like a turtle's. She wore white leather sneakers with pom-pom socks and a cotton crew-neck pullover with a plain gold circle pin. Her wraparound skirt was printed with roosters, like something from the children's department. In that outfit she seemed timeless, without complication.

Denise said, "Isn't it a shame the way blue jeans fall apart nowadays? It's because they're not made in the U.S.A. anymore."

More than once, Barbara has driven by the Morganfield house. "Imagine cleaning it," Kay said when they went past together one evening on their way out to eat. The house had two garages and a sloping, vacant lawn with grass as plush as the lining of a silverware box. Denise and Bob had two children and an Irish setter. "Think of the shoes they must have in her closets," Barbara said.

One hot night almost a year ago, Barbara and Bob drove to Cairo, Illinois, to eat. The restaurant, a restored Victorian house, was painted pea green, with black trim. They sat at a corner table on the porch and gazed out on the brown and turbulent Mississippi River. A barge, dark against the setting sun, glided by like a water bug. The hostess knew Bob, but she was discreet, and the waiter was just a teenager. The Bloody Marys had stalks of celery planted in them. The salad bar offered unlimited servings of boiled shrimp, and Bob kept going in for more. Barbara asked for extra lemon wedges. She felt happy, as though she were doing something extraordinary. She was deeply in love with him—and scared at what that meant.

"Did you know this place used to be a whorehouse?" he asked her.

"How do you know?"

He laughed teasingly. "I just know. Every young boy in western Kentucky comes to Cairo sooner or later."

"I always heard about Cairo." She smiled. "When I was little I thought it was where they made Karo syrup."

Bob scooted his drink around on a scalloped pasteboard coaster. "When the Egyptian explorers paddled up the Mississippi in their canoes and discovered this place, it reminded them of their hometown on the Nile River, so they settled here and called it Cairo. And then they started building pyramids."

"No Egyptians ever came up the Mississippi River!" Barbara said, giggling.

"But it's true. Haven't you heard about the pyramids?"

"No. I've seen the Indian mounds, though." The Ancient Buried City was just down the highway from the restaurant.

"This is different. There really were pyramids, but they've fallen down. The weeds have grown up around the ruins and the snakes have taken over. You know how Cleopatra was bitten by a snake? She was Egyptian."

"I saw that movie. Liz Taylor, with black Magic Marker eyes."

"These pyramids weren't high-quality pyramids because it was the wrong kind of rock, so they collapsed." Bob lifted his glass. Chunks of ice flipped out onto the tablecloth and splashed red drops among the scattered shrimp peelings. "But that's what the young boys come to Cairo for—to learn the secret of the pyramids."

Images of secret maps and treasures, hidden away in safe places, came to Barbara's mind. The house they were in would have such hiding places. "What's the secret?" she asked.

He grinned. "It wouldn't be a secret if I told you."

"But I want to know."

"The secret is how to handle women," he said with a grin.

"That's no big secret." Barbara leaned back and studied him. He was tanned a caramel color. He wore a short-sleeved blue cotton shirt, and his pen had leaked slightly into the seam of the pocket.

"You think I'm silly, don't you?" he asked.

"No, I don't. You like to have fun. I like that." She crunched the last of her celery. She said, "But you hide your real self. That's what keeps me interested."

"There you go," he said. "Maybe that's the secret."

The sunset was quick—like a tiddlywink that had been skipped across the river. The waiter lit a candle in a mesh-covered glass. When the food arrived, Bob was on his fourth Bloody Mary. He shoveled out his baked potato as though he were fashioning a canoe from a log. The Egyptians didn't really have canoes, she thought.

"I must be nuts," he said, growing serious. "Sometimes I just don't know what to make out of my life."

"What do you mean?"

"This morning I got to the mall early, and there was nobody there. You could just about roller-skate down the corridors—and I had this happy feeling. I was in the center of the mall, by the fountain, and everything looked so fresh and new, like the whole place was about to bust open like a flower as soon as the stores opened. Then I saw this girl who cashiers at the drugstore coming to work. She had on a yellow dress. Just then I had one of those realizations—one of those moments you know you'll remember all your life?" He tried to snap his fingers, but they were slippery from the shrimp peelings. He said, "I just suddenly knew where I was and who I was and where I'd always be. It felt funny. I hated myself."

"But you should be proud," Barbara said, puzzled. "You have a lot of respect around town. You've worked hard for what you've got."

"But all of a sudden I felt like dropping everything." He paused, as if waiting for a revelation from Barbara, but she didn't know what to say. "What I wanted to do was roller-skate down the mall, and I knew I couldn't get away with that because of my reputation—and it made me terribly depressed."

"That would be fun," she said wistfully, skating-rink music rushing through her head. "But you're right. Nobody would understand."

His voice rose. He said, "Right then, I hated the store. I hated the whole town. Do you know what I mean?"

"Hey, you're doing all right," Barbara said soothingly, reaching for his hand.

"When I was little I wanted to be a cowboy, or a policeman, or a sailor," he said. "It never would have occurred to me to run a shoe store."

The waiter cleared the dishes. The candle flickered out and Bob's face dimmed. He said, "And then standing there this morning, I thought, Who the hell do you think you're kidding? The store has been fantastic. I've been really lucky."

"You can take a lot of credit for that," said Barbara. The waiter slapped dessert menus on the table, but it was too dark to read them.

"That's true," said Bob thoughtfully. "It's knowing when to take chances, when to bring in a new line, knowing how to buy. You have to know how to trust your instincts." He laughed. "I told you I was crazy. Didn't I tell you?"

She laughed, and they clung to each other for a moment in the dark corner of the porch. He had planned to take her on a buying trip to New York that spring, but at the last minute Denise had decided to go with him because she wanted to see *Cats*. Barbara was still disappointed, thinking of all the sights she wanted to see. In New York they could have felt free as teenagers on a date.

On the way home on the lonely, dark highway toward Paducah, he drove badly, hitting curves too fast. He had grown silent. At a four-way stop, she jerked up the parking brake. "I'm going to drive," she said, grabbing his hand from the wheel.

Obediently, he got out of the car and staggered to the passenger side, then turned and threw up into the kudzu-lined ditch. She opened the door for him and he clambered in. "Are you going my way?" he said, pretending to be a hitchhiker. At that moment, for once, she was in charge.

Steadily, Barbara sells socks, shorts, T-shirts, sweatshirts. She is afraid to break her concentration: punching the cash register codes, tearing the sales tags in half, stapling the packages, writing up the charge slips. It is satisfying to roll the credit cards in the machine. The store is so busy that Sue Ann does not touch the taco salad Barbara brought her. The molded tortilla basket sits in the employees' lounge like a grotesque, wilting flower. At four o'clock Barbara sneaks a bite of cold beans and a sliver of tomato. At five-thirty she gathers her things.

The mall is crowded with weekend shoppers and sightseers. It is the only quality mall for more than a hundred miles, and people from the country and the small towns congregate here on the weekend. The farm boys amble along self-consciously, and young couples, dressed alike in denim, cling to each other. Everyone looks dazed. The mall crowd has supermarket eyeballs—something funny Bob said. The last time he took her out to eat, they had to wait for their table, and Bob gave the name "Beach" so the hostess would call out on the microphone, "Beach Party."

Barbara loves the lighting in the mall—the way it is broken by the variegated greenery around the fountain and the rainbow colors of the merchandise in the store windows. The dark flow of pedestrians against the brilliant fluorescence makes her think of that sunset on the Mississippi River last year. Something is always happening; it is never the same, like the churning river. Two new stores have opened recently—menswear and electronics. Barbara and Kay hope to open a crafts boutique here someday. Kay is good at ceramics and Barbara, who has always liked working with her hands, is learning to weave. Opening a store here is not a far-fetched ambition, she keeps insisting to Kay, who is dubious. It just takes a little imagination, Barbara believes. At Bob's shoe store, the children's section is always crammed with posters and enormous stuffed animals. Once he had the old woman who lived in a shoe. The shoe was a cardboard sneaker large enough for children to climb inside. He won an award for that display.

She pauses at his store. It is closed, with a black ribbon on the door. Pink ribbons hung on this door at the grand opening two years ago, when he moved out here from downtown. His employees had a dinner on big-band night at a luxury hotel.

She read about it in the newspaper. That was before she got to know him. Today, reading the news of his death was like reading about the grand opening; in print, he was a distant figure, like a celebrity. As she stands in front of his store, she sees a fat woman in a cowboy hat pass by, then two teenagers in Coca-Cola Classic T-shirts, and a sinister couple in black jackets decorated with dozens of doodads—medallions, charms, buttons with the slogans "CYCLE KILLER" and "WASTE." The woman has brittle reddish hair and a harsh complexion. The man is lean-faced but has a potbelly. Their wrists are wrapped in chains. They look old, but hopeful.

Walking to her car out in the sun, Barbara spots the brightly colored hot-air balloons heading toward the mall—six of them, like gigantic football mums. Once, at his store, Bob gave her a balloon with the store logo on it. He was passing them out to kids that day. He joked around with her in front of the other employees, teasing her about being a kid because she sold children's clothing. The balloon was a private signal, a way to communicate their feelings in public. That day, she thought he was saying he loved her.

At home, she punches on the air conditioning and opens the refrigerator—yogurt, baloney, some chocolate cheesecake Glenda brought to work recently. Glenda's cheesecake is worse than her coffee. Barbara opens a ginger ale and drinks from the can. Her bed is unmade, the sheet and quilt wadded tightly, like the dough ball in her food processor when she makes pie crust.

Kay telephones at six-thirty. "I'll come by and get you and we'll go to the funeral home," she says. "I just got off work and I'm getting in the shower."

"I can't. I forgot I've got a date with Ed Boone. I don't know what else to do but go. I put him off twice before."

"Well! Ed's a sweet person, and he'd do *anything* for you. Like I told you last night, you don't need Bob Morganfield. Sometimes we just have to trust that God knows what's best for us."

"I know." Barbara doesn't know, actually. Kay makes no sense. Barbara says, "If Bob had known he was going to die, I believe he would have apologized to me."

"You can't think like that, Barbara. It doesn't do you any good."

"It just breaks my heart that he missed those balloons today. He would have loved them."

Kay doesn't respond to that. She says, "You go on out with Ed and have a good time. We'll go to the funeral home tomorrow. And, hey, Barbara?"

"What?"

"Don't stay out too late. I know you're dead on your feet."

That evening Barbara is so fatigued Ed Boone can't get her to laugh or talk. She always had to pretend she wasn't having an affair with Bob, and she's afraid if she goes to the funeral home, she will make a scene, embarrassing Denise. It would be a terrible thing to do, but Barbara can imagine what it would be like to go berserk—tearing a wreath of flowers to bits and strewing them everywhere. It would feel good to go running down the street, screaming and tearing her clothes off. She's reminded of that old fad of running nude through public places.

"I'm having a hard time today," she says, when Ed asks about the red-tag sale.

They're driving to the cinema complex. Hot air blasts through the dashboard vents. The big balloons hang pretty in the sky.

"I know just what you mean," Ed says. "Thank God it's Friday."

Ed is the most careful driver she has ever seen. He slows down for the caution light instead of trying to beat the red. He's divorced, with two children. There's a baby seat in the back of the car. He's thirty-four, drives an oversized car, and belongs to a rod-and-gun club.

At the movie, Ed buys her a tub of popcorn, and she takes it absentmindedly. He says, as the light dims, "I hope this movie's good. I heard it was."

"I heard that too."

He clutches her hand. His body is large and cuddly, like the stuffed animals in Bob's store. It occurs to her that if a child died, the mother would be left with the child's ridiculous teddy bear to hug. The air conditioning is freezing, and Ed helps her pull on her denim jacket. The movie is *Peggy Sue Got Married*. It's about a middle-aged woman who goes to her high-school reunion and then finds herself time-traveling back to high school, knowing what she knows now. She tries to invent panty hose and warns people against red dye, but then she seems to forget that she comes from the eighties, and she gets caught up once again in her teenage problems. If Barbara were in that situation, she'd try to change the outcome, but Peggy Sue seems trapped in time, forced to repeat the same mistakes. The best thing in the movie is when Peggy Sue gets a chance to see her old grandparents come to life again. Barbara's grandparents died when she was in high school.

"Did you like the movie?" Ed says in the car afterward.

"No. She shouldn't have married the same guy again. She could have changed her whole life and started over."

"But if she had, she wouldn't have had her beautiful children."

"But you don't know what she might have had instead," says Barbara. "Did you like the movie?"

"Yeah. I thought it was great." He eases out of the parking lot. Barbara has the impression that he is steering a cabin cruiser. He says, "If I had it to do over again, there are some things I might consider changing—but if it came right down to it, I don't think I'd change a thing."

The next morning Barbara picks up Kay and they drive downtown. The funeral home is a sprawling white stucco building with black limousines crowded around like dung beetles. In a pastel parlor filled with soberly dressed strangers, Barbara and Kay creep through the crowd, toward Bob's body lying in the casket like a store display. Barbara doesn't see Denise, but she recognizes the children, a girl and a boy of about eight and ten. Their hair shimmers like the interiors of oyster shells. Barbara remembers how Bob loved raw oysters. The flowers are arranged around his body protectively in a small parlor, and the crowd spills over into an adjoining room. Barbara stares but doesn't feel tears coming. She doesn't recognize him—the wax-fruit complexion, the arched eyebrows, the glossy hair, the crude set of his jaw.

"They did a good job," a man says to a woman Barbara figures out is Bob's mother. She's wearing burgundy lipstick and ropes of pearls and a hat with a sharp-pointed feather.

"At first Denise wanted to have a closed casket," the woman says. "But then they told her they could fix him up like new, and we're glad they went ahead, because we knew everybody would want to see him."

"He looks real nice," the man's wife says, grasping Bob's mother's hand. "You can't tell a thing. He looks like he's taking a nap."

"Or passed out drunk," Barbara whispers to Kay.

Barbara fingers a long white ribbon on a wreath. The message on the ribbon, in glitter writing, says "With Sympathy from BAWK—the Business Association of West Kentucky." A man in the corridor laughs loudly. A siren screams outside. She shouldn't have worn the yellow jumpsuit, but it was something Bob loved on her.

They sign the guest register. In a week or so, they will receive little printed thank-you notes, provided by the funeral home, signed "Mrs. Robert (Denise) Morganfield."

Roaming her apartment, Barbara locates his traces. The balloon from his store. A snapshot taken by a tourist of the two of them at a restaurant in Carbondale, Illinois. A matchbook from the Holiday Inn in Cape Girardeau, Missouri. A bar of soap from the Marriott in Nashville. A shower cap, still sealed in its plastic envelope, from a Best Western somewhere in Tennessee. A sample of his handwriting on a napkin. Some slingback heels she never liked that he gave her from his store. Methodically, she collects all these items in a plastic bag from work. She takes them out to the car, gets in, and snaps her harness. She points the key at the ignition.

Then she remembers the clock. She gets out of the car, climbs the stairs again, and unlocks her door. For her birthday last year, as a gag, he gave her a pink Elvis Presley clock shaped like a guitar. Each of the twelve letters of Elvis's name represents a number on the clock. She takes the clock down from the wall and examines it. When Bob gave it to her, she opened the box and burst out laughing. They fell into each other's arms, laughter turning to passion. That's the way she wants to remember him. It is an absurd clock, but a good one. It runs on a quartz battery, and it keeps time perfectly. She replaces the clock on its hook, and as she tilts it into position, Elvis's figure at the center seems to gyrate suggestively. The hands of the clock read L-V, ten past three.

Piano Fingers

*A*fter "The Equalizer," the weather news is on, and Dean switches off the program when the radar display appears. He's tired but not sleepy. He's sick of the garbage on TV. For some time, he has been thinking about an idea for a television series, a show about an amateur detective, an ordinary guy who drives a delivery van. Each week he goes to a different house and finds himself caught up in solving some fascinating crime: cocaine rings, kidnapped heiresses. Dean has a wonderful name for his detective: Ballinger. It's a glamorous name, yet the detective is a down-to-earth guy people can relate to. His van is flashy—bright red with purple lettering. All of the stories Dean imagines take place in California.

In bed, he watches his wife reading. Nancy zooms through a new novel from the library almost every evening. The covers of the books picture sexy women sprawling in the clutches of virile, dark-haired men. The women wear long, low-cut dresses, with their breasts bulging out the tops. Nancy calls the books "Bodice Busters," and for a long time Dean thought that was a brand name. Nancy is wittier than he gives her credit for.

With a peep of satisfaction, she finishes the last page and shuts the book, almost in a single motion. She reads books the way she irons clothes—snappy and efficient. She zips the iron up and down sleeves, across cuffs and around collars, in fluid movements.

"Did it have a happy ending?" he asks as she sets the book on her bedside table and flips off the light. Another one of her combination moves.

"If it didn't, I'd slam it up against the wall," she says.

In the dark, testing his powers of observation, he tries to picture her at the moment she turned out the light. What is she wearing? Her blue gown with the white trim, he thinks, the one she wears with the T-shirt underneath. She probably has on leg warmers, the pink fuzzy ones. He reaches his foot across the bed and runs his toes up and down her leg warmers. They're trying to save money on the oil bill by burning wood, and the house is always too cold for her.

"I read in the paper where women who read those books have better sex lives than anybody," she says as she rolls over to him.

"Is that true?" He holds her close, feeling her warm layers.

"You better believe it."

When Dean graduated from high school, he and Nancy already had a baby on the way. His father wanted him to go into the Army, to learn a trade, but Nancy didn't want to live at some strange military post with a new baby. She needed her mother at a time like that, she insisted. They had a difficult time starting out on Dean's wages at the filling station where he had worked throughout high school. Later, he worked at a garage and then for a while at the tire plant, where he made good money (nine dollars an hour). When Nancy started working, they were able to buy a two-bedroom brick ranch. The tire plant laid off half its force two years ago, and Dean started working as assistant manager at the downtown drugstore on the courthouse square. It was less money, but Nancy said she was glad, because the machinery at the tire plant was dangerous. "I was a nervous wreck," she told him. "But I wasn't going to get hurt," Dean insisted. "I knew what I was doing." The harsh rubber fumes at the tire plant burned his eyes, though, and the drugstore is more pleasant. Mr. Palmer, the owner of the drugstore, has treated Dean well, giving him a generous discount and free ice cream from the soda fountain for the kids. Medical advice from the pharmacist has saved them countless doctor bills. But before long, the drugstore will close, as soon as Mr. Palmer can sell it, and Dean will have to find a new job.

When he was laid off from the tire plant, Dean drew enough unemployment to keep up his house payments, but that may not be the case now. Somehow he believes everything will be O.K., because things have worked out in the past, but he can feel Nancy's dread, and he knows she expects more of him than he has been able to give. "I'm not asking for the moon," she is fond of saying. He takes that as a hint for him to be a better provider. Dean has a lot of ideas—including training to be an electrician, or a real estate agent, or even a travel agent—but she just laughs at some of his notions. He can never seem to do what's expected of him. It's as though he has a built-in mechanism that steers him in another direction. In school, his grades weren't great. He was intelligent but easily diverted. If he had to write a report on worms for biology, he'd look up worms in the encyclopedia but then get distracted by something more interesting, like wombats. Even now, his mother nags him about what he is going to do with his life, and his dad keeps saying Dean should have gone into the Army. Dean is only twenty-six, and people still call him a kid. But he feels suspended somewhere between childhood and old age, not knowing which direction he is facing.

"My head feels like a basketball," Mr. Palmer says, barging into the back of the drugstore, where Dean is filling out order forms for baby products. "I'm getting out of this goddamn climate." He grabs Dean's clipboard. "Baby formula. Shoot. They can buy that by the case out at Super X for twenty percent less than what I have to charge."

Mr. Palmer takes a bottle, seemingly at random, from a medicine shelf and pops a pill into his mouth. He says, "My head commenced to swell in the middle of the night and I had to set up to breathe. I'm going to move to Florida and junk this whole goddamn mess before I go broke." He stalks out the door. This is his regular morning appearance. No one dares ask him what is going on with the sale of the store.

"He's got a burr up his tail," Dean says to Lexie Thomas, the cashier. Lexie is applying eye makeup. She always uses testers from the cosmetics counter, and her face changes colors like swirls of oil in a puddle.

"I'm sure Mrs. Palmer's a dope addict," Lexie says, smudging her eyeliner with a sponge-tipped pencil. "I know for a fact he takes her gobs of Valium from the store."

"If they sell the store, I wonder where she'll get her drugs."

"Well, I ain't going to worry about it none," Lexie says. "I'm sure there's plenty down in Florida."

Dean gazes at a palette of eye shadows. Lexie's makeup always makes him sad. She's prettier without it. She has delicate freckles, unusual with dark hair. In high school, a couple of years ago, she got kicked off the girls' softball team for throwing too many bean balls.

As a courtesy, the drugstore delivers orders to some of its regular customers and to new members of the community. In the store car, Dean goes out to make a few deliveries—kidney medicine for Mrs. Aubrey on Lincoln Street, special-ordered horehound drops and some toiletries for Mr. Palmer's uncle, and a case of Diet Pepsi and a prescription that Dean suspects is a container of birth-control pills for an unfamiliar name in the Birch Hills subdivision. Making deliveries is his favorite part of the job. He likes driving around town, noticing all the changes— new paint jobs, new additions, an out-of-state car in someone's driveway, a business relocating. Behind the wheel today, he speculates about what might become of the store—a women's shop, maybe, or an office, lined with computers. If Dean took over the store, he would open an ice-cream parlor, with a jukebox and a place to dance to old sixties records. He'd call it Oldies but Goodies and decorate the walls with album covers. Sunday night would be Motown night, with two sundaes for the price of one. He would get a waffle iron and make some of those huge handcrafted crater cones like the kids got at the fair. He could even have curb service and send Jason and Jennifer out with trays. Waiting at a stoplight, Dean pictures Mrs. Palmer in an episode of

"Miami Vice." In her finger waves and wedgies, she would be hilarious, as out of place as a dog in church.

When Dean drops off the kidney medicine, a maid at the door says Mrs. Aubrey is just home from the hospital. Dean imagines the old woman dead in her bed. Suspicion is placed on Ballinger, who had access to the medicine. It would be like the Tylenol murders.

Dean drives on to the next place on his list. The Birch Hills subdivision—no birches, no hills—is a new development of medium-priced houses on the east edge of town. Dean and Nancy looked at lots here a few years ago, when it was a corn-field, but they were too expensive. Dean recalls that day. They went to the Sunday-afternoon open house at the single finished house in the development. That night Nancy wasn't able to sleep. She kept imagining dream-house floor plans. But Dean could see only the harvested cornfield, so bare and clean it would be a shame to disturb it.

"You must be the drugstore," says the woman at the door. She has on a sweater with a large parrot appliquéd on the front and tight pants, the stretchy kind with straps under the feet. Dean knows they have straps under the feet because they are a new fashion. Nancy bought a pair for herself and one for Jennifer. He used Jennifer's for a slingshot one day and made her angry.

"I have to find my checkbook," the woman says. She scurries away, moving like Dean's brother's ferret, slinky and fast. Dean stands in the kitchen. It is shiny and modern, something Nancy would drool over. The appliances are almond, and the floor is orange and tan blocks of flowerlike designs.

"Did you see a cat outside?" the woman asks when she returns.

"No, I didn't notice one, ma'am."

She laughs. "Everybody around here says 'ma'am.' And 'sir.' I think that's great." After examining the bill, she starts scribbling in her checkbook. "I just moved down here last summer. I teach second grade at the elementary school."

"My little girl's in the third grade."

"What's her name?"

"Jennifer. Jennifer Harris."

"How many Jennifers are in her class?"

"Three."

"I've got four Jennifers in my class."

He glances at the check she hands him. Stephanie R. Morgan. She has large teeth, a wide face, with pale eyebrows and a gaunt nose. She's vaguely pretty, but she has an odd figure—a small waist with disproportionately large hips, as though she were wearing a bustle. He wonders if she wears a T-shirt under her nightgown. Probably not. The heat in her house is even and pleasant. Electric heat, he is sure.

He says, "Where did you move here from? You've got a brogue."

"Michigan. I thought I told you. Michigan." Her smile is attractive, activating a set of dimples.

"Do you like it down here?"

"Oh, yes. The people are friendly, but there are some things that are just *different*. I guess I'll get used to it, though."

"What things?"

She relaxes against the door facing, her checkbook poised level with her tilted chin. "Well, the day I moved in, it was about ninety degrees. About six o'clock, I was dying for a beer, and I didn't have any food either, so I went to the supermarket. I couldn't find the beer, so I asked the stock boy, 'Where's the beer?' and he said to me, 'This county's dry.' I couldn't figure out why he was talking about the weather instead of showing me the beer!" Stephanie laughs. She speaks dramatically, waving her arms, with the parrot jumping around on her chest. "I was shocked," she says.

"I guess it takes a while to get used to our ways." He shifts his weight uncomfortably. "People don't approve of drinking around here."

"But everybody drinks anyway, I've noticed," she says with a sarcastic laugh.

"Well, yes, that's true, I guess." Dean feels embarrassed.

"Nice to meet you," she says as he opens the door to leave. "But I didn't catch your name."

"Dean. Dean Harris."

"Nice to know you, Dean." Her hair plunges over her brow, and she swishes it back. "Oh, there's my cat. Come here, Lonesome," she says, rushing out to pick up the cat. The long-haired white cat, with its stony stare, is more like Dean's image of a Northerner than Stephanie is.

After work Dean picks up Jennifer at her piano lesson. She takes lessons from Mrs. Addison, on Spring Street. He waits in his car—not the store car—for Jennifer to finish. The car heater is warm and cozy, and the radio is playing a sixteen-song music marathon. The sky is getting dark, and leaves are blowing off the trees. Wet leaves swirl down from a large maple in Mrs. Addison's yard. The sound of wet leaves against the car on a late-autumn day makes him feel nostalgia for something, he can't remember what. He realizes that there are such moments, such sensations, that are maybe not memory but just things happening now, things that come into focus suddenly and can be either happy or sad. The flutter of wet leaves in the gathering dark is a moment to notice, he thinks, like the sounds on the radio, the glowing light that just switched on in Mrs. Addison's upstairs. Probably Jennifer is going to the bathroom before she leaves.

"Hi, sweetpea," he says when Jennifer flings open the car door.

"She gave me some new music," Jennifer says, handing him a piece of sheet music—"The Fox and the Bee."

"She didn't *give* it to you," says Dean, seeing the price on the cover—two dollars and twenty-five cents.

"Can we stop at the grocery?" Jennifer asks as they drive away.

"What for?"

"I need a new notebook for school."

"We just got you a new notebook the other day."

"I want another one. I don't like that one we got."

"Why not?"

"The lines are too wide. They're baby lines." She unzips her book pack and shows him the notebook. It is thick, with at least a hundred pages.

"You'll have to use that one up first. When I was little, I didn't get to waste paper that way."

Jennifer frowns and crams the notebook into her pack. She's like Nancy, the way she whips objects around. Dean says to his daughter, "Do you know a teacher at school named Miss Morgan?"

"Oh, yeah, she's new. What do you want to know for?"

"Oh, nothing. I delivered some stuff to her house today." It hadn't occurred to Dean to wonder why the woman was home during the day. Playing hooky? He feels sorry for the schoolteacher. Being unmarried in such a small town must be depressing. What can she do except go to the singles mixers at the Methodist church? He wonders what those birth-control pills mean. Maybe she has a boyfriend back in Michigan. Dean is sure she was coming on to him. Or maybe Northerners really are genuinely friendly. But he has always heard how rude they are.

Jennifer plays with the radio dial, switching to an AM Top 40 station. Dean says, "She had a nice big cat you'd like."

"What's his name?"

"Lonesome," says Dean.

"Lonesome," repeats Jennifer. "That's how I feel. Lonesome."

"Oh, come on, Jennifer. You don't either."

Later, when he turns onto their street, Dean says, "Mom's already home." Wood smoke is puffing out of their chimney. The smoke drifts across the neighborhood and disappears. That's the way Dean sees himself when he leaves home in the morning to go out into the world.

In the kitchen, Nancy says, "My feet hurt so bad today at work I couldn't stand it any longer. My shoes were killing me. Finally, I had to sneak right out the door and down to the Shoe Village and get this pair of flats to last out the day. Do you like them?" The shoes are in their box, and she is already in her house shoes.

"They're nice," he says. They are tan, with bows.

"It's crazy to wear high heels when you have to stand up all day," she says, replacing the shoes in the box. "I like high heels better, though. They make me feel better about myself."

Dean snatches up the shoes and holds them like a walkie-talkie—one against his ear, the other in front of his mouth. "Hello?" he says. "Testing."

"They were on sale," she says defensively.

After supper, Nancy, wearing her fleece-lined vest, settles on the couch to read. "Get your lessons, Jennifer, and stop watching TV," she says.

"Daddy's watching it."

"You don't have to. I thought I was setting a good example, reading a book." Nancy flips a page, reading as she talks.

Jason tears into the room, skidding on a throw rug and sliding on scraps of wood into the woodpile. He has an F-18 fighter jet in his hand. The living room doubles as an aircraft carrier.

"What did I say about getting in that bathtub, Jason?" Nancy says, not even looking up from her book.

"I'm going to," says Jason. "I have to finish my landings. I have thirty-nine more to go."

"You can't even count to thirty-nine," says Jennifer.

"Dean, are you going to set there and let the kids get away with murder?"

Dean says, "Jason, go get in the bathtub before I have to get me a switch." He trembles with the authority of his voice.

He usually ignores the commercials, but he's deliberately watching this one, about some people having a good time just because they bought a certain kind of breath mint. Probably with the breath mint all their inhibitions will be gone and they can all go jump in some hot tub together—in California. They put anything on TV to make a buck. Dean can imagine ten ideas for TV shows better than this evening's lineup alone. He has been thinking about a new plot for "Ballinger." He sees the schoolteacher's house, her warm orange-and-tan kitchen floor, her sweater with the parrot, her white cat: a perfect setup for an intriguing mystery. Back home, she was suspected of having murdered her lover. She came to this small town and took a new identity just to avoid the talk. She is innocent, but she knows who the real murderer is and he is after her. In the souped-up van, Ballinger rescues her from her pursuer. The van does wheelies around the courthouse square.

Earlier, in the kitchen, Nancy said to Dean, "People tell me things that are important and I can't remember them. I must be getting old." She seemed puzzled, almost forlorn. Dean wasn't sure what she meant.

"Jennifer said she was lonesome," he said.

When he married Nancy, she was slim and flirtatious, with long bangs. They swore they would always be happy together. It's not that they don't love each other as much, Dean realizes, but stuff gets in the way. She is always so busy. She has worked out certain ways she does things—routines and methods. She is often short-tempered with the kids, and she sometimes seems frantic for no reason, despite her peculiar sense of order. On Halloween, recently, while Dean and two little unidentifiable space-movie monsters went trick-or-treating, Nancy was in the bathtub, reading, not answering the door when the neighbor kids came by.

After Jennifer and Jason are in bed, Dean shoves a couple of slender logs onto the fire so that the large log in the stove will burn out faster and he can shut it down. It is very warm in the living room now, and Nancy has removed her vest.

She says, "The guy in this book reminds me of you."

"How?"

"The way you were when I first knew you."

"Was that better or worse than now?"

"Different." She laughs and draws her opened book to her chest as if to catch an overwhelming burst of laughter. "When I first met you, you were the cutest thing in the world. But you didn't know your ass from your elbow!"

"I think I've got that figured out now," he says with a slow smile.

Dean works at his woodpile on Saturday. It is a bright day, and the blue blares through the remaining leaves on the maple tree like something important Dean should notice. He loves to split firewood. He loves everything about creating a woodpile—sectioning logs with a chain saw, setting the pieces on a stump and whacking at them with an ax, then stacking the wood in perfect rows. He can get an effortless, satisfying split in three out of four swings. It is like karate—concentrating energy at one precise point. When he worked at the tire plant, the machinery required such concentration and precision that he was exhausted at the end of his shift. The supervisor would say, "You stop thinking for one second and it's chop suey, Louie." Dean was never sure exactly what would happen if he miscalculated the position of the spinning rubber on the tire-builder, but he wouldn't let his mind wander. He felt like the captain of a ship steering through a storm. The hum and clack of the machinery was hypnotic, and operating it was like being in one of those frantic dreams where you are late for something.

The chain saw has been running rough lately. The muffler may need cleaning. He yanks the cord on the saw, and the sound splits the air. He always tries to use the chain saw early on Saturdays, so the noise won't cause interference in a ball game on the neighbors' TV sets. Instead, he zaps the children's cartoons.

Every weekend Nancy makes a list of things for Dean to do— errands in town, making repairs, cleaning out gutters. She never wants him to help her with housework, although sometimes he volunteers to fold the laundry or do the vacuuming. She says it makes her feel powerless not to be in charge of certain things, but he feels she has drawn a line between them, as though she doesn't want him to meddle in her life. This weekend her list, wadded in his pocket, includes a P.S.—emergency economy measures. That sounds like something from the federal government. No new clothes. No processed food. No eating out. Cancel the newspaper.

He attacks a pile of logs, large chunks of oak his brother dumped in the yard. His brother, a successful carpenter, has a yard large enough for trees to die in. Dean should see Bill about assisting him in his shop, but they've never been able to work together. Bill, who is five years older, is so bossy. Dean can't even saw a two-by-four without Bill telling him how he should have done it. Dean sets the chain saw, still running, on the ground and works a log loose from the pile. He hoists it onto the sawbuck and picks up the chain saw. But the chain is loose, so he turns the saw off and tightens it. He jerks the cord again and zeros in on the cut, working methodically. Lost in the noise, which turns into the cheering section at a ball game, Dean saws on, log after log, and when Nancy and the kids come home with the groceries and new library books, he doesn't hear them turn in the driveway behind him.

On Tuesday, the radio predicts snow flurries, with the low tonight in the thirties. Dean picks up Jennifer at Mrs. Addison's and goes inside to pay. Piano lessons are on Nancy's list of economy measures, but when Mrs. Addison praises Jennifer's progress and says she has long piano fingers, Dean cannot bring himself to cancel the lessons. Piano fingers mean a God-given talent, like being able to draw or sing. In the car, he takes Jennifer's hand. "I want to see them piano fingers," he says admiringly.

She slides off her glove and holds out her hand for him to see. "Mrs. Addison's acting a little funny," says Jennifer.

Her hand is growing slender, with smooth, hard fingernails. "What did Mrs. Addison do?" he murmurs.

"She played this song, and her hands jumped up and down like those little puppies Grandma had."

"Springers."

"I don't know. They just bounced up and down, like that was part of the song. It was funny." Jennifer laughs as she talks.

"I wish I'd seen it," Dean says.

"I'll get her to do it for you next time if you promise not to giggle."

"Of course I won't giggle. I bet *you* giggled."

"No, I didn't!" Jennifer loses control then, giggling until her face is red, and Dean laughs with her.

After they stop laughing, he drives out to his brother's and tells Jennifer to sit in the car while he talks business with Uncle Bill.

"I always have to wait in the car," she protests.

"Well, I wait in the car for you at Mrs. Addison's. Now, I won't be long."

Part of the truth is that he doesn't want Jennifer to play with Bill's ferret. He's afraid it might bite her beautiful fingers.

Bill is custom-building a bathroom vanity in the shop attached to the side of his house. His wife hasn't come home from work yet. The shop is cold, and Dean keeps his gloves on, declining Bill's offer of a beer. Bill knows very well that Dean never drinks. Dean comes right to the point and asks to borrow three hundred dollars for a real-estate investment seminar—a whole weekend at a big hotel. He shows Bill a pamphlet about it.

"They won't take a charge card, and I can't cash in my CD till February," Dean says. "I figured I'd take about half the CD and put it into this real estate. In seven years you can triple your investment."

Bill barely glances at the pamphlet. Like a magician, he whips out a rag and rubs the dust off the hunk of chipboard he has been sawing. He shakes his head skeptically. "I smell a rat," he says.

"Well, I know a guy who comes in the drugstore, and he went to one of these seminars and said it was real helpful."

Bill unties his tool apron. He examines all the pockets and hangs the apron on a nail. Out of the corner of his eye, Dean sees the ferret glide by and disappear behind some paint cans. Bill says, "Why are these people holding this seminar? Why ain't they out there getting rich on real-estate investments themselves? Why do they want you in on it?"

The ferret pokes his nose above a can. He resembles a hairy snake. The ferret's name is Crapola.

"Real estate's not moving around here," Bill is saying.

"Forget it," says Dean.

"I say this for your own good, Dean," says Bill. "I just happen to know that's a racket. I saw it on '20/20.' It's not illegal, but you know why they ain't out there hustling real estate if that's the way to get rich? It's because they're getting rich running these weekends."

"I said forget it." Dean backs toward the door.

"Don't give up so easy, Dean," says Bill. "You always give up. I'll help you out when you need it. I just don't want to see you spend three hundred dollars on something you'll be sorry for."

"So what if it's a rip-off?" Dean blurts out. "Why can't I be the judge of that? Nobody ever thinks I can do something on my own."

"I can't see throwing good money away," Bill says.

Dean worries at the zipper on his jacket, sliding it up and down. "It's not just me you don't have confidence in," he says. "You're just like everybody around here—scared to do anything risky. They won't go outside if it's raining, afraid they'll get their feet wet. I'm sick and tired of that attitude. It's stupid."

"No, you're wrong," Bill says. "Some people don't have sense enough to get in out of the rain."

"You're full of crapola!" Dean shouts as he charges out the door. He yanks down the earflaps on his cap.

After his outburst, Dean feels the way Ballinger feels when he has wrapped up the case. Ballinger leaves the victim's house, gratified that he has been able to solve the mystery. He modestly calls it "helping out." He always manages to turn up the key piece of evidence the authorities have missed; it's usually something subtle: a pattern in the floor tiles that's repeated in the victim's shirt; a clue in the refrigerator; or just the way a man unties his tool apron and inspects the pockets—as if he's afraid of leaving incriminating evidence. Quick cut to the company where Ballinger works. The employees are joking around, celebrating Ballinger's victory. The receptionist has brought a cake with "Way to Go!" written on the top. They tease Ballinger about his habit of pulling down his earflaps as he leaves the scene. It's not cold in California, Dean reminds himself. More cuts: Bill watching Dean from the window, Jennifer looking at him walk down the flagstone path from Bill's shop. They see the spring in his step, his air of confidence. Nancy will be thrilled that Dean finally told off his brother. She often says, "Why is it the most obnoxious people have the most money?"

"You weren't gone long," says Jennifer. "I didn't get cold. I didn't even get bored."

Dean sits at the wheel a moment before starting the car. It is turning colder. It is maybe ten degrees colder than it was an hour ago. A cinnamon-colored Oldsmobile pulls into the driveway next to Bill's house. There's a plastic stork in the yard—a new baby at that house. The neighborhood is one of the older subdivisions. A post-office official and a tire-plant manager live across the street; other neighbors run small businesses or work in the downtown stores. Dean knows that on this street in the last couple of years one man, a school-board member, was arrested for molesting a child at the playground; a young woman tried to commit suicide; a child died of leukemia.

Dean doesn't take the direct route home. He drives randomly, up and down streets so familiar he could drive them in his sleep. Downtown, the street lights bleach the sidewalk into a shore of sand. The drugstore is closed, the lights illuminating the window display: a wheelchair, a bedpan, some metal walkers and splatter canes. A funny scene runs through Dean's mind—Mrs. Palmer, just off the bus from Florida, crazed and desperate, breaking the glass door, after drugs. He's glad the drugstore is being sold. Why would he want to work there forever?

"I'm going to buy you a piano," he says to Jennifer as they turn onto Broadway.

"Last week you wouldn't even buy me a notebook," she says with a pout.

He laughs. "You're just like your mom, for the world!" He reaches over and pats her hands—the fuzzy, tender worms of her purple wool gloves. "I'm real proud of you," he says. She shrugs, and he says, "Someday you'll be in a band. Why, I bet you'll go platinum with your very first release."

"I already learned 'The Fox and the Bee.' "

"Good for you! What did I tell you?"

The downtown lights reflect on the dark plate-glass windows of the corner bank. Some of the lights in the window are reflections of reflections, like a kaleidoscope of possibilities for his life. His trouble, he realizes, is that there are too many choices. So many directions are imaginable, it is hard to settle on just one. He's afraid to narrow his options the way most people do. It would mean missing out on almost everything.

Dean tells his daughter, "We can't buy a real piano, but we can buy one of those little portable keyboards that just about fit in your lap."

"Oh, boy, those are neat!" she cries. "A girl at school has one. She brought it to show-and-tell and played 'California Girls.' She wouldn't let anybody else touch it, though."

"If you had one, you wouldn't have to stay late at school to practice your music," Dean says as he turns down the highway leading out to the shopping center.

At the Wal-Mart, Dean steers Jennifer to the electronics department. He has seen the keyboards advertised, and he is fascinated by how simple and small they are. He likes the way so many things are miniaturized these days—concentrated power, like vitamin tablets.

Jennifer, awed, tests several keyboards. She prefers the one with forty-eight keys and some extra sound effects—vibrato, reverberation, and something called cosmic tone. She plays "Minuet," which she says she earned a gold star on. The keyboard sounds surprisingly like a real piano, but it has volume control.

"It hadn't got but three octaves each way," she says.

"Does that make any difference?"

"It's short, is all."

The thing looks like trick false teeth flattened out into a big grin. Jennifer laughs and squeals gleefully at the sounds she is making. Sometimes Dean is so full of love for his children he feels giddy. To steady himself, he stares at a stack of videotapes on a sale table.

"I want to be able to hear you play at home," he says. "I never get to hear you play."

Jennifer frowns. "Is this my Christmas present? 'Cause if it is, I want to wait, 'cause I don't want to not have any presents at Christmas."

"Don't worry, punkinhead," he says, tousling her hair. "Santa Claus knows where we live."

The keyboard is only eighty-nine dollars, and Dean charges it on his credit card. He'll forgo the investment seminar. That was just an idea.

"This little girl can play up a storm. We're talking major talent," Dean brags to the cashier.

"I bet you can really play this thing, can't you, hon?" the woman says, grinning indulgently at Jennifer. "My little nephew's got one and he's just crazy about it."

Outside, Dean helps Jennifer zip up her jacket and find her

gloves. A sporty car careens through the parking lot as though it is being chased. When they reach their car, Dean opens the hatchback and places the package inside. Jennifer wants to open it right away and hold the keyboard in her lap on the way home, but Dean reminds her about her seat belt.

After getting into the car, he says, "When Mommy throws a fit over this, you just stay out of it, sugar. I'll do the explaining. I'll tell her we've got plans. Anybody with your fingers has to have something decent to practice on."

"Traci Malone can play twice as good as me, and she hasn't been taking as long as me. Why do you think I'm so good?"

Dean remembers a poster he saw recently on somebody's wall —one of his customers. It showed a mother and three kids. The mother was saying, "Because I'm the mommy. That's why." So he answers Jennifer now, "Because I'm the daddy. That's why."

He stares at his daughter. The little girl sitting expectantly beside Dean seems like someone he has suddenly dreamed into reality. He can hardly believe his eyes.

"Hey, look," she says, pointing to the windshield.

It is starting to snow: big, beautiful splotches—no two alike.

Bumblebees

*F*rom the porch, Barbara watches her daughter, Allison, photographing Ruth Jones out in the orchard. Allison is home from college for the summer. Barbara cannot hear what they are saying. Ruth is swinging her hands enthusiastically, pointing first to the apricot tree and then to the peach tree, twenty feet away. No doubt Ruth is explaining to Allison her notion that the apricot and the peach cross-pollinate. Barbara doesn't know where Ruth got such an idea. The apricot tree, filled with green fruit, has heart-shaped leaves that twirl in clusters on delicate red stems. Earlier in the year, the tree in bloom resembled pink lace.

Allison focuses the camera on Ruth. Ruth's hand is curled in her apron. Her other hand brushes her face shyly, straightening her glasses. Then she lifts her head and smiles. She looks very young out there among the dwarf trees.

Barbara wonders if Ruth is still disappointed that one of the peach trees, the Belle of Georgia, which Barbara chose, is a freestone. "Clingstones are the best peaches," Ruth said when they planted the trees. It is odd that Ruth had such a definite opinion about old-fashioned clingstones. Barbara agrees that clingstones are better; it was just an accident that she picked Belle of Georgia.

They were impatient about the trees. Goebel Petty, the old man Barbara and Ruth bought the small farm from two years before, let them come and plant the trees before the sale was final. It was already late spring. Barbara chose two varieties of peach trees, the apricot, two McIntoshes, and a damson plum, and Ruth selected a Sweet Melody nectarine, two Redheart plums, and a Priscilla apple. Ruth said she liked the names.

The day they planted the trees was breezy, with a hint of rain—a raw spring day. Mr. Petty watched them from the porch as they prepared the holes with peat moss. When they finished setting the balled-and-burlapped roots into the hard clay, he called out, "Y'all picked a bad place—right in the middle of that field. I had fescue planted there." Later, he said to them, "The wind will come rip-roaring down that hill and blow them trees over."

Barbara could have cried. It had been so long since she had planted things. She had forgotten that Georgia Belles were freestones. She didn't notice the fescue. And she didn't know about the wind then. After they moved in, she heard it rumble over the top of the hill, sounding like a freight train. There were few real hills in this part of Kentucky, but the house was halfway up a small one, at the end of a private road. The wind whipped across the hickory ridge. Barbara later discovered that particular kind of wind in a Wordsworth poem: "subterraneous music, like the noise of bagpipers on distant Highland hills."

Now, as Ruth and Allison reach the porch, Ruth is laughing and Allison is saying, "But they never teach you that in school. They keep it a secret and expect you to find it out for yourself." Allison tosses her hair and Barbara sees that several strands stick to the Vaseline she always has on her lips to keep them from chapping. Allison brushes the hair away.

"Ruth, do you remember what you said that day we planted those trees?" asks Barbara.

"No. What?" Ruth has a lazy, broad smile, like someone who will never lose her good humor—like Amelia Earhart, in one of those photographs of her smiling beside her airplane.

Barbara says, "You said you wondered if we'd last out here together long enough to see those trees bear."

"I reckon we're going to make it, then," Ruth says, her smile fading.

"Y'all are crazy," says Allison, picking a blade of grass from her bare knee. "You could go out and meet some men, but here you are hanging around a remote old farm."

Barbara and Ruth both laugh at the absurdity of the idea. Barbara is still bitter about her divorce, and Ruth is still recovering from the shock of the car accident three years before, when her husband and daughter were killed. Barbara and Ruth, both teachers at the new consolidated county high school, have been rebuilding their lives. Barbara took the initiative, saying Ruth needed the challenge of fixing up an old farmhouse. Together, they were able to afford the place.

"We're not ready for men yet," Ruth says to Allison.

"Maybe in the fall," Barbara says idly.

"Maybe a guy will come waltzing up this road someday and you can fight over him," Allison says.

"I could go for that Tom Selleck on 'Magnum, P.I.,' " Ruth says.

"Maybe he'll come up our road," Barbara says, laughing. She feels good about the summer. Even Allison seems cheerful now. Allison had a fight with her boyfriend at the end of the school year, and she has been moody. Barbara has been worried that having Allison around will be too painful for Ruth, whose daughter, Kimberly, had been Allison's age. Barbara knows that Ruth can't sleep until Allison arrives home safely at night. Allison works evenings at McDonald's, coming home after midnight. The light under Ruth's door vanishes then.

"I never heard of two women buying a farm together," Mr. Petty said when they bought the farm. They ignored him. Their venture was reckless—exactly what they wanted at that time. Barbara was in love with the fields and the hillside of wild apples, and she couldn't wait to have a garden. All her married life she had lived in town, in a space too small for a garden. Once she got the farm, she envisioned perennials, a berry patch, a tall row of nodding, top-heavy sunflowers. She didn't mind the dilapidated condition of the old house. Ruth was so excited about remodeling it that when they first went indoors she didn't really mind the cracked linoleum floors littered with newspapers and Mr. Petty's dirty clothes. She was attracted by the Larkin desk and the upright piano. The barn was filled with Depression-style furniture, which Ruth later refinished, painstakingly brushing the spindles of the chairs to remove the accumulated grime. The house was filthy, and the floor of an upstairs room was covered with dead bumblebees. Later, in the unfinished attic they found broken appliances and some unidentifiable automobile parts. Dirt-dauber nests, like little castles, clung to the rafters.

On the day they planted the fruit trees, they explored the house a second time, reevaluating the work necessary to make the place livable. The old man said apologetically, "Reckon I better get things cleaned up before you move in." As they watched, he opened a closet in the upstairs room with the bumblebees and yanked out a dozen hangers holding forties-style dresses—his mother's dresses. He flung them out the open window. When Barbara and Ruth took possession of the property two weeks later, they discovered that he had apparently burned the dresses in a trash barrel, but almost everything else was just as it had been—even the dead bumblebees littering the floor. Their crisp, dried husks were like a carpet of autumn leaves.

Ruth would not move in until carpenters had installed new plasterboard upstairs to keep bees from entering through the cracks in the walls. In the fall, Barbara and Ruth had storm windows put up, and Barbara caulked the cracks. One day the following spring, Ruth suddenly shrieked and dropped a skillet of grease. Barbara ran to the kitchen. On the windowpane was a black-and-yellow creature with spraddled legs, something like a spider. It was a huge bumblebee, waking up from the winter and sluggishly creeping up the pane. It was trapped between the window and the storm pane. When it started buzzing, Barbara decided to open the window. With a broom, she guided the bee out the door, while Ruth hid upstairs. After that, bees popped up in various windows, and Barbara rescued them. Ruth wouldn't go outdoors bareheaded. She had heard that a sting on the temple could be fatal. Later, when the carpenters came to hang Masonite siding on the exterior of the house, the bees stung them. "Those fellows turned the air blue with their cussing!" Ruth told friends. In the evenings, Barbara and Ruth could hear the wall buzzing, but the sounds gradually died away. One day after the carpenters left, Barbara heard a trapped bird fluttering behind the north wall of the living room, but she did not mention it to Ruth. This summer, Barbara has noticed that the bees have found a nook under the eaves next to the attic. Sometimes they zoom through the garden, like truck drivers on an interstate, on their way to some more exotic blossoms than her functional marigolds, planted to repel insects from the tomatoes.

Barbara's daughter has changed so much at college that having her here this summer is strange—with her cigarettes, her thick novels, her box of dog biscuits that she uses to train the dog. The dog, a skinny stray who appeared at the farm in the spring, prowls through the fields with her. Allison calls him Red, although he is white with brown spots. He scratches his fleas constantly and has licked a place raw on his foreleg. Allison has bandaged the spot with a sanitary napkin and some wide adhesive tape. Allison used to be impatient, but now she will often go out at midday with the dog and sit in the sun and stare for hours at a patch of weeds. Barbara once asked Allison what she was staring at. "I'm just trying to get centered," Allison said with a shrug.

"Don't you think Ruth looks good?" Barbara asks Allison as they are hoeing the garden one morning. Allison has already chopped down two lima bean plants by mistake. "I like to see her spending more time out-of-doors."

"She still seems jittery to me."

"But her color looks good, and her eyes sparkle now."

"I saw her poking in my things."

"Really? I'm surprised." Barbara straightens up and arches her back. She is stiff from stooping. "What on earth did she think she was doing?"

"It made me feel crummy," Allison says.

"But at least she's coming out of her shell. I wish you'd try to be nice to her. Just think how I'd feel if you'd been killed in a wreck."

"If you caught me snooping, you'd knock me in the head."

"Oh, Allison—"

Allison lights a cigarette in the shade of the sumac, at the edge of the runoff stream that feeds into the creek below. She touches a thistle blossom.

"Come and feel how soft this flower is, Mom," she says. "It's not what you'd expect."

Barbara steps into the shade and caresses the thistle flower with her rough hands. It is a purple powder puff, the texture of duck down. Honeybees are crawling on some of the flowers on the stalk.

Allison picks a stalk of dried grass with a crisp beige glob stuck on it. "Here's another one of those funny egg cases," she says. "It's all hatched out. I think it's from a praying mantis. I saw it in my biology book." She laughs. "It looks like a hot dog on a stick."

Every day Allison brings in some treasure: the cracked shell of a freckled sparrow egg, a butterfly wing with yellow dust on it, a cocoon on a twig. She keeps her findings in a cigar box that has odd items glued on the lid: screws, thimbles, washers, pencils, bobbins. The box is spray-painted gold. Allison found it in the attic. Barbara has the feeling that her daughter, deprived of so much of the natural world during her childhood in town, is going through a delayed phase of discovery now, at the same time she is learning about cigarettes and sex.

Now Allison crushes her cigarette into the ground and resumes her hoeing, scooping young growth from the dry dirt. Barbara yanks pigweed from the carrot row. It hasn't rained in two weeks, and the garden is drying up. The lettuce has shot up in gangly stalks, and the radishes went to seed long ago.

Barbara lays down her hoe and begins fastening up one long arm of a tomato plant that has fallen from its stake. "Let me show you how to pinch suckers off a tomato vine," she says to Allison.

"How do you know these things, Mom? Did you take biology?"

"No. I was raised in the country—don't you remember? Here,

watch. Just pinch this little pair of leaves that's peeping up from where it forks. If you pinch that out, then there will be more tomatoes. Don't ask me why."

"Why?" says Allison.

In her garden diary, Barbara writes, "Thistles in bloom. Allison finds praying mantis egg carton." It is midmorning, and the three of them are having Cokes on the porch. Ruth is working on quilt pieces, sewing diamonds together to make stars. Her hands are prematurely wrinkled. "I have old-people hands and feet," she once told Barbara merrily. Ruth's face doesn't match. Even at forty, she has a young woman's face.

A moment ago, Allison said something to Ruth about her daughter and husband, and Ruth, after pausing to knot a thread and break it with her teeth, says now, "The reason I don't have their pictures scattered around the house is I overdid it at first. I couldn't read a book without using an old school picture of Kimberly for a bookmark. I had her pictures everywhere. I didn't have many pictures of him, but I had lots of her. Then one day I realized that I knew the faces in the pictures better than I knew my memories of their faces. It was like the pictures had replaced them. And pictures lie. So I put away the pictures, hoping my memories would come back to me."

"Has it worked?"

"A little bit, yes. Sometimes I'll wake up in the morning and her face will come to me for a second, and it's so vivid and true. A moment like that is better than seeing the pictures all the time. I'm thinking the memory will get clearer and clearer if I just let it come." Ruth threads her needle in one purposeful jab and draws the ends of the thread together, twisting them into a knot. "I was at my sister's in Nashville that night and we stayed out late and they couldn't get in touch with us. I can't forgive myself for that."

"You couldn't help it, Ruth," Barbara says impatiently. Ruth has told the story so many times Barbara knows it by heart. Allison has heard it, too.

As Ruth tells about the accident, Allison keeps her book open, her hand on the dog. She is reading *Zen and the Art of Motorcycle Maintenance*. It isn't just about motorcycles, she has told them.

Her needle working swiftly, Ruth says, "It was still daylight, and they had pulled up to the stop sign and then started to cross the intersection when a pickup truck carrying a load of turnips rammed into them. He didn't stop and he just ran into them. There were turnips everywhere. Richard was taking Kimberly to baton practice—she was a third-place twirler at the state championships the year before." Ruth smooths out the star she has completed and creases open the seams carefully with her thumbnail. "He died instantly, but she just lingered on for a week, in a coma. I talked to that child till I was blue in the face. I read stories to her. They kept saying she never heard a word, but I had to do it anyway. She might have heard. They said there wasn't any hope." Ruth's voice rises. "When Princess Grace died and they turned off her machines? They never should have done that, because there might have been a miracle. You can't dismiss the possibility of miracles. And medical science doesn't know everything. For months I had dreams about those turnips, and I never even saw them! I wasn't there. But those turnips are clearer in my mind than my own child's face."

The mail carrier chugs up the hill in his jeep. Allison stays on the porch, shaded by the volunteer peach tree that sprang up at the corner of the porch—probably grown from a seed somebody spit out once—until the jeep is gone. Then she dashes down to the mailbox.

"Didn't you hear from your boyfriend, hon?" Ruth asks when Allison returns.

"No." She has a circular and a sporting-goods catalogue, with guns and dogs on the front. She drops the mail on the table and plops down in the porch swing.

"Why don't you write him a letter?" Ruth asks.

"I wrote him once and he didn't answer. He told me he'd write me."

"Maybe he's busy working," Ruth says kindly. "If he's working construction, then he's out in the hot sun all day and he probably doesn't feel like writing a letter. Time flies in the summer." Ruth fans herself with the circular. "He's not the only fish in the sea, though, Allison. Plenty of boys out there can see what a pretty girl you are. The sweetest girl!" She pats Allison's knee.

Barbara sees the three of them, on the porch on that hillside, as though they are in a painting: Allison in shorts, her shins scratched by stubble in the field, smoking defiantly with a vacant gaze on her face and one hand on the head of the dog (the dog, panting and grinning, its spots the color of ruined meat); Ruth in the center of the arrangement, her hair falling from its bobby pins, saying something absurdly cheerful about something she thinks is beautiful, such as a family picture in a magazine; and Barbara a little off to the side, her rough hands showing dirt under the fingernails, and her coarse hair creeping out from under the feed cap she wears. (Her hair won't hold curl, because she perspires so much out in the sun.) Barbara sees herself in her garden, standing against her hoe handle like a scarecrow at the mercy of the breezes that barrel over the ridge.

In the afternoon, Barbara and Ruth are working a side dressing of compost into the soil around the fruit trees. The ground is so hard that Barbara has to chop at the dirt. The apricot is the only tree in the orchard with fruit, and some of the apricots are beginning to blush with yellow. But the apple leaves are turning brown. Caterpillars have shrouded themselves in the outermost leaves and metamorphosed already into moths.

Ruth says, "Imagine a truckload of apricots. It almost seems funny that it would be turnips. You might think of apples or watermelons. You see trucks of watermelons all the time, and sometimes you hear about them rolling all over the highway when there's a wreck. But turnips!" She picks up her shovel and plunges it into the ground. "God was being original," she says.

"The nectarine tree looks puny," Barbara says abruptly. "I had my doubts about growing nectarines."

"That man that ran into them in his turnip truck? They said he didn't look. He just plowed right into them. The police swore he hadn't been drinking, but I believe he was on dope. I bet you anything—"

Suddenly screams waft up from the house. It is Allison shriek-
ing. Barbara rushes down the path and sees her daughter in front
of the house shaking her head wildly. Then Allison starts running, circling the house, pulling at her hair, following her own
voice around the house. Her hair was in ponytail holders, but
when she reappears it is falling down and she is snatching the
bands out of her hair. As she disappears around a corner again,
Barbara yells, "Mash it, Allison! Mash that bee against your
head!"

Allison slams to a stop in front of the porch as Barbara catches
her. In a second Barbara smacks the bumblebee against the back
of her daughter's head.

"He was mad at me," sobs Allison. "He was chasing me."

"It's that perfume you've got on," says Barbara, searching
through Allison's hair.

"It's just bath oil. Oh, my head's stung all over!"

"Be still."

Barbara grabs one of Allison's cigarettes from the package in
her shirt pocket. She pushes Allison up onto the porch, where she
sits down, trembling, in the wicker rocker. Barbara tears the paper
of the cigarette and makes a paste out of tobacco shreds and spit
in the palm of her hand. She rubs the paste carefully into the red
spots on Allison's scalp.

"That will take the sting out," she says. "Now just relax."

"Oh, it hurts," says Allison, cradling her head in her hands.

"It won't last," Barbara says soothingly, pulling her daughter
close, stroking her hair. "There, now."

"What's wrong with Allison?" asks Ruth, appearing from behind the lilac bush as though she has been hiding there, observ-
ing the scene. Barbara keeps holding Allison, kissing Allison's
hair, watching the pain on Ruth's face.

After that, Ruth refuses to wear her glasses outdoors, because the
tiny gold R decorating the outer corner of the left lens makes her
think a bee is trying to get at her eye. But now the bees are hiding
from the rain. For two days, it has been raining steadily, without
storming. It rarely rains like this, and Barbara's garden is drowning. In the drizzle, she straightens the Kentucky Wonder vines,

training them up their poles. The peppers and peas are turning yellow, and the leaves of the lima beans are bug-eaten. The weeds are shooting up, impossible to hoe out in the mud. The sunflowers bend and break.

With the three of them cooped up, trying to stay out of each other's way, Barbara feels that the strings holding them together are both taut and fragile, like the tiny tendrils on English-pea vines, which grasp at the first thing handy. She's restless, and for the first time in a long while she longs for the company of a man, a stranger with sexy eyes and good-smelling aftershave. The rain brings out nasty smells in the old house. Despite their work on the place, years of filth are ingrained in it. Dust still settles on everything. Ruth discovers a white mold that has crept over the encyclopedia. "An outer-space invasion," Allison says gleefully. "It's going to eat us all up." Ruth bakes cookies for her, and on Friday evening, when Allison has to work, Ruth videotapes "Miami Vice" for her. Allison's tan is fading slightly in the gloomy weather, and her freckles remind Barbara of the breast of a thrush.

The creek is rising, and the dog whines under the front porch. Allison brings him onto the enclosed back porch. His bandage is muddy and shredded. She has the mail with her, including a letter from her father, who lives in Mobile. "Daddy wants me to come down this fall and live," she tells Barbara.

"Are you going?"

"No. I've made a decision," Allison says in the tone of an announcement.

"What, honey?" Ruth asks. She is mixing applesauce cake, from a recipe of her grandmother's she promised to make for Allison.

"I'm going to quit school for a year and get a job and an apartment in Lexington."

"Lexington?" Barbara and Ruth say simultaneously. Lexington is more than two hundred miles away.

Allison explains that her friend Cindy and she are going to share an apartment. "It'll be good for us to get out in the real world," she says. "School's a drag right now."

"You'll be sorry if you don't finish school, honey," Ruth says.

"It doesn't fit my needs right now." Allison picks up her music and heads for the piano. "Look, think of this as junior year abroad, O.K.? Except I won't be speaking French."

Barbara jerks on her rain slicker and galoshes. In the light drizzle, she starts digging a trench along the upper side of the garden, to divert the water away from it. The peppers are dying. The cabbages are packed with fat slugs. She works quickly, fighting the rivulets of water that seep through the garden. The task seems useless, but belligerently she goes on, doing what she can.

Ruth comes slogging up the muddy path in her galoshes, blinking at the rain. She's not wearing her glasses. "Are you going to let her go to Lexington?" Ruth asks.

"She's grown," Barbara says.

"How can you let her go?"

"What can I do about it?"

Ruth wipes the raindrops from her face. "Don't you think she's making a mistake?"

"Of course, God damn it! But that's what children are—people with a special mission in life to hurt their parents."

"You don't have to tell me about hurt, Barbara. Do you think *you* know anything about that?"

Furiously, Barbara slaps the mud with her hoe. Next year she will relocate the garden above the house, where the drainage will be better.

The next day, the rain lets up, but it is still humid and dark, and a breeze is stirring over the ridge, as though a storm is on its way. Allison is off from work, and she has been playing the piano, picking out nonsense compositions of her own. Barbara is reading. Suddenly, through the picture window, Barbara sees Ruth in the orchard, pumping spray onto a peach tree. Barbara rushes outside, crying, "Ruth, are you crazy!"

The cloud of spray envelops Ruth. Barbara yells, "No, Ruth! Not on a windy evening! Don't spray against the wind!"

"The borers were going to eat up the peach tree!" Ruth cries, letting the sprayer dangle from her hand. She grabs a blob of peach-tree gum from the bark and shows it to Barbara. "Look!"

"The wind's blowing the spray all over *you*, not the tree," Barbara says sharply.

"Did I do wrong?"

"Let's go inside. The storm's coming."

"I wanted to help," Ruth says, in tears. "I wanted to save the tree."

Later, when Barbara and Allison are preparing supper and Ruth is in the shower washing off the insecticide, Allison says, "Mom, when did you realize you weren't in love with Daddy anymore?"

"The exact moment?"

"Yeah. Was there one?"

"I guess so. It might have been when I asked him to go have a picnic with us over at the lake one day. It was the summer you were a lifeguard there, and I thought we could go over there and be together—go on one of those outdoor trails—and he made some excuse. I realized I'd been married to the wrong man all those years."

"I think I know what you mean. I don't think I'm in love with Gerald anymore." Studiously, Allison chops peppers with the paring knife.

Barbara smiles. "You don't have to be in a hurry. That was my trouble. I was in a hurry. I married too young." Hastily, she adds, "But that's O.K. I got you in the bargain."

Allison nods thoughtfully. "What if you wanted to get married again? What would you do about Ruth?"

"I don't know."

"You'd have to get a divorce from *her* this time," Allison says teasingly.

"It would be hard to sell this place and divide it up." Barbara is not sure she could give it up.

"What's going on with Ruth, anyway?" Allison is asking. "She's so weird."

"She used to be worse," Barbara says reassuringly. "You remember how she was at first—she couldn't even finish the school year."

"I didn't want to tell you this, but I think Ruth's been pilfering," Allison says. "I can't find my purple barrette and that scarf

Grandma gave me. I bet Ruth took them." Allison looks straight out the window at the water washing down the runoff stream, and a slight curl of satisfaction is on her lips. Barbara stares at the dish of bread-and-butter pickles she is holding and for a moment cannot identify them. Images rush through her mind—chocolate chips, leftover squash, persimmons.

That night, Allison has gone out to a movie, and Barbara cannot sleep. The rain is still falling lightly, with brief spurts of heavy rain. It is past midnight when Allison's car drives up. The dog barks, and Ruth's light switches off, as if this were all some musical sequence. Earlier in the evening, Barbara glimpsed Ruth in her room, shuffling and spreading her pictures on the bed like cards in a game of solitaire. She keeps them in a box, with other mementos of Kimberly and Richard. Barbara wanted to go to her with some consolation, but she resisted, as she resisted mothering Allison too closely. She had the feeling that she was tending too many gardens; everything around her was growing in some sick or stunted way, and it made her feel cramped. As she hears Allison tiptoeing down the hall, Barbara closes her eyes and sees contorted black motorcycles, shiny in the rain.

Early the next morning, Allison calls them outdoors. "Look how the creek's up," she cries in a shrill voice.

The creek has flooded its banks, and the bridge is underwater, its iron railing still visible.

"Oh, wow," Allison says. "Look at all that water. I wish I was a duck."

"It's a flood," Barbara says matter-of-factly. Her garden is already ruined, and she has decided not to care what happens next.

At breakfast, a thunderous crack and a roar send them out to the porch. As they watch, the bridge over the creek tears loose and tumbles over, the railing black against the brown, muddy stream. The violence of it is shocking, like something one sees in the movies.

"Oh, my God," Ruth says quietly, her fingers working at her shirt.

"We're stranded!" says Allison. "Oh, wow."

"Oh, Lord, what will we do?" Ruth cries.

"We'll just have to wait till the water goes down," Barbara says, but they don't hear her.

"I won't have to work," Allison says. "I'll tell McDonald's I can't get there, unless they want to send a rescue helicopter for me. Or they could send the McDonald's blimp. That would be neat."

"Isn't this sort of thrilling?" Barbara says. "I've got goose bumps." She turns, but Ruth has gone indoors, and then Allison wanders off with the dog.

Barbara heads out through the field. From the edge of the woods, she looks out over the valley at the mist rising. In the two years Barbara and Ruth have lived here, it has become so familiar that Barbara can close her eyes and see clearly any place on the farm—the paths, the stand of willows by the runoff stream that courses down the hill to feed the creek. But sometimes it suddenly all seems strange, like something she has never seen before. Today she has one of those sensations, as she watches Allison down by the house playing with the dog, teaching him to fetch a stick. It is the kind of thing Allison has always done. She is always toying with something, prodding and experimenting. Yet in this light, with this particular dog, with his frayed bandage, and that particular stick and the wet grass that needs mowing—it is something Barbara has never seen before in her life.

She continues up the hill, past the woods. On the path, the mushrooms are a fantastic array, like a display of hats in a store —shiny red Chinese parasols, heavy globular things like brains, prim flat white toadstools. The mushrooms are so unexpected, it is as though they had grown up in a magical but clumsy compensation for the ruined garden. Barbara sidesteps a patch of dangerous-looking round black mushrooms. And ahead on the path lies a carpet of bright-orange fungi, curled like blossoms. She reaches in the pocket of her smock for her garden diary.

On Tuesday the sun emerges. The yard is littered with rocks washed out of the stream, and the long grass is flattened. The bumblebees, solar-activated, buzz through the orchard.

From the orchard, Barbara and Ruth gaze down the hill. The runoff stream still rushes downhill, brown and muddy, and Barbara's trench above the garden has widened.

"The apricots are falling off," Ruth says, picking up a sodden, bug-pocked fruit.

"It's O.K.," Barbara says, toeing the humps of a mole tunnel.

"I thought I'd fix up a room for Allison so she won't have to sleep in the living room," Ruth says. "I could clean out the attic and fix up a nice little window seat."

"You don't need to do that, Ruth. Don't you have something of your own to do?"

"I thought it would be nice."

"Allison won't be around that long. Where is she, anyway? I thought she was going to try to wade the creek and meet her ride to work."

"She was exploring the attic," Ruth says, looking suddenly alarmed. "Maybe she's getting into something she shouldn't."

"What do you mean, Ruth? Are you afraid she'll get in your box?"

Ruth doesn't answer. She is striding toward the house, calling for Allison.

Allison appears on the porch with a dusty cloth bundle she says she has found under a loose floorboard in the attic.

"Burn it!" Ruth cries. "No telling what germs are in it."

"I want to look inside it," Allison says. "It might be a hidden treasure."

"You've been reading too many stories, Allison," says Barbara.

"Take it out in the driveway where you can burn it, child," Ruth says anxiously. "It looks filthy."

Allison fumbles with the knot, and Ruth stands back, as though watching someone light a firecracker.

"It's just a bunch of rags," says Barbara skeptically. "What we used to call a granny bag."

"I bet there's a dead baby in here," says Allison.

"Allison!" Ruth cries, covering her face with her hands. "Stop it!"

"No, let her do it, Ruth," says Barbara. "And you watch."

The rags come apart. They are just stockings wound tightly around each other—old stockings with runs. They are disintegrating.

"My old granny used to wear her stockings till they hung in shreds," Barbara says breezily, staring at Ruth. Ruth stares back with frightened eyes. "Then she'd roll them up in a bundle of rags, just like this. That's all it is."

"Oh, crap," says Allison, disappointed. "There's nothing in here."

She drops the stockings on the damp gravel and reaches in her pocket for a cigarette. She strikes a match, holds it to her cigarette and inhales, then touches the match to the rags. In the damp air, the flame burns slowly, and then the rags suddenly catch. The smell of burning dust is very precise. It is like the essence of the old house. It is concentrated filth, and Allison is burning it up for them.

Big Bertha Stories

Donald is home again, laughing and singing. He comes home from Central City, near the strip mines, only when he feels like it, like an absentee landlord checking on his property. He is always in such a good humor when he returns that Jeannette forgives him. She cooks for him—ugly, pasty things she gets with food stamps. Sometimes he brings steaks and ice cream, occasionally money. Rodney, their child, hides in the closet when he arrives, and Donald goes around the house talking loudly about the little boy named Rodney who used to live there—the one who fell into a septic tank, or the one stolen by gypsies. The stories change. Rodney usually stays in the closet until he has to pee, and then he hugs his father's knees, forgiving him, just as Jeannette does. The way Donald saunters through the door, swinging a six-pack of beer, with a big grin on his face, takes her breath away. He leans against the door facing, looking sexy in his baseball cap and his shaggy red beard and his sunglasses. He wears sunglasses to be like the Blues Brothers, but he in no way resembles either of the Blues Brothers. I should have my head examined, Jeannette thinks.

The last time Donald was home, they went to the shopping center to buy Rodney some shoes advertised on sale. They stayed at the shopping center half the afternoon, just looking around. Donald and Rodney played video games. Jeannette felt they were a normal family. Then, in the parking lot, they stopped to watch a man on a platform demonstrating snakes. Children were petting a twelve-foot python coiled around the man's shoulders. Jeannette felt faint.

"Snakes won't hurt you unless you hurt them," said Donald as Rodney stroked the snake.

"It feels like chocolate," he said.

The snake man took a tarantula from a plastic box and held it lovingly in his palm. He said, "If you drop a tarantula, it will shatter like a Christmas ornament."

"I hate this," said Jeannette.

"Let's get out of here," said Donald.

Jeannette felt her family disintegrating like a spider shattering as Donald hurried them away from the shopping center. Rodney squalled and Donald dragged him along. Jeannette wanted to stop for ice cream. She wanted them all to sit quietly together in a booth, but Donald rushed them to the car, and he drove them home in silence, his face growing grim.

"Did you have bad dreams about the snakes?" Jeannette asked Rodney the next morning at breakfast. They were eating pancakes made with generic pancake mix. Rodney slapped his fork in the pond of syrup on his pancakes. "The black racer is the farmer's friend," he said soberly, repeating a fact learned from the snake man.

"Big Bertha kept black racers," said Donald. "She trained them for the 500." Donald doesn't tell Rodney ordinary children's stories. He tells him a series of strange stories he makes up about Big Bertha. Big Bertha is what he calls the huge strip-mining machine in Muhlenberg County, but he has Rodney believing that Big Bertha is a female version of Paul Bunyan.

"Snakes don't run in the 500," said Rodney.

"This wasn't the Indy 500 or the Daytona 500—none of your well-known 500s," said Donald. "This was the Possum Trot 500, and it was a long time ago. Big Bertha started the original 500, with snakes. Black racers and blue racers mainly. Also some red-and-white-striped racers, but those are rare."

"We always ran for the hoe if we saw a black racer," Jeannette said, remembering her childhood in the country.

In a way, Donald's absences are a fine arrangement, even considerate. He is sparing them his darkest moods, when he can't cope with his memories of Vietnam. Vietnam had never seemed such a meaningful fact until a couple of years ago, when he grew depressed and moody, and then he started going away to Central City. He frightened Jeannette, and she always said the wrong thing in her efforts to soothe him. If the welfare people find out he is spending occasional weekends at home, and even bringing some money, they will cut off her assistance. She applied for welfare because she can't depend on him to send money, but she knows he blames her for losing faith in him. He isn't really working regularly at the strip mines. He is mostly just hanging around there, watching the land being scraped away, trees coming down, bushes flung in the air. Sometimes he operates a steam shovel, and when he comes home his clothes are filled with the clay and it is caked on his shoes. The clay is the color of butterscotch pudding.

At first, he tried to explain to Jeannette. He said, "If we could have had tanks over there as big as Big Bertha, we wouldn't have lost the war. Strip mining is just like what we were doing over there. We were stripping off the top. The topsoil is like the culture and the people, the best part of the land and the country. America was just stripping off the top, the best. We ruined it. Here, at least the coal companies have to plant vetch and loblolly pines and all kinds of trees and bushes. If we'd done that in Vietnam, maybe we'd have left that country in better shape."

"Wasn't Vietnam a long time ago?" Jeannette asked.

She didn't want to hear about Vietnam. She thought it was unhealthy to dwell on it so much. He should live in the present. Her mother is afraid Donald will do something violent, because she once read in the newspaper that a veteran in Louisville held his little girl hostage in their apartment until he had a shootout with the police and was killed. But Jeannette can't imagine Donald doing anything so extreme. When she first met him, several

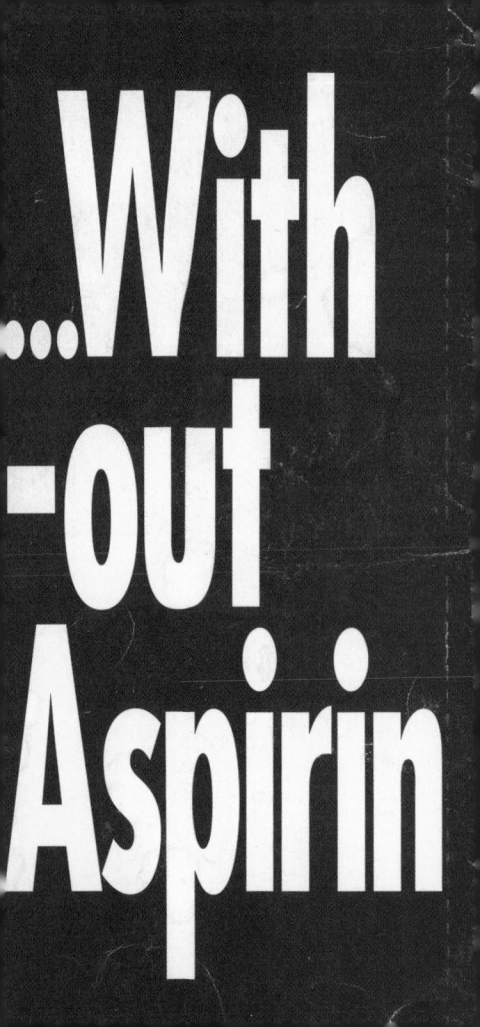

...With-out Aspirin

years ago, at her parents' pit-barbecue luncheonette, where she was working then, he had a good job at a lumberyard and he dressed nicely. He took her out to eat at a fancy restaurant. They got plastered and ended up in a motel in Tupelo, Mississippi, on Elvis Presley Boulevard. Back then, he talked nostalgically about his year in Vietnam, about how beautiful it was, how different the people were. He could never seem to explain what he meant. "They're just different," he said.

They went riding around in a yellow 1957 Chevy convertible. He drives too fast now, but he didn't then, maybe because he was so protective of the car. It was a classic. He sold it three years ago and made a good profit. About the time he sold the Chevy, his moods began changing, his even-tempered nature shifting, like driving on a smooth interstate and then switching to a secondary road. He had headaches and bad dreams. But his nightmares seemed trivial. He dreamed of riding a train through the Rocky Mountains, of hijacking a plane to Cuba, of stringing up barbed wire around the house. He dreamed he lost a doll. He got drunk and rammed the car, the Chevy's successor, into a Civil War statue in front of the courthouse. When he got depressed over the meaninglessness of his job, Jeannette felt guilty about spending money on something nice for the house, and she tried to make him feel his job had meaning by reminding him that, after all, they had a child to think of. "I don't like his name," Donald said once. "What a stupid name. Rodney. I never did like it."

Rodney has dreams about Big Bertha, echoes of his father's nightmare, like TV cartoon versions of Donald's memories of the war. But Rodney loves the stories, even though they are confusing, with lots of loose ends. The latest in the Big Bertha series is "Big Bertha and the Neutron Bomb." Last week it was "Big Bertha and the MX Missile." In the new story, Big Bertha takes a trip to California to go surfing with Big Mo, her male counterpart. On the beach, corn dogs and snow cones are free and the surfboards turn into dolphins. Everyone is having fun until the neutron bomb comes. Rodney loves the part where everyone keels over dead. Donald acts it out, collapsing on the rug. All the dolphins and the surfers keel over, everyone except Big Bertha. Big Bertha is so big she is immune to the neutron bomb.

"Those stories aren't true," Jeannette tells Rodney.

Rodney staggers and falls down on the rug, his arms and legs akimbo. He gets the giggles and can't stop. When his spasms finally subside, he says, "I told Scottie Bidwell about Big Bertha and he didn't believe me."

Donald picks Rodney up under the armpits and sets him upright. "You tell Scottie Bidwell if he saw Big Bertha he would pee in his pants on the spot, he would be so impressed."

"Are you scared of Big Bertha?"

"No, I'm not. Big Bertha is just like a wonderful woman, a big fat woman who can sing the blues. Have you ever heard Big Mama Thornton?"

"No."

"Well, Big Bertha's like her, only she's the size of a tall building. She's slow as a turtle and when she crosses the road they have to reroute traffic. She's big enough to straddle a four-lane highway. She's so tall she can see all the way to Tennessee, and when she belches, there's a tornado. She's really something. She can even fly."

"She's too big to fly," Rodney says doubtfully. He makes a face like a wadded-up washrag and Donald wrestles him to the floor again.

Donald has been drinking all evening, but he isn't drunk. The ice cubes melt and he pours the drink out and refills it. He keeps on talking. Jeannette cannot remember him talking so much about the war. He is telling her about an ammunitions dump. Jeannette had the vague idea that an ammo dump is a mound of shotgun shells, heaps of cartridge casings and bomb shells, or whatever is left over, a vast waste pile from the war, but Donald says that is wrong. He has spent an hour describing it in detail, so that she will understand.

He refills the glass with ice, some 7-Up, and a shot of Jim Beam. He slams doors and drawers, looking for a compass. Jeannette can't keep track of the conversation. It doesn't matter that her hair is uncombed and her lipstick eaten away. He isn't seeing her.

"I want to draw the compound for you," he says, sitting down at the table with a sheet of Rodney's tablet paper.

Donald draws the map in red and blue ballpoint, with asterisks and technical labels that mean nothing to her. He draws some circles with the compass and measures some angles. He makes a red dot on an oblique line, a path that leads to the ammo dump.

"That's where I was. Right there," he says. "There was a water buffalo that tripped a land mine and its horn just flew off and stuck in the wall of the barracks like a machete thrown back-handed." He puts a dot where the land mine was, and he doodles awhile with the red ballpoint pen, scribbling something on the edge of the map that looks like feathers. "The dump was here and I was there and over there was where we piled the sandbags. And here were the tanks." He draws tanks, a row of squares with handles—guns sticking out.

"Why are you going to so much trouble to tell me about a buffalo horn that got stuck in a wall?" she wants to know.

But Donald just looks at her as though she has asked something obvious.

"Maybe I *could* understand if you'd let me," she says cautiously.

"You could never understand." He draws another tank.

In bed, it is the same as it has been since he started going away to Central City—the way he claims his side of the bed, turning away from her. Tonight, she reaches for him and he lets her be close to him. She cries for a while and he lies there, waiting for her to finish, as though she were merely putting on makeup.

"Do you want me to tell you a Big Bertha story?" he asks playfully.

"You act like you're in love with Big Bertha."

He laughs, breathing on her. But he won't come closer.

"You don't care what I look like anymore," she says. "What am I supposed to think?"

"There's nobody else. There's not anybody but you."

Loving a giant machine is incomprehensible to Jeannette. There must be another woman, someone that large in his mind. Jeannette has seen the strip-mining machine. The top of the crane is visible beyond a rise along the parkway. The strip mining is kept just out of sight of travelers because it would give them a poor image of Kentucky.

For three weeks, Jeannette has been seeing a psychologist at the free mental health clinic. He's a small man from out of state. His name is Dr. Robinson, but she calls him The Rapist, because the word *therapist* can be divided into two words, *the rapist*. He doesn't think her joke is clever, and he acts as though he has heard it a thousand times before. He has a habit of saying, "Go with that feeling," the same way Bob Newhart did on his old TV show. It's probably the first lesson in the textbook, Jeannette thinks.

She told him about Donald's last days on his job at the lumberyard—how he let the stack of lumber fall deliberately and didn't know why, and about how he went away soon after that, and how the Big Bertha stories started. Dr. Robinson seems to be waiting for her to make something out of it all, but it's maddening that he won't tell her what to do. After three visits, Jeannette has grown angry with him, and now she's holding back things. She won't tell him whether Donald slept with her or not when he came home last. Let him guess, she thinks.

"Talk about yourself," he says.

"What about me?"

"You speak so vaguely about Donald that I get the feeling that you see him as somebody larger than life. I can't quite picture him. That makes me wonder what that says about you." He touches the end of his tie to his nose and sniffs it.

When Jeannette suggests that she bring Donald in, the therapist looks bored and says nothing.

"He had another nightmare when he was home last," Jeannette says. "He dreamed he was crawling through tall grass and people were after him."

"How do *you* feel about that?" The Rapist asks eagerly.

"I didn't have the nightmare," she says coldly. "Donald did. I came to you to get advice about Donald, and you're acting like I'm the one who's crazy. I'm not crazy. But I'm lonely."

Jeannette's mother, behind the counter of the luncheonette, looks lovingly at Rodney pushing buttons on the jukebox in the corner. "It's a shame about that youngun," she says tearfully. "That boy needs a daddy."

"What are you trying to tell me? That I should file for divorce and get Rodney a new daddy?"

Her mother looks hurt. "No, honey," she says. "You need to get Donald to seek the Lord. And you need to pray more. You haven't been going to church lately."

"Have some barbecue," Jeannette's father booms, as he comes in from the back kitchen. "And I want you to take a pound home with you. You've got a growing boy to feed."

"I want to take Rodney to church," Mama says. "I want to show him off, and it might do some good."

"People will think he's an orphan," Dad says.

"I don't care," Mama says. "I just love him to pieces and I want to take him to church. Do you care if I take him to church, Jeannette?"

"No. I don't care if you take him to church." She takes the pound of barbecue from her father. Grease splotches the brown wrapping paper. Dad has given them so much barbecue that Rodney is burned out on it and won't eat it anymore.

Jeannette wonders if she would file for divorce if she could get a job. It is a thought—for the child's sake, she thinks. But there aren't many jobs around. With the cost of a baby-sitter, it doesn't pay her to work. When Donald first went away, her mother kept Rodney and she had a good job, waitressing at a steak house, but the steak house burned down one night—a grease fire in the kitchen. After that, she couldn't find a steady job, and she was reluctant to ask her mother to keep Rodney again because of her bad hip. At the steak house, men gave her tips and left their telephone numbers on the bill when they paid. They tucked dollar bills and notes in the pockets of her apron. One note said, "I want to hold your muffins." They were real-estate developers and businessmen on important missions for the Tennessee Valley Authority. They were boisterous and they drank too much. They said they'd take her for a cruise on the *Delta Queen*, but she didn't believe them. She knew how expensive that was. They talked about their speedboats and invited her for rides on Lake Barkley, or for spins in their private planes. They always used the word *spin*. The idea made her dizzy. Once, Jeannette let an electronics salesman take her for a ride in his Cadillac, and they breezed down the wilderness road through the Land Between the Lakes. His car had automatic windows and a stereo system and lighted computer-screen numbers on the dash that told him how many miles to the gallon he was getting and other statistics. He said the numbers distracted him and he had almost had several wrecks. At the restaurant, he had been flamboyant, admired by his companions. Alone with Jeannette in the Cadillac, on The Trace, he was shy and awkward, and really not very interesting. The most interesting thing about him, Jeannette thought, was all the lighted numbers on his dashboard. The Cadillac had everything but video games. But she'd rather be riding around with Donald, no matter where they ended up.

While the social worker is there, filling out her report, Jeannette listens for Donald's car. When the social worker drove up, the flutter and wheeze of her car sounded like Donald's old Chevy, and for a moment Jeannette's mind lapsed back in time. Now she listens, hoping he won't drive up. The social worker is younger than Jeannette and has been to college. Her name is Miss Bailey, and she's excessively cheerful, as though in her line of work she has seen hardships that make Jeannette's troubles seem like a trip to Hawaii.

"Is your little boy still having those bad dreams?" Miss Bailey asks, looking up from her clipboard.

Jeannette nods and looks at Rodney, who has his finger in his mouth and won't speak.

"Has the cat got your tongue?" Miss Bailey asks.

"Show her your pictures, Rodney." Jeannette explains, "He won't talk about the dreams, but he draws pictures of them."

Rodney brings his tablet of pictures and flips through them silently. Miss Bailey says, "Hmm." They are stark line drawings, remarkably steady lines for his age. "What is this one?" she asks. "Let me guess. Two scoops of ice cream?"

The picture is two huge circles, filling the page, with three tiny stick people in the corner.

"These are Big Bertha's titties," says Rodney.

Miss Bailey chuckles and winks at Jeannette. "What do you like to read, hon?" she asks Rodney.

"Nothing."

"He can read," says Jeannette. "He's smart."

"Do you like to read?" Miss Bailey asks Jeannette. She glances at the pile of paperbacks on the coffee table. She is probably going to ask where Jeannette got the money for them.

"I don't read," says Jeannette. "If I read, I just go crazy."

When she told The Rapist she couldn't concentrate on anything serious, he said she read romance novels in order to escape from reality. "Reality, hell!" she had said. "Reality's my whole problem."

"It's too bad Rodney's not here," Donald is saying. Rodney is in the closet again. "Santa Claus has to take back all these toys. Rodney would love this bicycle! And this Pac-Man game. Santa has to take back so many things he'll have to have a pickup truck!"

"You didn't bring him anything. You never bring him anything," says Jeannette.

He has brought doughnuts and dirty laundry. The clothes he is wearing are caked with clay. His beard is lighter from working out in the sun, and he looks his usual joyful self, the way he always is before his moods take over, like migraine headaches, which some people describe as storms.

Donald coaxes Rodney out of the closet with the doughnuts.

"Were you a good boy this week?"

"I don't know."

"I hear you went to the shopping center and showed out." It is not true that Rodney made a big scene. Jeannette has already explained that Rodney was upset because she wouldn't buy him an Atari. But she didn't blame him for crying. She was tired of being unable to buy him anything.

Rodney eats two doughnuts and Donald tells him a long, confusing story about Big Bertha and a rock-and-roll band. Rodney interrupts him with dozens of questions. In the story, the rock-and-roll band gives a concert in a place that turns out to be a toxic-waste dump and the contamination is spread all over the country. Big Bertha's solution to this problem is not at all clear. Jeannette stays in the kitchen, trying to think of something original to do with instant potatoes and leftover barbecue.

"We can't go on like this," she says that evening in bed. "We're just hurting each other. Something has to change."

He grins like a kid. "Coming home from Muhlenberg County is like R and R—rest and recreation. I explain that in case you think R and R means rock and roll. Or maybe rumps and rears. Or rust and rot." He laughs and draws a circle in the air with his cigarette.

"I'm not that dumb."

"When I leave, I go back to the mines." He sighs, as though the mines were some eternal burden.

Her mind skips ahead to the future: Donald locked away somewhere, coloring in a coloring book and making clay pots, her and Rodney in some other town, with another man—someone dull and not at all sexy. Summoning up her courage, she says, "I haven't been through what you've been through and maybe I don't have a right to say this, but sometimes I think you act superior because you went to Vietnam, like nobody can ever know what you know. Well, maybe not. But you've still got your legs, even if you don't know what to do with what's between them anymore." Bursting into tears of apology, she can't help adding, "You can't go on telling Rodney those awful stories. He has nightmares when you're gone."

Donald rises from bed and grabs Rodney's picture from the dresser, holding it as he might have held a hand grenade. "Kids betray you," he says, turning the picture in his hand.

"If you cared about him, you'd stay here." As he sets the picture down, she asks, "What can I do? How can I understand what's going on in your mind? Why do you go there? Strip mining's bad for the ecology and you don't have any business strip mining."

"My job is serious, Jeannette. I run that steam shovel and put the topsoil back on. I'm reclaiming the land." He keeps talking, in a gentler voice, about strip mining, the same old things she has heard before, comparing Big Bertha to a supertank. If only they had had Big Bertha in Vietnam. He says, "When they strip off the top, I keep looking for those tunnels where the Viet Cong hid. They had so many tunnels it was unbelievable. Imagine Mammoth Cave going all the way across Kentucky."

"Mammoth Cave's one of the natural wonders of the world," says Jeannette brightly. She is saying the wrong thing again.

At the kitchen table at 2 A.M., he's telling about C-5A's. A C-5A is so big it can carry troops and tanks and helicopters, but it's not big enough to hold Big Bertha. Nothing could hold Big Bertha. He rambles on, and when Jeannette shows him Rodney's drawing of the circles, Donald smiles. Dreamily, he begins talking about women's breasts and thighs—the large, round thighs and big round breasts of American women, contrasted with the frail, delicate beauty of the Orientals. It is like comparing oven broilers and banties, he says. Jeannette relaxes. A confession about another lover from long ago is not so hard to take. He seems stuck on the breasts and thighs of American women—insisting that she understand how small and delicate the Orientals are, but then he abruptly returns to tanks and helicopters.

"A Bell Huey Cobra—my God, what a beautiful machine. So

efficient!'' Donald takes the food processor blade from the drawer
where Jeannette keeps it. He says, "A rotor blade from a chopper
could just slice anything to bits."

"Don't do that," Jeannette says.

He is trying to spin the blade on the counter, like a top. "Here's
what would happen when a chopper blade hits a power line—
not many of those over there!—or a tree. Not many trees, either,
come to think of it, after all the Agent Orange." He drops the
blade and it glances off the open drawer and falls to the floor,
spiking the vinyl.

At first, Jeannette thinks the screams are hers, but they are his.
She watches him cry. She has never seen anyone cry so hard, like
an intense summer thundershower. All she knows to do is shove
Kleenex at him. Finally, he is able to say, "You thought I was
going to hurt you. That's why I'm crying."

"Go ahead and cry," Jeannette says, holding him close.

"Don't go away."

"I'm right here. I'm not going anywhere."

In the night, she still listens, knowing his monologue is being
burned like a tattoo into her brain. She will never forget it. His
voice grows soft and he plays with a ballpoint pen, jabbing holes
in a paper towel. Bullet holes, she thinks. His beard is like a bird's
nest, woven with dark corn silks.

"This is just a story," he says. "Don't mean nothing. Just
relax." She is sitting on the hard edge of the kitchen chair, her
toes cold on the floor, waiting. His tears have dried up and left a
slight catch in his voice.

"We were in a big camp near a village. It was pretty routine and
kind of soft there for a while. Now and then we'd go into Da
Nang and whoop it up. We had been in the jungle for several
months, so the two months at this village was a sort of rest—an R
and R almost. Don't shiver. This is just a little story. Don't mean
nothing! This is nothing, compared to what I could tell you. Just
listen. We lost our fear. At night there would be some incoming
and we'd see these tracers in the sky, like shooting stars up close,
but it was all pretty minor and we didn't take it seriously, after

what we'd been through. In the village I knew this Vietnamese family—a woman and her two daughters. They sold Cokes and beer to GIs. The oldest daughter was named Phan. She could speak a little English. She was really smart. I used to go see them in their hooch in the afternoons—in the siesta time of day. It was so hot there. Phan was beautiful, like the country. The village was ratty, but the country was pretty. And she was beautiful, just like she had grown up out of the jungle, like one of those flowers that bloomed high up in the trees and freaked us out sometimes, thinking it was a sniper. She was so gentle, with these eyes shaped like peach pits, and she was no bigger than a child of maybe thirteen or fourteen. I felt funny about her size at first, but later it didn't matter. It was just some wonderful feature about her, like a woman's hair, or her breasts."

He stops and listens, the way they used to listen for crying sounds when Rodney was a baby. He says, "She'd take those big banana leaves and fan me while I lay there in the heat."

"I didn't know they had bananas over there."

"There's a lot you don't know! Listen! Phan was twenty-three, and her brothers were off fighting. I never even asked which side they were fighting on." He laughs. "She got a kick out of the word *fan*. I told her that *fan* was the same word as her name. She thought I meant her name was banana. In Vietnamese the same word can have a dozen different meanings, depending on your tone of voice. I bet you didn't know that, did you?"

"No. What happened to her?"

"I don't know."

"Is that the end of the story?"

"I don't know." Donald pauses, then goes on talking about the village, the girl, the banana leaves, talking in a monotone that is making Jeannette's flesh crawl. He could be the news radio from the next room.

"You must have really liked that place. Do you wish you could go back there to find out what happened to her?"

"It's not there anymore," he says. "It blew up."

Donald abruptly goes to the bathroom. She hears the water running, the pipes in the basement shaking.

"It was so pretty," he says when he returns. He rubs his elbow absentmindedly. "That jungle was the most beautiful place in the world. You'd have thought you were in paradise. But we blew it sky-high."

In her arms, he is shaking, like the pipes in the basement, which are still vibrating. Then the pipes let go, after a long shudder, but he continues to tremble.

They are driving to the Veterans Hospital. It was Donald's idea. She didn't have to persuade him. When she made up the bed that morning—with a finality that shocked her, as though she knew they wouldn't be in it again together—he told her it would be like R and R. Rest was what he needed. Neither of them had slept at all during the night. Jeannette felt she had to stay awake, to listen for more.

"Talk about strip mining," she says now. "That's what they'll do to your head. They'll dig out all those ugly memories, I hope. We don't need them around here." She pats his knee.

It is a cloudless day, not the setting for this sober journey. She drives and Donald goes along obediently, with the resignation of an old man being taken to a rest home. They are driving through southern Illinois, known as Little Egypt, for some obscure reason Jeannette has never understood. Donald still talks, but very quietly, without urgency. When he points out the scenery, Jeannette thinks of the early days of their marriage, when they would take a drive like this and laugh hysterically. Now Jeannette points out funny things they see. The Little Egypt Hot Dog World, Pharaoh Cleaners, Pyramid Body Shop. She is scarcely aware that she is driving, and when she sees a sign, LITTLE EGYPT STAR-LITE CLUB, she is confused for a moment, wondering where she has been transported.

As they part, he asks, "What will you tell Rodney if I don't come back? What if they keep me here indefinitely?"

"You're coming back. I'm telling him you're coming back soon."

"Tell him I went off with Big Bertha. Tell him she's taking me on a sea cruise, to the South Seas."

"No. You can tell him that yourself."

He starts singing "Sea Cruise." He grins at her and pokes her in the ribs.

"You're coming back," she says.

Donald writes from the VA Hospital, saying that he is making progress. They are running tests, and he meets in a therapy group in which all the veterans trade memories. Jeannette is no longer on welfare because she now has a job waitressing at Fred's Family Restaurant. She waits on families, waits for Donald to come home so they can come here and eat together like a family. The fathers look at her with downcast eyes, and the children throw food. While Donald is gone, she rearranges the furniture. She reads some books from the library. She does a lot of thinking. It occurs to her that even though she loved him, she has thought of Donald primarily as a husband, a provider, someone whose name she shared, the father of her child, someone like the fathers who come to the Wednesday night all-you-can-eat fish fry. She hasn't thought of him as himself. She wasn't brought up that way, to examine someone's soul. When it comes to something deep inside, nobody will take it out and examine it, the way they will look at clothing in a store for flaws in the manufacturing. She tries to explain all this to The Rapist, and he says she's looking better, got sparkle in her eyes. "Big deal," says Jeannette. "Is that all you can say?"

She takes Rodney to the shopping center, their favorite thing to do together, even though Rodney always begs to buy something. They go to Penney's perfume counter. There, she usually hits a sample bottle of cologne—Chantilly or Charlie or something strong. Today she hits two or three and comes out of Penney's smelling like a flower garden.

"You stink!" Rodney cries, wrinkling his nose like a rabbit.

"Big Bertha smells like this, only a thousand times worse, she's so big," says Jeannette impulsively. "Didn't Daddy tell you that?"

"Daddy's a messenger from the devil."

This is an idea he must have gotten from church. Her parents have been taking him every Sunday. When Jeannette tries to reassure him about his father, Rodney is skeptical. "He gets that funny look on his face like he can see through me," the child says.

"Something's missing," Jeannette says, with a rush of optimism, a feeling of recognition. "Something happened to him once and took out the part that shows how much he cares about us."

"The way we had the cat fixed?"

"I guess. Something like that." The appropriateness of his remark stuns her, as though, in a way, her child has understood Donald all along. Rodney's pictures have been more peaceful lately, pictures of skinny trees and airplanes flying low. This morning he drew pictures of tall grass, with creatures hiding in it. The grass is tilted at an angle, as though a light breeze is blowing through it.

With her paycheck, Jeannette buys Rodney a present, a miniature trampoline they have seen advertised on television. It is called Mr. Bouncer. Rodney is thrilled about the trampoline, and he jumps on it until his face is red. Jeannette discovers that she enjoys it, too. She puts it out on the grass, and they take turns jumping. She has an image of herself on the trampoline, her sailor collar flapping, at the moment when Donald returns and sees her flying. One day a neighbor driving by slows down and calls out to Jeannette as she is bouncing on the trampoline, "You'll tear your insides loose!" Jeannette starts thinking about that, and the idea is so horrifying she stops jumping so much. That night, she has a nightmare about the trampoline. In her dream, she is jumping on soft moss, and then it turns into a springy pile of dead bodies.

State Champions

In 1952, when I was in the seventh grade, the Cuba Cubs were the state champions in high-school basketball. When the Cubs returned from the tournament in Lexington, a crowd greeted them at Eggner's Ferry bridge over Kentucky Lake, and a convoy fourteen miles long escorted them to the county seat. It was a cold day in March as twelve thousand people watched the Cubs ride around the courthouse square in convertibles. The mayor and other dignitaries made speeches. Willie Foster, the president of the Merit Clothing Company, gave the players and Coach Jack Story free suits from his factory. The coach, a chunky guy in a trench coat like a character in a forties movie, told the crowd, "I'm mighty glad we could bring back the big trophy." And All-Stater Howie Crittenden, the razzle-dazzle dribbler, said, "There are two things I'm proud of today. First, we won the tournament, and second, Mr. Story said we made him feel like a young mule."

The cheerleaders then climbed up onto the concrete seat sections of the Confederate monument and led a final fight yell.

> Chick-a-lacka, chick-a-lacka chow, chow, chow
> Boom-a-lacka, boom-a-lacka bow, wow, wow
> Chick-a-lacka, boom-a-lacka, who are we?
> Cuba High School, can't you see?

The next day the Cubs took off in the convertibles again, leading a motorcade around western Kentucky, visiting the schools in Sedalia, Mayfield, Farmington, Murray, Hardin, Benton, Sharpe, Reidland, Paducah, Kevil, La Center, Barlow, Wickliffe, Bardwell, Arlington, Clinton, Fulton, and Pilot Oak.

I remember the hoopla at the square that day, but at the time I felt a strange sort of distance, knowing that in another year another community would have its champions. I was twelve years old and going through a crisis, so I thought I had a wise understanding of the evanescence of victory.

But years later, in the seventies, in upstate New York, I met a man who surprised me by actually remembering the Cuba Cubs' championship. He was a Kentuckian, and although he was from the other side of the state, he had lasting memories of Howie Crittenden and Doodle Floyd. Howie was a great dribbler, he said. And Doodle had a windmill hook shot that had to be seen to be believed. The Cubs were inspired by the Harlem Globetrotters—Marques Haynes's ball-handling influenced Howie and Goose Tatum was Doodle's model. The Cuba Cubs, I was told, were, in fact, the most incredible success story in the history of Kentucky high-school basketball, and the reason was that they were such unlikely champions.

"Why, they were just a handful of country boys who could barely afford basketball shoes," the man told me in upstate New York.

"They were?" This was news to me.

"Yes. They were known as the Cinderella Cubs. One afternoon during the tournament, they were at Memorial Coliseum watching the Kentucky Wildcats practice. The Cubs weren't in uniform, but one of them called for a ball and dribbled it a few times and then canned a two-hand set shot from midcourt. Adolph Rupp happened to be watching. He's another Kentucky basketball legend—don't you know anything about Kentucky basketball? He rushed to the player at midcourt and demanded, 'How did you do that?' The boy just smiled. 'It was easy, Mr. Rupp,' he said. 'Ain't no wind in here.' "

Of course, that was not my image of the Cuba Cubs at all. I

hadn't realized they were just a bunch of farm boys who got together behind the barn after school and shot baskets in the dirt, while the farmers around complained that the boys would never amount to anything. I hadn't known how Coach Jack Story had started them off in the seventh grade, coaching the daylights out of those kids until he made them believe they could be champions. To me, just entering junior high the year they won the tournament, the Cuba Cubs were the essence of glamour. Seeing them in the gym—standing tall in those glossy green satin uniforms, or racing down the court, leaping like deer—took my breath away. They had crew cuts and wore real basketball shoes. And the cheerleaders dressed smartly in Crayola-green corduroy circle skirts, saddle oxfords, and rolled-down socks. They had green corduroy jackets as well as green sweaters, with a C cutting through the symbol of a megaphone. They clapped their hands in rhythm and orchestrated their elbows in a little dance that in some way mimicked the Cubs as they herded the ball down the court. "Go, Cubs, Go!" "Fight, Cubs, Fight!" They did "Locomotive, locomotive, steam, steam, steam," and "Strawberry shortcake, huckleberry pie." We had pep rallies that were like revival services in tone and intent. The cheerleaders pirouetted and zoomed skyward in unison, their leaps straight and clean like jump shots. They whirled in their circle skirts, showing off their green tights underneath.

I never questioned the words of the yells, any more than I questioned the name Cuba Cubs. I didn't know what kind of cubs they were supposed to be—bear cubs or wildcats or foxes—but I never thought about it. I doubt if anyone did. It was the sound of the words that mattered, not the meaning. They were the Cubs. And that was it. Cuba was a tiny community with a couple of general stores, and its name is of doubtful origin, but local historians say that when the Cuba post office opened, in the late 1850s, the Ostend Manifesto had been in the news. This was a plan the United States had for getting control of the island of Cuba in order to expand the slave trade. The United States demanded that Spain either sell us Cuba at a fair price or surrender it outright. Perhaps the founding fathers of Cuba, Kentucky (old-time pronunciation: Cubie), were swayed by the fuss with Spain. Or maybe they just had romantic imaginations. In the Jackson Purchase, the western region of Kentucky and Tennessee that Andrew Jackson purchased from the Chickasaw Indians in 1818, there are other towns with faraway names: Moscow, Dublin, Kansas, Cadiz, Beulah, Paris, and Dresden.

The gymnasium where the Cuba Cubs practiced was the hub of the school. Their trophies gleamed in a glass display case near the entrance, between the principal's office and the gymnasium, and the enormous coal furnace that heated the gym hunched in a corner next to the bleachers. Several classrooms opened onto the gym floor, with the study hall at one end. The lower grades occupied a separate building, and in those grades we used an outhouse. But in junior high we had the privilege of using the indoor rest rooms, which also opened onto the gym. (The boys' room included a locker room for the team, but like the outhouses, the girls' room didn't even have private compartments.) The route from the study hall to the girls' room was dangerous. We had to walk through the gym, along the sidelines, under some basketball hoops. There were several baskets, so many players could practice their shots simultaneously. At recess and lunch, in addition to the Cuba Cubs, all the junior high boys used the gym, too, in frantic emulation of their heroes. On the way to the rest room you had to calculate quickly and carefully when you could run beneath a basket. The players pretended that they were oblivious of you, but just when you thought you were safe and could dash under the basket, they would hurl a ball out of nowhere, and the ball would fall on your head as you streaked by. Even though I was sort of a tomboy and liked to run—back in the fifth grade I could run as fast as most of the boys—I had no desire to play basketball. It was too violent.

Doodle Floyd himself bopped me on the head once, but I doubt if he remembers it.

The year of the championship was the year I got in trouble for running in the study hall. At lunch hour one day, Judy Howell and I decided to run the length of the gym as fast as we could, daring ourselves to run through the hailstorm of basketballs flying at us. We raced through the gym and kept on running, unable to slow down, finally skidding to a stop in the study hall. We were giggling because we had caught a glimpse of what one of the senior players was wearing under his green practice shorts (different from the satin show shorts they wore at the games), when Mr. Gilhorn, the history teacher, big as a buffalo, appeared before us and growled, "What do you young ladies think you're doing?"

I had on the tightest Levi's I owned. When they were newly washed and ironed, they fit snug. My mother had ironed a crease in them. I had on a cowboy shirt and a bandanna.

Mr. Gilhorn went on, "Now, girls, do we run in our own living rooms? Peggy, does your mama let you run in the house?"

"Yes," I said, staring at him confidently. "My mama always lets me run in the house." It was a lie, of course, but it was my habit to contradict whatever anybody assumed. If I was supposed to be a lady, then I would be a cowboy. The truth in this instance was that it had never occurred to me to run in our house. It was too small, and the floorboards were shaky. Therefore, I reasoned, my mother had never laid down the law about not running in the house.

Judy said, "We won't do it again." But I wouldn't promise.

"I know what would be good for you girls," said Mr. Gilhorn in a kindly, thoughtful tone, as if he had just had a great idea.

That meant the duckwalk. As punishment, Judy and I had to squat, grabbing our ankles, and duckwalk around the gym. We waddled, humiliated, with the basketballs beating on our heads and the players following our progress with loud quacks of derision.

"This was your fault," Judy claimed. She stopped speaking to me, which disappointed me because we had been playmates since the second grade. I admired her short blond curls and color-coordinated outfits. She had been to Detroit one summer.

During study-hall periods, we could hear the basketballs pounding the floor. We could tell when a player made a basket —that pause after the ball hit the backboard and sank luxuriously into the net before hitting the floor. I visited the library more often than necessary just to get a glimpse of the Cubs practicing as I passed the door to the gym. The library was a shelf at one end of the study hall, and it had a couple of hundred old books—mostly hand-me-downs from the Graves County Library, including outdated textbooks and even annuals from Kentucky colleges. That year I read some old American histories, and a biography of Benjamin Franklin, and the "Junior Miss" books. On the wainscoted walls of the study hall were gigantic framed pictures, four feet high, each composed of inset portraits of all the faculty members and the seniors of a specific year. They gazed down at us like kings and queens on playing cards. There was a year for each frame, and they dated all the way back to the early forties.

In junior high, we shared the study hall with the high-school students. The big room was drafty, and in the winter it was very cold. The boys were responsible for keeping the potbelly stove filled with coal from the coal pile outside, near where the school buses were parked. In grade school during the winter, I had worn long pants under my dresses—little starched print dresses with gathered skirts and puffed sleeves. But in junior high, the girls wore blue jeans, like the boys, except that we rolled them up almost to our knees. The Cuba Cubs wore Levi's and green basketball jackets, and the other high-school boys—the Future Farmers of America—wore bright-blue FFA jackets. Although the FFA jackets didn't have the status of the basketball jackets, they were beautiful. They were royal-blue corduroy, and on the back was an enormous gold eagle.

I had a crush on a freshman named Glenn in an FFA jacket. He helped manage the coal bucket in the study hall. Glenn didn't ride my bus. He lived in Dukedom, down across the Tennessee line. Glenn was one of the Cuba Cubs, but he wasn't one of the major Cubs—he was on the B team and didn't yet have a green jacket. But I admired his dribble, and his long legs could travel that floor like a bicycle. When I waited at the edge of the gym for my chance to bolt to the girls' room, I sometimes stood and watched him dribble. Then one day as I ran pell-mell to the rest room, his basketball hit me on the head and he called to me flirtatiously. "I got a claim on her," he yelled out to the world. If a boy had a claim on a girl, it meant she was his girlfriend. The next day in study hall he showed me an "eight-page novel." It was a Li'l Abner comic strip. In the eight-page novel, Li'l Abner peed on Daisy Mae. It was disgusting, but I was thrilled that he showed me the booklet.

"Hey, let me show you these hand signals," Glenn said a couple of days later, out on the playground. "In case you ever need them." He stuck his middle finger straight up and folded the others down. "That's single *F*," he said. Then he turned down his two middle fingers, leaving the forefinger and the little finger upright, like horns. "That's double *F*," he said confidently.

"Oh," I said. At first I thought he meant hand signals used in driving. Cars didn't have automatic turn signals then.

There were other hand signals. In basketball, the coach and the players exchanged finger gestures. The cheerleaders clapped us on to victory. And with lovers, lightly scraping the index finger on the other's palm meant "Do you want to?" and responding the same way meant "Yes." If you didn't know this and you held hands with a boy, you might inadvertently agree to do something that you had no intention of doing.

Seventh grade was the year we had a different teacher for each subject. Arithmetic became mathematics. The English teacher paddled Frances High and me for stealing Jack Reed's Milky Way from his desk. Jack Reed had even told us he didn't mind that we stole it, that he wanted us to have it. "The paddling didn't hurt," I said to him proudly. He was cute, but not as cute as Glenn, who had a crooked grin I thought was fascinating and later found reincarnated in Elvis. In the study hall I stood in front of the stove until my backside was soaked with heat. I slid my hands down the back of my legs and felt the sharp crease of my Levi's. I was in a perpetual state of excitement. It was 1952 and the Cuba Cubs were on their way to the championship.

Judy was still mad at me, but Glenn's sister Willowdean was in my class, and I contrived to go home with her one evening, riding her unfamiliar school bus along gravel roads far back into the country. Country kids didn't socialize much. To go home with someone and spend the night was a big event, strange and unpredictable. Glenn and Willowdean lived with three brothers and sisters in a small house surrounded by bare, stubbled tobacco fields. It was a wintry day, but Willowdean and I played outdoors, and I watched for Glenn to arrive.

He had stayed late at school, practicing ball, and the coach brought him home. Then he had his chores to do. At suppertime, when he came in with his father from milking, his mother handed him a tray of food. "Come on and go with me," he said to me. His Levi's were smudged with cow manure.

His mother said, "Make sure she's got her teeth."

"Have you got your teeth, Peggy?" Glenn asked me with a grin.

His mother swatted at him crossly. "I meant Bluma. You know who I meant."

Glenn motioned with a nod of his head for me to follow him, and we went to a tiny back room, where Glenn's grandmother sat in a wheelchair in a corner with a heater at her feet. She had dark hair and lips painted bright orange and a growth on her neck.

"She don't talk," Glenn said. "But she can hear."

The strange woman jerked her body in a spasm of acknowledgment as Glenn set the supper tray in her lap. He fished her teeth out of a glass of water and poked them in her mouth. She squeaked like a mouse.

"Are you hungry?" Glenn asked me as we left the room. "We've got chicken and dumplings tonight. That's my favorite."

That night I slept with Willowdean on a fold-out couch in the living room, with newspaper-wrapped hot bricks at our feet. We huddled under four quilts and whispered. I worked the conversation around to Glenn.

"He told me he liked you," Willowdean said.

I could feel myself blush. At supper, Glenn had tickled me under the table.

"I'll tell you a secret if you promise not to tell," she said.

"What?" I loved secrets and usually didn't tell them.

"Betty Jean's going to have a baby."

Willowdean's sister Betty Jean was a sophomore. On the school bus her boyfriend, Roy Matthews, had kept his arm around her during the whole journey, while she cracked gum and looked pleased with herself. That evening at the supper table, Glenn and his brothers had teased her about Roy's big feet.

Willowdean whispered now, "Did you see the way she ate supper? Like a pig. That's because she has to eat for two. She's got a baby in her stomach."

"What will she do?" I asked, scared. The warmth of the bricks was fading, and I knew it would be a freezing night.

"Her and Roy will live with us," said Willowdean. "That's what my sister Mary Lou did at first. But then she got mad and took the baby off and went to live with her husband's folks. She said they treated her better."

The high-school classes were small because kids dropped out, to have babies and farm. They seemed to disappear, like our calves going off to the slaughterhouse in the fall, and it was creepy.

"I don't want to have a baby and have to quit school," I said.

"You don't?" Willowdean was surprised. "What do you want to go to school for?"

I didn't answer. I didn't have the words handy. But she didn't seem to notice. She turned over and pulled the quilts with her. In the darkness, I could hear a mouse squeaking. But it wasn't a mouse. It was Willowdean's grandmother, in her cold room at the back of the house.

That winter, while basketball fever raged, a student teacher from Murray State College taught Kentucky history. She was very pretty and resembled a picture of Pocahontas in one of the library books. One time when she sat down, flipping her large gathered skirt up, I saw her panties. They were pink. She was so soft-spoken she didn't know how to make us behave well enough to accomplish any classwork. Daniel Boone's exploits were nothing, compared to Doodle Floyd's. During the week the Cubs were at the tournament, Pocahontas couldn't keep us quiet. The school was raising money for next year's basketball uniforms, and each class sold candy and cookies our mothers had made. Frequently there was a knock at the door, and some kids from another grade would be there selling Rice Krispies squares wrapped in waxed paper, or brownies, or sometimes divinity fudge. One day, while Pocahontas was reading to us about Daniel Boone and the Indians, and we were throwing paper wads, there was a sudden pounding on the door. I was hoping for divinity, and I had a nickel with me, but the door burst open and Judy Howell's sister Georgia was there, crying, "Judy Bee! Mama's had a wreck and Linda Faye's killed."

Judy flew out of the room. For one moment the class was quiet, and then it went into an uproar. Pocahontas didn't know what to do, so she gave us a pop quiz. The next day we learned that Judy's little sister Linda Faye, who was three years old, had been thrown into a ditch when her mother slammed into a truck that had pulled out in front of her. The seventh-grade class took up a collection for flowers. I was stunned by the news of death, for I had never known a child to die. I couldn't sleep, and my mind went over and over the accident, imagining the truck plowing into the car and Linda Faye pitching out the door or through the window. I created various scenes, ways it might have happened. I kept seeing her stretched out stiff on her side, like the dead animals I had seen on our farm. At school I was sleepy, and I escaped into daydreams about Glenn, imagining that I had gone to Lexington, too, to watch him in triumph as he was called in from the sidelines to replace Doodle Floyd, who had turned his ankle.

It was a sober, long walk from the study hall to the rest room. The gymnasium seemed desolate, without the Cubs practicing. I walked safely down the gym, remembering the time in the fourth grade when I was a flower girl in the court of the basketball queen. I had carried an Easter basket filled with flower petals down the center of the gym, scattering rose petals so the queen could step on them as she minced slowly toward her throne.

I was too scared to go to the funeral, and my parents didn't want me to go. My father had been traumatized by funerals in his childhood, and he didn't think they were a good idea. "The Howells live so far away," Mama said. "And it looks like snow."

That weekend, the tournament was on the radio, and I listened carefully, hoping to hear Glenn's name. The final game was crazy. In the background, the cheerleaders chanted:

> *Warren, Warren, he's our man*
> *If he can't do it*
> *Floyd can—*
> *Floyd, Floyd, he's our man*
> *If he can't do it*
> *Crittenden can—*

The announcer was saying, "Crittenden's dribbling has the crowd on its feet. It's a thrilling game! The Cubs were beaten twice by this same Louisville Manual squad during the season, but now they've just inched ahead. The Cubs pulled even at 39–39 when Floyd converted a charity flip, and then Warren sent them ahead for the first time with a short one-hander on Crittenden's pass. The crowd is going wild!"

Toward the end of the game, the whole Coliseum—except for a small Manual cheering section—was yelling, "Hey, hey, what do you say? It looks like Cuba all the way!"

As I listened to the excited announcer chatter about huddles and time-outs and driving jumps and hook shots, I forgot about Judy, but then on Sunday, when I went to the courthouse square to welcome the Cubs home, her sister's death struck me again like fresh news. Seeing so many people celebrating made me feel uncomfortable, as if the death of a child always went unnoticed, like a dead dog by the side of the road. It was a cold day, and I had to wear a dress because it was Sunday. I wanted to see Glenn. I had an audacious plan. I had been thinking about it all night. I wanted to give him a hug of congratulations. I would plant a big wet kiss on his cheek. I had seen a cheerleader do this to one of the players once after he made an unusual number of free throws. It was at a home game, one of the few I attended. I wanted to hug Glenn because it would be my answer to his announcement that he had a claim on me. It would be silent, without explanation, but he would know what it meant.

I managed to lose my parents in the throng and I headed for the east side of the square, where the dime store was. Suddenly I saw Judy, with her mother, in front of a shoe store. I knew the funeral had been the day before, but here they were at the square, in the middle of a celebration. Judy and her mother were still in their Sunday church clothes. Judy saw me. She looked straight at me, then turned away. I pretended I hadn't seen her, and I hurried to the center of the square, looking for Glenn.

But when I finally saw him up ahead, I stopped. He looked different. The Cubs, I learned later, had all gone to an Army-surplus store and bought themselves pairs of Army fatigue pants and porkpie hats. Glenn looked unfamiliar in his basketball jacket—now he had one—and the baggy Army fatigues instead of his Levi's. The hat looked silly. I thought about Judy, and how her sister's death had occurred while Glenn was away playing basketball and buying new clothes. I wanted to tell him what it was like to be at home when such a terrible thing happened, but I couldn't, even though I saw him not thirty feet from me. As I hesitated, I saw his parents and Willowdean and one of his brothers crowd around him. Playfully, Willowdean knocked his hat off.

The tournament was over, but we were still wild with our victory. Senior play practice started then, and we never had classes in the afternoon because all the teachers were busy coaching the seniors on their lines in the play. Maybe they had dreams of Broadway. If the Cubs could go to the tournament, anything was possible. Judy returned to school, but everyone was afraid to speak to her. They whispered behind her back. And Judy began acting aloof, as though she had some secret knowledge that lifted her above us.

On one last cool day in early spring we had cleanup day, and there were no classes all day. Everyone was supposed to help clean the school grounds, picking up all the discarded candy wrappers and drink bottles. There was a bonfire, and instead of a plate lunch in the lunchroom—too much like the plain farm food we had to eat at home—we had hot dogs, boiled outside in a kettle over the fire. The fat hot dogs in the cold air tasted heavenly. They steamed like breath.

Just as I finished my hot dog and drank the last of my RC (we had a choice between RC Cola and Orange Crush, and I liked to notice which people chose which—it seemed to divide people into categories), Judy came up behind me and whispered, "Come out there with me." She pointed toward the graveyard across the road.

I followed her, and as we walked between solemn rows of Wilcoxes and Ingrahams and Morrisons and Crittendens, the noise of the playground receded. Judy located a spot of earth, a little brown heap that was not grassed over, even though the dandelions had already come up and turned to fluff. She knelt beside the dirt pile, like a child in a sandbox, and fussed with a pot of artificial flowers. She straightened them and poked them down into the pot, as if they were real. As she worked tenderly but firmly with the flowers, she said, "Mama says Linda Faye will be waiting for us in heaven. That's her true home. The preacher said we should feel special, to think we have a member of our family all the way up in heaven."

That was sort of how I had felt about Glenn, going to Lexington to the basketball tournament, and I didn't know what to say. I couldn't say anything, for we weren't raised to say things that were heartfelt and gracious. Country kids didn't learn manners. Manners were too embarrassing. Learning not to run in the house was about the extent of what we knew about how to act. We didn't learn to congratulate people; we didn't wish people happy birthday. We didn't even address each other by name. And we didn't jump up and spontaneously hug someone for joy. Only cheerleaders claimed that talent. We didn't say we were sorry. We hid from view, in case we might be called on to make appropriate remarks, the way certain old folks in church were sometimes called on to pray. At Cuba School, there was one teacher who, for punishment, made her students write "I love you" five hundred times on the blackboard. "Love" was a dirty word, and I had seen it on the walls of the girls' rest room—blazing there in ugly red lipstick. In the eight-page novel Glenn had showed me, Li'l Abner said "I love you" to Daisy Mae.

Private Lies

I f you don't want to hear about it, why don't you say so?"
Mickey asked his wife. He was lying in bed with a glass of
Scotch balanced on his navel.

"I thought I made myself plain," Tina said. "If you want to go
find your long-lost daughter, please just leave me out of it. I don't
want the kids to find out about your past."

"What if she needs a kidney transplant? Or has a hereditary
disease?"

"What disease?" Tina asked. She snapped off a length of den-
tal floss.

Mickey closed his eyes and breathed so that his drink tilted
slightly. He inched it to his lips. "I want to find her," he said.

"I don't know how you expect to find her. Those adoption
people guard them kids like the gold in Fort Knox."

"The gold in Fort Knox doesn't mean the same thing anymore," Mickey said, sipping his drink. "It's an outdated comparison."

He wasn't supposed to drink, because he was preulcerous, but
he compromised by drinking Scotch with half-and-half. His
brother swore a doctor had told him it was harmless that way—
Scotch tranquilized the stomach muscles; half-and-half blotted
out the acid. Tina told him he would have a heart attack from the
milk fat. She was a nurse. Mickey and Tina had been together for
more than a dozen years, and they had a boy and a girl, Ricky and

Kelly. The furniture was paid for, and the final installment on the car was due next month. Mickey sold real estate, and he hadn't sold a house in six weeks, but with interest rates going down, he was optimistic. If Mickey hadn't had a daughter born out of wedlock eighteen years ago next Tuesday, he'd have nothing on his mind now worse than the recession.

Tina turned down the corner of a page of her book, something called *Every Secret Thing*, and put it on the night table. She said, "What if she don't want to see you?"

"I think I've got a right."

"The law will tell you you lost your rights a long time ago."

Mickey saw the child once, through the window at the hospital. Donna, the mother, got to hold the baby, but he did not. No one was supposed to know he was the father. The little creature was shrimp-colored, with fuzzy black hair. Mickey could not believe what he had done. They let Donna hold her for about two minutes. Donna checked her all over, counted her fingers and toes, looked inside her diaper. "I wanted to make sure she was all there," Donna said later. "I didn't want to give away a defective baby."

Mickey sometimes felt that marriage to Tina was like riding a bus. She was the driver and he was a passenger. She made all the decisions—food, furniture, Kelly's braces, his socks. If he weren't married to Tina, he might be alone in a rented room, living on canned soup and Tang. Tina rescued him. With her, life had a regularity that was almost dogmatic. But now Tina was working a night shift, and her schedule was disrupted. She hated to miss "M*A*S*H," her favorite program. When she watched it, she always scrutinized the surgical procedures and pointed out when the action was inauthentic. "B.J. shouldn't ask for the retractor at that point," she would say.

Without Tina at night, Mickey had to keep the schedule rolling. One evening, before "M*A*S*H" came on, he helped Ricky with his arithmetic.

"I have to be in a special class," Ricky said suddenly, between problems.

"What class?"

"I have to have a tutor."

"What for? You're already in the Enrichment Class."

"I can't say my *s*'s right."

"What's wrong with your *s*'s? I don't hear anything wrong with your *s*'s."

"The teacher said so."

"Say something with an *s*. Say 'snake.' Say 'sports special.' "

"Snake. Sports special."

"That teacher has her head up her butt," said Mickey, tilting his glass of beer and then trying to peer at Ricky through the rim. It made him cross-eyed to do that.

Beer with half-and-half wasn't drinkable. It was too much like the barium milk shake he had had to drink when they X-rayed his stomach. The chalky liquid had made him gag. After swallowing it, he had watched on a screen as the dancing dots went through his system. Now he tried an experiment. First he took a swig of beer, then a sip of half-and-half. He leaned back in his La-Z-Boy and watched his children watching TV. When the commercial for Federal Express popped on, Mickey turned the volume up with the remote control. Ricky and Kelly loved the fast-talking businessman, making deals on the telephone. No one could talk that fast. Yet it didn't seem to be a trick, like a speeded-up tape, because the man didn't sound like a chipmunk.

"You should learn to talk that fast, Daddy," said Kelly.

"Why?"

"So you could sell lots of houses. It would save time."

Mickey rehearsed ways of telling Ricky and Kelly that they had a half-sister. Tina would kill him.

Mickey was uncomfortable whenever he appraised houses. The owners hovered over him while he measured the rooms and ran through his checklist of FHA-approved specifications. They resented the intrusion, but later, when he brought strangers in, the owners seemed resigned to their loss. The prospective buyers explored the houses, opening closets and cabinets. Tina snooped around like that, as a nurse, taking temperatures, washing people's private parts. Yet she wouldn't tolerate anyone knowing how much insurance they had, or how much they owed on their car. The ultimate in privacy, though, was guaranteed by adoption agencies. Like the CIA, they created new identities. Mickey didn't even know his daughter's name. If they were to meet, how would she view him? If she could appraise his life, as he would a house, she might find its dimensions too narrow, its ceilings too high, its basement cluttered and dank with memories and secrets. A dangerous basement. Not a good selling point. She would see a grouchy, preulcerous, balding bore. But that was not really true. He had his comic moments. He liked to clown around, singing "The Star-Spangled Banner" in a mock-operatic style; he would pretend to forget the words and then shift abruptly into "Carry Me Back to Old Virginny." He was a riot at parties.

Mickey and his ex-wife, Donna, had both stayed around the small town where they grew up, but he had not talked to her in three years, since the time they ran into each other at McDonald's. She was getting a hamburger and French fries to go. They made small talk. Not long after that, her second husband, Bill Jackson, died of a heart attack, and Mickey felt guilty about not sending her flowers. Mickey detested Bill Jackson—a loudmouthed fool with a violent streak—and he thought Donna was better off without him. Mickey had entertained the idea that finding their daughter would be more for Donna's sake than for his own, because she had never had other children. She had had only her husband, Bill, and, before him, three years of a bad marriage to Mickey. The marriage had dried up and died, without the baby. In fact, they did not marry until after the baby was gone. It all seemed like a cruel mistake, as though they lived in some fascist state where illegitimate babies were rounded up and taken away. When Donna got pregnant, her parents sent her to Florida to stay with her aunt temporarily. Her parents, who had money, pressured her into giving the baby up for adoption, arguing that if she kept the child, she would have to quit school in disgrace. Mickey worked after school at a feed mill to pay for a bus trip to Florida to see her when the baby was born. When he got there, Donna convinced him that giving up the baby was the only choice they had if they ever wanted to return to Kentucky. Later, after she graduated, they did marry—an afterthought, a desperate way of making amends or maybe just to spite her parents. For their honeymoon, they drove to Florida. It was the wrong time of year, unbearably hot. They stayed in an air-conditioned room in a cheap motel. Donna got her period. It seemed such a vicious irony. The marriage didn't work. Mickey often got drunk and left Donna alone at night. He blamed her for giving up the baby. After a while, he blamed her parents. In a later period, he blamed society. And more recently, he blamed himself.

Donna was expecting him. On the telephone, she seemed hesitant, but she agreed to see him. Her apartment was in a low brick building with sliding-glass entrances facing a patio and a pool, like a Holiday Inn. As he rang her bell, Mickey wondered if he could sell her a house.

"Come in if you can get in," she said, shoving away a large grocery box near the doorway. "Clothes for the Salvation Army," she said. She looked up, smiling at him. Her smile was different. "Bridgework," she explained, noticing his look.

As he sank into her white-wicker love seat, she stood over him expectantly. Her eyelids were blue. Her light-brown hair was cut in curly layers that stuck out in fluffy bunches. She worked at Lucille's Beauty Bar.

"Do you know why I'm here?" he asked, feeling suddenly weak.

"Let me guess."

"I bet you can."

"Mickey, I thought we settled everything years ago."

"Tomorrow's her birthday."

Donna went to the kitchen. She gave Mickey some lemon icebox pie and Coke. Both Coke and lemons were on his list of forbidden substances, so he picked at the pie and sipped the Coke. Donna watched him and smoked a cigarette. She never used to smoke. The dishes clattered on her glass coffee table. Mickey had to study her ashtray a long time before he realized that it was a model of Mount St. Helens. Maybe his daughter had been on a camping trip on that mountain when it blew up. He would never know.

Watching Donna emerge from the bathroom, looking stylish and aloof in pants and high heels, Mickey felt a burning pain in his stomach. Donna seemed different, prettier and more assured. Her voice had grown husky, as though she had spent years on the stage. She used to be a whiner. When they were married, she threw tantrums. When a friend gave them a starter set of stoneware as a wedding present, she grew so impatient to finish the set that she sometimes cried about it. She wasn't used to being poor, and she loathed living in a trailer.

"Do you want some more Coke?" Donna asked.

"No." He laid down the fork and blurted out, "I can't think about anything but her. Knowing she's eighteen now—it's made me stop and think. And I want to find her. Donna, they've got to tell us where she is."

"There's no way on God's green earth we can find her," said Donna. "You know that." She lit a cigarette and offered Mickey one, but he waved the pack away.

"I've been quit four years on July first," he said.

"You have everything measured."

Donna's smoke traveled in front of his face. "Anyone else would have praised me for quitting," he said. "Look, Donna. All I'm saying is, the girl's eighteen now, and she just might be wondering who her mama and daddy are. Why don't we try to find her? I can't afford a lawyer, but together we could—"

"I don't want to find her," said Donna, sucking deeply on her cigarette. "She wouldn't mean anything to me. I don't know her. That's all way in the past."

The pain seized Mickey's stomach. "I don't think you mean that, Donna."

"It would be just asking for trouble," she said, looking straight into his eyes. She stood up and took the plate with the unfinished pie into the kitchen. She even looked taller now, Mickey realized, amazed. "She wouldn't want to see us," Donna said from the kitchen. "Not after what we did."

"Here, sign this," Tina said, shoving a paper at Mickey.

"What is it?" asked Mickey suspiciously. On "M*A*S*H," Radar always tricked the colonel into signing for things.

"The permission to let Ricky take special classes for his *s*'s."

"I don't hear nothing wrong with his *s*'s."

"You don't? Did you hear him say 'Southside'?" Their street was Southside Drive. Tina went to the foot of the stairs and called Ricky.

Ricky obediently said "Southside."

"Say 'sports special,' " said Mickey.

"Sports special."

"Can't you hear it?" Tina asked.

"No. You never heard it either till the experts thought this up."

"Experts," said Ricky, lisping on both *s* sounds.

"You're exaggerating," Mickey said.

He signed the paper. Once, he had signed a kid away completely.

If Mickey had some money, he'd hire a detective. If he sold a house, he would go to Florida to search for his daughter. He would kidnap Donna and take her with him. He couldn't get over her bridgework. It made her smile sexy and mysterious. Nobody was thinking seriously of buying. Mickey had a feeling that the prime rate was going to go down, but when he took clients around in the big company Buick to view houses, he felt like a museum guide. People seemed to be looking at interiors aesthetically, as though the Formica counters and bay windows with imitation leaded glass were priceless antiquities. One day, Mickey showed a sixty-thousand-dollar house to a young couple who drove a ten-year-old Ford with a noisy muffler. They were spending an unusual amount of time in the house. The man was crawling around in the attic, inspecting the insulation, and the woman was measuring rooms. Mickey forgot where he was. He stared out the picture window. It was raining lightly. A bird was in the street, hopping just ahead of a downhill rivulet, then letting it overtake him and splashing his wings in it. "Are you on the way to loving me?" the woman with the tape measure asked. Mickey shook himself out of his trance. The woman was smiling. "I love that song, don't you?" She was referring to a song playing on the radio. She wasn't even talking to Mickey. She was talking to her husband, who had cobwebs on his nose.

When Mickey arrived at home that afternoon, after the couple had said they would think about the house, he punched the remote control for the garage door. Too late, he saw that the robin that had been building a nest on the ledge above the door was at it again. The vibration from the door sent sprigs of dry grass wafting to the ground. He turned around and drove to Donna's.

"You can't get rid of me that easy," he said. When she laughed, he said clumsily, "I like your apartment."

She smiled with her gums showing, like Lily Tomlin. "Try this tea," she said. "It's herb tea. It'll help you relax."

Donna had red-striped wallpaper that he could see on his eyelids when he closed his eyes. She said she had chartered a plane with some "crazy business types" and had flown over Mount St. Helens. That explained the ashtray. She had been out in Seattle at a hairdressers' convention. Beauticians were no longer called beauticians. Now they were called hairdressers, or, better still, cosmetologists, which sounded like a group Carl Sagan would be president of.

"Tell me what else you've been doing with your life," said Mickey, burning his tongue on his tea. He admired a woman who would charter a plane.

"Just crazy things," she said. "Since Bill died, I've been thrown back on my own resources, you might say. I run around with some girls and we go to Lexington and mess around. Or we go to Memphis and mess around."

Mickey listened, fascinated.

Donna said, "That tea's good for your stomach. I'm getting into herbs. Chamomile, tansy, chervil, lots of them. And mugwort!" She broke out laughing. "You put mugwort under your pillow to make you dream more intensely. But I had to take it out. With all those wild dreams, I wasn't getting any rest! It's a very *female* herb, they say." She laughed again. "Whatever that means."

"I dreamed somebody dumped forty newborn kittens at my house—all orange, with two black mamas. What do you think that means?"

"I'm not going to answer that." Donna turned her back on him and rummaged in a kitchen drawer. "I think you dreamed that deliberately," she said.

"Did you love Bill?"

"What kind of question is that? Do *you* love Tina?"

"Well, yes and no." Mickey sipped the tea. It was watery, with a taste of licorice.

"Let's change the subject," Donna said, almost whispering as she brushed past him.

"Do you have any half-and-half?"

"No, just milk."

"How about Scotch?"

"Are you still drinking? Isn't the tea any good?"

"It's too hot." He set the mug down. "I'll come back to it."

Donna gave him some gin, with a milk chaser. The tea grew cold. Donna had a drink with him, the first they had ever had together. Growing giggly, she told him several wacky episodes from her trips to Lexington and Memphis. She and a friend planned to move to Lexington and open a little teashop that sold gourmet items and herbs—*if* her friend could make up her mind about leaving her husband.

"It's a bad time to start a new business," Mickey warned her. "Are you going to buy or rent? Do you know how to do your own taxes?"

"I wasn't born yesterday," Donna said.

She gave him another drink and they watched *Hangar 18* on HBO. She sat beside him on the couch, so close he could smell her perfume. Mickey hardly noticed the movie. He was thinking about Donna's teeth, her formidable high-heeled boots, the way she stuck her cigarette in the volcano.

When the movie ended, Donna said, "I feel cheated. The idea

that human life originated on another planet is old stuff."

"I feel cheated, too," Mickey said, before realizing she was talking about the movie. But she was already in his arms.

Mickey and Donna got in the habit of talking on the telephone late at night, when Tina was working and the children were asleep. Tina complained about the line being busy when she tried to call from the hospital, but Mickey blamed it on the party line. Mickey didn't remember having conversations with Donna when they were married. Now he liked the way long silences on the telephone seemed so natural. Donna wouldn't say, "Are you still there?" She just waited for him to talk. She wouldn't talk about their daughter, though. When he brought up the subject, she said "Hush," in her new, throaty voice. Mickey reviewed his life for her. Tina and the kids. Houses. He said Tina was the sort of person who had separate garbage bags for everything, even tiny ones for scraps from each meal. He told her about Ricky's speech therapy, and Donna said authorities were trying to make everyone sound like John Chancellor. You couldn't make Tina see that, he said, feeling elated.

When he could get free in the afternoons, he went to Donna's apartment. There was nothing about making love with Donna that was familiar. She seemed to have learned all new techniques. Her body was different, lighter, more flexible. Her striped wallpaper burned his eyelids. They heard piano lessons coming from the floor above them, pupils jerking their way through John Thompson. Later, they watched HBO and drank herb tea.

On the news, the prime rate dropped half a percentage point. Housing starts were holding steady. Mickey expected to sell a house any day. He was sure he had fought off the ulcer.

One night at McDonald's with Ricky and Kelly, Mickey saw Donna with a blond woman in a back booth, and he felt a twinge in his duodenum. She waved, and the children stared at her. When Donna walked by their booth, he nodded and said, "How ya doing, Donna," as though she were any old secretary or store clerk he used to know. He bought a milk shake to go, so he could take it home and put Scotch in it.

When Mickey finally sold a house—a brick ranch with a two-car garage, owner-financed—he knew immediately that he wanted to take Donna to Florida. When he told Tina he wanted to go search for his daughter, she said, "I don't care, but I can't have the children knowing what you're up to. That's all I ask. The things they learn in school are bad enough."

Tina was trying to get the cellophane off a box containing a frozen deep-dish peach pie. Mickey stared at the uncharacteristically helpless way she was opening the package, pawing at the cellophane like a declawed cat. Kelly rushed in then, pummeling his stomach and saying, "You *have* to get me new sneakers for gym. I can't live like a grubbo!"

Mickey planned to leave Tina half the commission money. He told Donna, "We'll still have enough to have a blast. We'll stay in a fancy hotel this time."

He knew she loved to travel. She had been to Yosemite with Bill once, and on a package tour to New York with a girlfriend, as well as on the recent trip to Seattle, which she was still paying VISA for.

Donna said, "I'd go with you if you went to Hawaii instead."

"Too far. Too expensive."

"Bermuda, then. Or Acapulco."

"Those are all tropical resorts," he said. "I can tell that's where you really want to go. And Florida is the closest."

Donna studied the map of Florida that he gave her. She made a list of places she wouldn't mind seeing: Disney World, Sea World, anything with "world" in it. "Alligator Alley!" she sang out on the telephone when he said "Hello" one evening.

"I knew you'd see it my way," Mickey said.

"Why don't you get Tina a subscription to HBO?" Donna suggested. "That will keep her busy."

Mickey wondered if he was leaving Tina for good. He was not really making that clear. Kelly and Ricky didn't enter into his plans yet. It was too complicated. Tina was so orderly. She thought of all the details. She asked questions. Would he promise to stay in hotels that had smoke alarms? Did he know how ridiculous it was to set out for Florida with no inkling of how to find the girl? Tina followed him around as he tended to last-minute chores. He cleaned the leaves out of the gutters for her, then almost wept at the poignancy of that final gesture. He was up on the ladder and she was talking, talking. She told him that her niece, who had a paper route, was accosted on her bike by a weirdo who wanted her to stick a newspaper in his pants. He had on pants with a stretch waistband, and he pulled the band out for her to poke the rolled newspaper in. Tina's niece escaped, pedaling like crazy. Then Tina described an operation for breast cancer, explaining the way the doctors inserted a probe into a bleeding duct. Was that hereditary? Mickey wanted to know.

On the lawn, a robin fluttered its wings, rose in the air like a helicopter, and snatched a slim green caterpillar glinting in the sun.

"You can't just up and leave all you've worked so hard for," Tina said, finally breaking into tears.

"Tina's no fool," Donna said. "I bet she knows what's going on." They were driving her Mazda to the Nashville airport. Mickey had told Tina he had a ride with a client, and met Donna at his office.

"Don't worry," he said. "This is *our* trip. It's none of her business. We're going to have us some fun." He started singing "The Star-Spangled Banner" in his fake operatic style. Donna howled with laughter. He realized she had never heard his act before. When he pretended to forget the words and shifted into "Carry Me Back to Old Virginny," she went to pieces.

Florida was balmy, the right season this time. The plane ride was thrilling, and Mickey was giddy. He had graduated to Brandy Alexanders. The herb tea, he was convinced, had cured his stomach problem. The hotel was a beachfront high-rise with pink balconies—first class, to compensate for the depressing motel years ago. Mickey had intended to pay for Donna's trip, but at the hotel desk she slapped down her credit card.

"I insist on paying my own way," she said.

"No. I didn't mean for you to do that."

"I insist. Don't forget I owe you for that plane ticket."

The desk clerk ran the credit cards through the machine.

"This is the eighties," Donna said. "Nobody gives a hoot if we're not married."

From the balcony of their third-floor room, they watched the swarm of people on the beach. The sunshine felt like a warm glow of approval.

"Look at all the fat people," Donna said. "Some people just shouldn't be allowed to wear bathing suits."

"I'm glad I lifted weights this winter," said Mickey.

He brought a bucket of ice and a can of Coke to the balcony and sat down in a canvas chair. As he poured the Coke into plastic glasses, he said, "Cokes are sixty cents in that machine. I couldn't believe it."

When he handed Donna the glass, she burst into tears.

"All I can imagine is that we will just somehow run into her down here and recognize her," she sobbed. "I've heard of that happening with separated twins."

Mickey found a Kleenex and nervously dabbed at her cheeks. "She'd look just like you," he said.

"She had your mouth." Donna stopped crying and shed her beach jacket. Her skin was pale and freckled. Mickey thought of two springer spaniels he had known in his life, both named Freckles.

Donna blew her nose and said, "I should have gotten an abortion back then, but I was too chicken. I knew of a girl in Bowling Green who died suddenly from a strange hemorrhage. I was a sophomore. She was such a nice girl, and real popular. Everybody was so naive back then. They all believed she really died from a hemorrhage, out of the blue. I was terrified that any month I might bleed to death, without warning. But a couple of years later, when I got pregnant and my parents wanted me to have an abortion, I put two and two together, and I realized what had happened to her. That's why I wouldn't have an abortion. But later I thought I should have. Then the whole thing would have been over with."

"That's a terrible thing to say. You'd feel worse."

"I think death is a whole lot easier to get over than the mess people make of their lives. Bill's been dead three years. I'm over *him*." Donna lit a cigarette and blew out a deliberate cloud of smoke. "It's all so messy," she said. "I didn't want to dig up the past. She's got her own life."

"But we could find her."

"I don't see how."

"What if she wants to find us?" asked Mickey. "Where would she look?"

Donna didn't answer. Mickey watched a flock of sea birds fly between him and a palm tree, like a line crossing it out.

On the beach, Donna scooped up some sand and put it in Mickey's hand. "Feel," she said. "Feel how scratchy it is."

"Why's that?"

"It's teeny bits of coral. It's not smooth, the way other sand is. It's hell on your feet."

"I didn't know that." He had on tennis shoes and Donna had on flip-flops.

"I remember that from when we were in Florida before."

Mickey found a little white shell and handed it to Donna, but she wouldn't take it.

"I don't want to collect shells," she said. "When you look inside them, sometimes you find creepy little things living in there."

Mickey let the shell fall. He did not remember the sand from before. Looking out at the bright ocean coming to meet it, in whispers, he felt, with a sense of relief, that nothing private was left here. The thousands of people were all exposed—like underwear in the wrong room, like a lisp. Mickey saw himself and Donna years from now, holding hands, still walking on this beach. They stepped back, then forward, like dancers. They were moving like this along the beach, crunching the fragments of skeletons.

Coyotes

Cobb's fiancée, Lynnette Johnson, wasn't interested in bridal magazines or china patterns or any of that girl stuff. Even when he brought up the subject of honeymoons she would joke about some impossible place—Bulgaria, Hong Kong, Lapland, Peru.

"I just want to go no-frills," she said. "What kind of wedding do *you* want?" She was sitting astride his lap in a kitchen chair.

"I want the kinky-sex, thank-God-it's-Friday, double-Dutch-chocolate special," he said, playing with her hair. It smelled like peppermint.

She was warm and heavy in his lap, and she had her arms around him like a sleepy child. It bothered him that she hadn't even told her folks yet about him, but he had put off taking her to meet his mother, so he thought he understood.

It was the weekend, and they were trying to decide whether to go out for dinner. They were at his apartment at Orchard Acres —two-fifty a month, twice as much as he had paid for his previous apartment. His new place was nice, with a garbage disposal and a patio. He had moved out of his rathole when he began working with the soil-conservation service, but now he wished he had saved to buy a house instead of splurging on an expensive apartment with a two-year lease. She kept clothes in his closet and in the chest of drawers, and the bathroom was littered with her things, but she was adamant about holding on to her own place for the time being. Lynnette had such definite ways. She always got up early and ran six or eight miles, even in the winter. She ate peanut butter for breakfast—for protein, she told him. She claimed weeds were beautiful. She had arranged some dried brown weeds in a jug on the dining table. She had picked the weeds from a field when they went pecan-hunting back in the fall. Wild pecans were small, and the nuts were hard to pick out. Cobb still had most of them in a cracker box.

"You wouldn't believe the pictures I saw today," she said a bit later when they were lolling in bed, still undecided about going out to eat. Cobb was trying to lose weight.

Lynnette worked in a film-developing place that rushed out photos in twenty-four hours. The pictures rolled off the chain-drive assembly and through the cutter, and she examined and counted them before slipping them into envelopes.

"There was a man and a woman and a dog," she said. "A baby was asleep in a bassinet at the foot of the bed. Some of the pictures were of the man in bed with the dog—posed together like they were having breakfast in bed. The dog was sitting up on its haunches against the pillow. And in some of the pictures the woman was in bed with the dog. You couldn't really tell, but I don't think either of these people had a stitch of clothes on. They were laughing. The dog, I swear, was laughing, too."

"What kind of dog?"

"A big one. Blond, with his tongue hanging out."

"Sounds like a happy family scene," said Cobb, noticing that he and Lynnette were sitting up against their pillows the way she said the people in the photos were. "It was probably Sunday morning," he said. "And they were fooling around before the baby woke up."

"No, I think it was something really weird." She held her wrist up near the lamp and studied her watch. Getting out of bed, she said, "I saw the woman come in and pick up the pictures. A really nice woman—middle-aged, but still pretty. You'd never suspect anything. But she was too old to have a baby."

Some of the pictures Lynnette told him about frightened her.

She saw people posing with guns and knives, grinning and pointing their weapons at each other. But the nudes were more disturbing. The lab wasn't supposed to print them, but when she examined negatives for printing she saw plenty of nude shots, mostly close-ups of private parts or couples photographing themselves in the mirror in much the same pose they would have struck beside some monument on their vacation. Once, Lynnette saw a set of negatives that must have been from an orgy—a dozen or more naked people. One was a group shot, like a class picture, taken beside a barbecue grill. Cobb suggested that they might have been a nudist society, but Lynnette said nudists were too casual to take photographs of this kind. Those people weren't casual, she said.

Cobb was his real name, but people assumed it was a nickname —implying "rough as a cob." Rough in that sense, he thought, meant prickly, touchy, capable of great ups and downs. But Cobb knew he wasn't really like that. He guessed he hadn't lived up to his name, or grown into it, as people were said to do, and this left him feeling a little vague about himself. Cobb was twenty-eight, and he had had a number of girlfriends, but none like Lynnette. Ironically, he first met her when he took in a roll of film to be developed—his trip to Florida with Laura Morgan. He had dated Laura for about a year. They had driven down in her Thunderbird, spending a week at Daytona and then a couple of days at Disney World. They took pictures of the motels, the palm trees, the usual stuff. When he went to get the pictures, he struck up a conversation with Lynnette. From something she said, he realized she had seen his photos. He suddenly realized how trite they were. She saw pictures like that come through her machine every day. He felt his life take a turn, a hard jolt. They started going out—at first secretly, because it took Cobb a few weeks to work matters out with Laura. Laura wouldn't speak to him now when he ran into her in the hall at work. She was the type who would have wanted a wedding reception at the Holiday Inn, a ranch house in a cozy subdivision, church on Sunday. But Lynnette made him feel there were different ways to look at the world. She brought out something fresh and unexpected in him. She made him see that anything conventional—Friday-night strolls at the mall or an assortment of baked-potato toppings at a restaurant—was funny and absurd. They went around town together trading on that feeling, finding the unusual in the everyday, laughing at things most people didn't see the humor in. "You're just in love," his older brother, George, said when Cobb tried to explain his excitement.

Cobb went to his mother's for supper on Tuesdays, when his stepfather, Jim Dance, an accountant, was out at his Optimist Club meetings. Their house made Cobb uncomfortable. The furnishings defied classification. He hadn't grown up with any of it; it was all acquired after his mother, Gloria, married Jim. The walls were covered with needlepoint scenes of castles and reproductions of paintings of Amish families in buggies. The dining room had three curio cabinets, as well as Gloria's collection of souvenir coasters, representing all fifty states. In the living room, Early American clashed with low modern chairs upholstered with fat pillows. The room was filled with glass paperweights and glass globes and ashtrays, all swirling with colors like the planet Jupiter.

Cobb had come over to tell her he was going to marry Lynnette. His mother was overjoyed and gave him a hug. He could feel the flour on her hands making prints on his sweater.

"Is she a good cook?" she wanted to know.

"I don't know. We always eat out. I don't want any ham," he said, indicating the platter of ham on the table. "Do you want me to marry a good cook who will fatten me up or a lousy cook who'll keep me trim? What's your standard, Mom?"

Gloria forked a piece of ham onto his plate. "What are her people like?" She tore into the ham on her own plate.

"They're not in jail. They're not on welfare. They don't walk around with knives. They're not cross-eyed or anything."

"Why am I surprised?" she said.

"I don't even know them," Cobb said. "They're not from

around here. She moved down here from Wisconsin when she was in high school. Her daddy worked at Ingersoll, but now he's been transferred to Texas."

Gloria smiled. "It'll be awful hot in Texas by June. Are they going to have a big shindig?"

"I don't think we'll get married there." Hesitantly, he said, "Lynnette's different, Mom. She's real serious and she doesn't like anything fancy."

"You ought to learn something about her people," Gloria said anxiously. "You never know."

"She's real nice. You'll like her."

Gloria poured more iced tea into her tall blue glass. "Well, it's about time you married," she said. "You know, when you were a baby you walked and talked earlier than any of the others. I had faith that you'd turn out fine, no matter what I did. But when you were about thirteen you went through a stage. You got real moody, and you slept all the time. After that, you never were the same lively boy again." Gloria bowed her head. "I never did understand that."

"That was probably when I found out about nuclear war. That's a real downer when it dawns on you."

"I never worry about nuclear war and such as that! The evil of the day is enough to keep me busy." Sullenly, she chomped on a biscuit.

"The evil of the day is where it's at, Mom," said Cobb.

After supper, when he returned from the bathroom, she was standing by a lamp, consulting the *TV Guide*, with the magazine's cover curled back. "On 'Moonlighting' they just talk-talk-talk," she said. "It drives you up the wall."

He flipped through her coffee-table books: *The Book of Barbecue, The Art of Breathing, The Perils of Retirement.* Everything was either an art or a peril these days. When he was growing up, his mother didn't read much. She was always too tired. She worked at a clothing store, and his dad drove a bread truck. There were four children. Nobody ever did anything especially outrageous or strange. Once, they went to the Memphis zoo, their only over-night family trip. In a petting-zoo area, a llama tried to hump his sister. Now his sister was living in Indiana, and his daddy was in Chicago with some woman.

Cobb noticed how people always seemed to be explaining them-selves. If his stepfather was eating a hamburger, he'd immedi-ately get defensive about cholesterol, even though no one had commented on it. Cobb never felt he had to explain himself. He was always just himself. But he was beginning to think there was a screwy little note, like a wormhole, in that attitude of his. He had a sweatshirt that said "PADUCAH, THE FLAT SQUIRREL CAPITAL OF THE WORLD." Lynnette was giving him a terrible time about it. The sweatshirt showed a flattened squirrel. It wasn't realistic, with fur and eyes and a fluffy tail or anything; it was just a black abstract shape.

"It's in extremely bad taste," Lynnette said. "I can't even stand to mash a bug. So I can't begin to laugh at a steamrollered creature."

It was the first thing that had really come between them, so he apologized and stopped wearing the sweatshirt. The shirt was just stating a fact, though. Driving down Broadway one day in the fall, Cobb counted three dead squirrels in three blocks. It was all those enormous oak trees.

"You're sweet," Lynnette said, forgiving him. "But sometimes, Cobb, you just don't think."

The incident made him wonder. It startled him that he had done something others would instantly consider so thoughtless. He wondered how much of his behavior was like that, how much Lynnette would discover about him that was questionable. He felt defenseless, in the dark. He didn't know how serious she was about getting married. She told him she couldn't ask her folks to throw a big wedding. It would make them nervous, she said. He figured they couldn't afford it, so he didn't press her. She never asked for much from him, but her reaction to the sweatshirt seemed blown out of proportion. He did not tell her he'd been out rabbit hunting a few times with his brother George.

Cobb saw a strange scene in the Wal-Mart. He had gone in to

buy rubber boots to wear hunting on George's property, which was certain to be muddy after the recent thaw. Cobb was trying to find a pair of size-9 boots when he noticed one of the clerks, a teenager, calling to a couple over in the housewares aisle. "I've got something to tell y'all," she said. The boy and girl came over. They were about the same age as the clerk and were dressed alike in flannel shirts and new jeans. The clerk had on a pale-blue sweater and jeans and pink basketball shoes. She wore a work smock, unbuttoned, over her sweater.

"Well, we got married," she said in a flat tone, holding her hand up to show them her ring.

"I thought y'all were going to wait," said the girl, fiddling with a package of cassette tapes she was holding.

"Yeah, we got tired of waiting and we were setting around and Kevin said why not, this weekend's as good as any, so we just went ahead and did it."

"Kevin never could stand to wait around," said the boy, smiling faintly.

His girlfriend asked, "Did y'all go anywhere?"

"Just to the lake. We stayed all night in one of those motels." She pushed and pulled at her ring awkwardly, as if she was trying to think of something interesting to say about the trip. The boy and girl said they were going to Soul Night at Skate City, even though it was always so crowded. Another explanation, Cobb realized. They drifted off, the girl tugging at the boy's belt loop.

Cobb momentarily forgot what he had come for. His eyes roamed the store. A bargain table of snow boots, a table of tube socks. His mother and the CPA had been to Gatlinburg, where they saw tube socks spun in a sock store. She said it was fascinating. At a museum there, she saw a violin made from a ham can. Cobb was confused. Why weren't these three young people excited and happy? Why would anybody go all the way to Gatlinburg to see how tube socks were made?

George's place used to be in the country, but now a subdivision was working its way out in his direction, and a nearby radio transmitter loomed skyward. When Cobb arrived, the dog, Ruffy, greeted him lazily from a sunny spot on the deck George had built onto the back of his house. Above a patch of grass beside a stump, a wind sock shaped like a goose was bobbing realistically, puffed with wind.

"Hey, Cobb," said George, opening the back door. "That thing fooled you, didn't it?" He laughed uproariously.

George worked a swing shift and didn't have to go in till four. His wife, Ceci, was at work, waitressing at the Cracker Barrel. Toys and clothes and dirty dishes were strewn about. Cobb stepped around a large aluminum turkey-roasting pan caked with grease.

After George put on his boots and jacket and located a box of shotgun shells, they headed through the fields back to a pond where George had set some muskrat traps. It was a biting, damp day. Cobb's new boots were too roomy inside, and the chill penetrated the rubber. Tube socks, he thought.

"I hate winter," George said. "I sure will be glad when it warms up."

Cobb said, "I like it O.K. I like all weather."

"You would."

"I like not knowing what it's going to be. Even when they say what it's going to be, you're still not sure."

"You ain't changed a bit, Cobb. I thought you were getting serious about that Johnson girl. I thought you were ready to settle down."

"What does that mean? Settle down?"

George just laughed at Cobb. George was nine years older, and he had always treated him like a child.

"If you're going to get married, my advice is not to expect too much," George said. "It's give-and-take. As long as you understand that, maybe you won't screw it up."

"What makes you think I might screw it up?"

George whooped loudly. "My God, Cobb, you could fuck up an *anvil*."

"Thanks for the vote of confidence."

A car horn sounded in the direction of George's house. "Hell. There she is, home early, wanting me to go after that shoulder we had barbecued at It's the Pits. Well, she can wait till we check these traps."

There was nothing in the traps. One of them had been sprung, apparently by a falling twig. Cobb felt glad. He thought he would tell Lynnette how he felt. Then he wondered if he was trying too hard to please her.

George said, "I was half expecting to catch a coyote."

"I thought coyotes lived out West." George pronounced "coyote" like "high oat," but Cobb pronounced the *e*. He didn't know which was right.

"They're moving this way," George said. "A fellow down the street shot one, and there was one killed up on the highway. I haven't seen any, but when an ambulance goes on, they howl. I've heard 'em." George formed his lips in a circle and howled a high "woo-woo" sound that gave Cobb chill bumps.

Cobb couldn't stop thinking about the teenage bride at the Wal-Mart. He invented some explanations for the behavior of those three teenagers: Maybe the girl wasn't great friends with the couple and so she was shy about telling them her news. Or maybe the guy was her former boyfriend and so she felt awkward telling about her marriage. Cobb remembered the smock she was wearing and the gray-green color of the cheap boots lined up on the wall behind her. When he told Lynnette about the girl and how empty she had seemed, Lynnette said, "She probably doesn't get enough exercise. Teenagers are in notoriously bad shape. All that junk food."

Lynnette was never still. She did warm-up and cool-down stretches. Even talking, she used her whole body. She was always ready to make love, even after the late movie on TV. At his apartment that weekend, they watched *The Tomb of Ligeia*. She wanted to make love during the scary parts.

It was almost one in the morning when the movie ended. She got up and brought yogurt back from the refrigerator—blueberry for him, strawberry for her. He liked to watch her eat yogurt. He shook his carton up until the yogurt was mixed and liquefied enough to drink, but she ate hers carefully—plunging her spoon into the cup vertically, all the way to the bottom, then bringing it up coated with plain yogurt and a bit of the fruit at the tip. He liked to watch her lick the spoon. George would probably say that this was a pleasure that wouldn't last, but Cobb felt he could watch Lynnette eat yogurt every day of their lives. There would be infinite variety in her actions.

Each of them seemed to have an off-limits area, a place they were afraid to reveal. He couldn't explain to her what it felt like to get up before dawn to go deer hunting—to feel for his clothes in the dark, to fortify himself with hot oats and black coffee, and then to plunge out in the cold, quiet morning, crunching frost with his hard boots. Hardly daring to breathe, he crouched in the blind, listening for a telltale snort and quiver, leaves rustling, a blur of white in the growing dawn, then a sudden clatter of hooves and a flash of joy.

There were some new pictures from work that Lynnette was telling him about now. "It was a Florida vacation," she said. "Old couple. Palm trees, blue water. But no typical shots—no Disney World, no leaping dolphins. Instead, there are these pictures of mud, pictures of tree roots and bark. Trees up close. And all these views of a small stucco house. Pictures of cars at motels, cars on the beach, cars in a parking lot at a supermarket. A sort of board-walk trail in the woods. Then a guy holding up something small. You can't tell what it is."

"How small?" Cobb was trying to follow her description with his eyes closed.

"Like a quarter he's about to flip."

"Tell me one of your stories about the pictures."

"Let's see, they used to live there long ago. They raised their kids there, then moved far away. Now . . . they're retired now and so they go back, but everything's changed. The trees are bigger. There are more cars. The old motels look—well, old. Someone else owns their house, and the crepe myrtle and the azaleas she planted have grown into monsters. But she recognizes them—the same shade of purple, the same place she planted them by the driveway. They go and spy on the house and get chased away. Then they go to one of the parks where there's a boardwalk through the woods. A man raped her there once, when she was young and pretty, but after all these years going back there doesn't mean much. Then she loses her wedding ring and they retrace their steps, looking for it. They look through cracks in the boardwalk. They take all these pictures, in case the ring shows up in the pictures and they'll be able to tell later. Like in that old movie we saw, *Blow-Up?* Then they find the ring, and she photographs him holding it up. But it doesn't show up in the picture."

"That didn't happen to you, did it?"

"What?"

"Getting raped."

"No. I just made it up."

Turning over and opening his eyes, he said, "The way you do that, make up stories—you wouldn't change that, would you? When we're old, you should still do that."

"I hope I have a better job by then."

"No, I mean the way you can look at something and have a take on it. Not just take it for granted."

"It's no big deal," she said, squirming.

"It is to me."

She set her yogurt on the lamp table and suddenly pounded her pillow. "You know what I hate the most?" she said. "Those spread shots guys take of their wives or girlfriends. I think about those whenever I do my stretches for running." She shuddered. "It's disgusting—like something a gynecologist would see. It's not even sexy."

"Maybe you shouldn't look at them."

She ate some yogurt, and a strange look came on her face, as though she had just tasted a spot of mold. "You don't expect a nurse or a doctor to go to pieces when they see blood, so I should at least be able to look at those negatives. It's not personal. It's not my life—right?"

"Right. It's like TV or movies. It's not real." Cobb tried to comfort her, but she wriggled out of his grasp.

"It *is* real," she said.

Cobb kicked at the bedspread, rearranging it. "I don't always understand you," he said, reaching for her again. "I'm afraid I'll screw things up between us. I'm afraid I'll make some mistake and not know it till it's too late."

"What are you talking about?"

"I don't know, something my brother said."

"It's a mistake to listen to your relatives," she said, spooning the last of her yogurt. "They always believe the worst."

That weekend, he took Lynnette to his mother's for Sunday dinner. His mother would have liked it better if he had taken Lynnette to Sunday-morning church services first, but he couldn't do that to her. And he didn't want to start something false he'd have to keep up indefinitely.

"You're not going to believe her house," said Cobb on the way.

Lynnette was wearing a black miniskirt, yellow tights, short black boots, a long yellow sweater. She looked great in yellow, like a yellow-legged shorebird with black feet he'd sometimes seen at the lake.

"Why are you so nervous about her house?" she asked. "All women have a unique way of relating to their house. I think it's interesting."

"This is more than interesting. It's a case study."

His mother was in the kitchen frying chicken. She wore an apron over her church clothes, a gray ensemble with flecks of pink scattered all over it. She said, "I would have stayed here this morning and had dinner ready for you, but we had this new young man at church giving a talk before the service. He came to work with the youth. He was so nice! The nicest young man you'd ever want to meet. He's called a Christian communicator." She laughed and rolled her hands in her apron.

Cobb tried to see his mother's house through Lynnette's eyes. All the glass objects made him suddenly see his mother's fragility. She was almost sixty years old, but she had no gray hair. It dawned on him that she must have been dyeing it for years. His mother didn't look at Lynnette or talk to her directly. She spoke to Lynnette through Cobb—a strange way to carry on a conversation, but something he had often noticed that people did.

Jim, the CPA, shooed them into the living room while Gloria cooked. Smoking a pipe, he fired questions at Lynnette as though he were interviewing her for the position of Cobb's wife: "Are you related to the Johnsons out on Jubilee Road? What does your daddy do? Who does your taxes?"

"I always do my own taxes," Lynnette said. "It's pretty simple."

"She's not but twenty-three," Cobb said to his stepfather. "You think she's into capital gains and tax shelters?"

At the table, Cobb remarked, "George called this morning and said he saw one of those coyotes out at his place. We're going out this afternoon."

"We're going to look for coyotes," Lynnette said enthusiastically. She pronounced "coyotes" with an *e* at the end, the way he did, so Cobb figured that was the correct way.

"Lynnette likes to go walking out in the fields," Cobb said. "She's a real nature girl."

Gloria said, "George is after me every summer to go back on that creek and look for blackberries, but now I wouldn't go for love nor money—not if there's wild coyotes."

"George says they're moving in because of all the garbage around," Cobb explained. "They catch rabbits out in the fields and then at night scoot into town and raid the garbage cans. They've got it made in the shade."

"Y'all better be careful," Gloria said.

"They don't attack people," Lynnette said. During the meal, she talked about her job. She said, "Sometimes I'll read about a wreck in the paper and then the pictures show up and I recognize the victim. The sheriff brings a roll in now and then when their equipment isn't working."

"I sure would hate that," said Gloria.

Lynnette, spearing a carrot slice, said, "We get amazing pictures—gunshot wounds and drownings, all mixed in with vacations and children. And the thing is, they're not unusual at all. They're everywhere, all the time. It's life."

Jim and Gloria nodded doubtfully, and Lynnette went on, "I couldn't sleep last night, thinking about some pictures that came in Friday—a whole roll of film of a murder victim on a metal table. The sheriff brought the roll in Friday morning and picked them up after lunch. I recognized the body from the guy's picture in the newspaper. I couldn't keep from looking."

"I saw that in the paper!" said Cobb's stepfather. "He owed money and the other guy got tired of waiting for it. So he got drunk and blasted him out. That's the way it is with some of these people—scum."

Lynnette dabbed her mouth with a mustard-yellow napkin and said, "It was weird to see somebody's picture in the newspaper and then see the person all strung out on a table with bullet holes in his head, and still be able to recognize the person. The picture they ran in the paper was a school picture. That was really sad. School pictures are always so embarrassing."

"Would you like some more chicken?" Gloria asked her. "Cobb, do you mean you're eating squash? I thought I'd never see the day."

That afternoon was pleasant and sunny, still nippy but with a springlike feel to the air. Cobb and Lynnette drove out to George's, stopping at Lynnette's apartment first so that she could change clothes. Cobb was glad to get out of his mother's house. He thought with a sinking feeling what it might be like in the coming years to go there regularly for Sunday dinner. He had never seen Lynnette seem so morbid, as though her whole personality had congealed and couldn't be released in its usual vivacious way.

George popped out on the deck as soon as they pulled up. The dog barked, then sniffed Lynnette.

"Ruffy was barking last night about eleven," George told them, before Cobb could introduce Lynnette. "I turned on the outside light, and Ruffy come running up to the deck, scared to death. There was this damned coyote out in the yard stalking that goose! It was fluttering in the wind and the coyote had his eye on it. Ruffy didn't know what to think." George pointed at the wind sock and made hulking, stalking motions with his body. He laughed.

"The goose looks absolutely real," Lynnette said, stooping to pet the dog. "I can see why a coyote would make a mistake."

"I tell you, it was the funniest thing," George said, overcome with his news. He stood up straight, containing his laughter, and then said, "Damn, Cobb, where'd you get such a good-looking girl?"

"At the gittin' place," Cobb said with a grin.

Ceci was there, along with the three kids. "Don't look at this mess," Ceci said when they went inside. "I gave up a long time ago trying to keep house." Ceci shoved at her two-year-old, Candy, who was tugging at her elbow. The little girl had about ten rubber bands wound tightly around her arm. As Ceci methodically worked them off, she said, "We're still eating on that shoulder, Cobb. I'll fix y'all a sandwich to take back to the creek if you want me to."

Cobb shook his head no. "Mom just loaded us up with fried chicken and I can't hardly walk."

Lynnette, who must have spotted the gun rack in the den, asked George, "Are you going to shoot the coyote?"

George shook his head. "Not on Sunday. I can't shoot him with a shotgun anyway. I'd need a high-powered rifle."

"I'd love to see a coyote," Lynnette said.

"Well, you can have him," said Ceci. "I don't want to see no coyotes."

"Maybe we'll run into one back at the creek," Cobb said to Lynnette in an assuring voice. He caressed her back protectively.

"They're probably all laying up asleep at this time of day," said George. "If I could get out there about six in the morning, then I might see one. But I can't get out of bed that early anymore."

"Lynnette gets up and runs six miles at daylight," Cobb said.

"That must be why she's so skinny," said George to Cobb, grinning to include Lynnette but not looking at her.

Ceci said, "I couldn't run that far if my life depended on it."

"You have to work up to it," said Lynnette.

Ceci finished removing the rubber bands from Candy's arm

and said to the child, "We don't want to see no old coyote, do we, sugar?"

Ceci's tone with Lynnette bothered Cobb. It implied that Ceci felt superior for *not* being able to run six miles. Cobb hated the way people twisted around their own lack of confidence to claim it as a point of pride. Agitated, he hurried Lynnette on out to the fields for their walk.

George yelled after them, "Be sure to keep count of how many coyotes y'all see."

Lynnette hooked her hand onto Cobb's elbow, and they started out through a bare cornfield spotted with stubble. "I wish we'd see one," she said. "I'd talk to it. I bet you could tame it if you were patient enough. I could see myself doing that."

"I wouldn't be surprised if you could." He laughed and draped his arm around her shoulders.

Lynnette said, "I used to know a family that had a tame deer that came to a salt lick they put out. The deer got so tame it would come in the house and watch TV with them."

"I don't believe you!" Cobb said. "You're joking."

"No, I'm not! During hunting season they'd tie a big red ribbon around her neck."

The mud from earlier in the week had dried, but Cobb was wearing his new rubber boots. Lynnette had changed into black high-top shoes and jeans. She wasn't wearing a cap. He loved her for the way she could take the cold.

"Are you O.K.?" he said. "Is it too windy?"

"It's fine. It's just—" She gave a sigh of exasperation. "I shouldn't have talked about those pictures at your mother's."

"Yes, you should. It was exactly what she needed to hear."

"No, I should've kept my mouth shut. But her house brought out something in me. I wanted to shock her."

"I know what you mean. I always want to break all that glass." He booted a clod of dirt. "Families," he said disgustedly.

"It's all right," she said. "It's just one of those things." She bent to pick up a blue-jay feather. She twirled it in her fingers.

George had bush-hogged a path along the creek, and they followed it. When they started down into the creek, Cobb held on to Lynnette, drawing aside branches so they wouldn't slap her face. The water had subsided, and there were a few places of exposed gravel where they could walk. They made their way along the edge of the water for a while, then came to a part of the creek where the water was a few inches deep. Cobb carried Lynnette across, piggyback. She squealed and started to laugh. He sloshed through the puddle and carefully let her loose on the other side. She took a few steps, then squatted to examine some footprints.

"A coyote has been here!" she said excitedly. "Or maybe a fox."

The prints, like dog-paw rosettes, were indistinct. Cobb remembered seeing a red fox running through a field of winter wheat one spring when he was a child. The wheat was several inches high, and the fox made a path through it, leaving a wake like a boat. All Cobb could see was the path through the wheat and the tail surfacing occasionally. He had never seen a small animal travel so fast. It was like watching time, the fastest thing there was.

They sat down on a fallen log next to an animal den in the bank, beneath the exposed roots of a sycamore tree. Dried, tangled vines hung down near the opening, and a dirt path led down the bank to the creek bed.

"What did you really think of my mom?" Cobb asked, taking Lynnette's hand.

"The knickknacks made me sad." Lynnette pulled at some tough vines on the ground. Cobb made sure the vine wasn't poison ivy; he watched her slender fingers worry and work with the flexible stems as she spoke. She said, "I don't want my mom to have to deal with a wedding."

"Why not?"

"She couldn't handle it."

"We don't have to have anything big."

Lynnette pulled away from him. "She's one of these people who have to make lists and check and recheck things," she said. "You know—the type of person who has to go back and make sure they turned off the oven when they left the house? She's that way, only real bad. It prevents her from functioning. She can't make a phone call without checking the number ten times."

Lynnette's mother sounded nuts, Cobb decided. He had seen her picture. She was pretty, with a generous smile. Cobb had imagined her, somehow, as a delicate woman who nevertheless had strong ideas. Her smile reminded him of Dolly Parton before she lost all that weight.

Lynnette said, "When I was a senior in high school, my mom tried to kill herself. She took a lot of Valium. I was at band practice and I got a call at the principal's office to go to the hospital. It was a total surprise. I never would have imagined she'd do that." Lynnette was still twiddling the feather as she talked, even though Cobb had her hand, squeezing it.

"Why did she do it?" he asked.

"For a long time I blamed myself. I thought I hadn't shown her enough love. I was always so busy with band practice and all that teenage shit. And I remembered that I had upset her once when I said something mean about Dad. But then only a couple of years ago I found out my dad was shacking up back then with some woman from the country club. And looking back, I realized that all Mom had was that house. She used to work before we moved here, but then she couldn't get a job, and she didn't have many friends, and her house was all she had. I remember coming home and she'd be dusting all her knickknacks or pasting up wallpaper or arranging artificial flowers. I used to make fun of it, and I'd never help out. That's when it started, the way she'd pick over things and count them and try to keep track of them. I didn't think it was strange then." Lynnette shuddered in disgust. "I remember when the Welcome Wagon came—these two grinning fat women. They brought us some junk from the stores, coupons and little things. There was a tiny cedar chest from a furniture store. Your mother has one something like it, on that whatnot in the hall."

"One of her Gatlinburg souvenirs," Cobb said.

"I hated the Welcome Wagon. I thought they just came to check us over, to see if we were the country-club type. And we weren't. And then to think my dad would fool around with one of those country-club women—a golfer. I could have died of shame."

Cobb held Lynnette closely. "Every day I get to know you better," he said. "This is just the beginning." He flailed around for some comparison. "This is just the yogurt on top, and there's the fruit to come."

She giggled. "That's the silliest thing I ever heard! That's why I care about you. You're not afraid to say something that ridiculous. And you really mean it, too." She dropped the blue-jay feather, and it swirled in the water for a moment, then caught on a leaf. "But I'm afraid, Cobb. I'm afraid I might do something like she did—for different reasons."

"What reasons?"

"I don't know."

"But you're not like that."

"But I might get like that."

"No, you won't. That's crazy." Cobb caught himself saying the wrong word. "No, that's ridiculous," he said. "You won't get like that."

"When I started seeing those pictures at work I'd imagine pictures of my—if my mother had succeeded that day."

Cobb watched the feather loosen from the leaf and begin to float away in the little trickle of water in the creek bed. He tried to comprehend all that might happen to that feather as it wore away to bits—a strange thought. In a dozen years, he thought, he might look back on this moment and know that it was precisely when he should have stopped and made a rational decision to go no further, but he couldn't know that now.

She said, "Do you have any idea how complicated it's going to be?"

Cobb nodded. "That's what I like," he said confidently. "Down here, we just call that taking care of business."

Tufts of her hair fluttered slightly in the breeze, but she didn't notice. She couldn't see the way the light came through her hair like the light in spring through a leaving tree.

Airwaves

When Jane lived with Coy Wilson, he couldn't listen to rock music before noon or after supper. In the morning, it was too jarring; at night, the vibrations lingered in his head and interfered with his sleep. But now that they are apart, Jane listens to Rock-95 all the time. Rock-95 is a college station—"your station for kick-ass rock and roll." She sets the radio alarm every night for 8 A.M., and when it goes off she dozes and dreams while the music blasts in her ears for an hour or more. Women rock singers snarl and scream their independence. The sounds are numbing. Jane figures if she can listen to hard rock in her sleep, she won't care that Coy has gone.

Jane stands in the window in pink shortie pajamas, watching her landlady, Mrs. Bush, hang out her wash. Today is white things: sheets, socks, underwear, towels. Jane's mother used to say, "Always separate your colored things from your white things!" as though there were something morally significant about the way you do laundry. Jane never follows the rules. All her sheets have flowers on them, and her underwear is bright colors. Anything white is outnumbered. The men's shorts on Mrs. Bush's wash line flap in the breeze like flags of surrender.

The coffee is bitter. She bought the store brand, because Mrs. Bush gave her a fifty-cent coupon and the store paid double coupons. Mrs. Bush, who is a waitress at the Villa Romano, keeps asking Jane when she is going to get a job. When Coy lived there, Mrs. Bush was always asking him when he was going to marry

Jane. Six weeks ago, not long after she split up with Coy, Jane was laid off from the Holiday Clothing Company. First she was a folder, then a presser. Folding was more satisfying than pressing —the heat from the presser took the curl out of her hair—but when she was switched to the pressing room, she got a fifty-cents-an-hour raise. She was hoping to go to the Villa Romano that night with Coy and have a spaghetti supper to celebrate, but he chose that day to move back home with his mother. His unemployment had run out two weeks before, and he had been at loose ends. He thought he was getting an ulcer. When Jane got home, he had lined up their joint possessions on the floor—the toaster, the blender, the records, the TV tables, a whatnot, even the kitchen utensils.

"The TV's mine," he said apologetically. "I had it when we started out."

"I told you I'd pay the rent," she said, as he punched his jeans into a duffel bag. When he wouldn't answer, she set the coffeepot in the cabinet and shut the door. "I got the coffeepot with Green Stamps," she said.

"I'm going to cut out coffee anyway."

"Good. It makes you irritable."

Coy set the toaster in a grocery box with some shaving cream and socks—all his mateless socks from what Jane called his Lonely Sock Drawer. Jane tried to keep from crying as she pleaded with him to stay.

"I can't let you go on supporting me," he said. "I wasn't raised that way."

"What's the difference? Your mother will support you. You could even watch her TV."

He divided the record albums as though he were dealing out cards. "One for you and one for me." He left his favorite Willie Nelson record in her pile.

When he left, she said, "You just let me know when you get yourself straightened out, and we'll take it from there."

"That's my whole point," said Coy. "I have to work things out."

Jane knew she should have been more understanding. He was appreciative of delicate, fine things most men wouldn't notice, such as flowers and pretty dishes. Coy was tender in his love-making, with more sensitivity than men were usually given credit for. On Phil Donahue's show, when the topic was sex, the women in the audience always said they wanted men who were gentle and considerate and involved in a lot of touching during the day instead of "wham-bam-thank-you-ma'am" at the end of the day. Coy was the answer to those women's prayers, but he went too far. He was so fragile, with his nervous stomach. He couldn't watch meat being cut up. Jane still finds broken rolls of Tums stashed around the apartment.

Unemployed, Jane is adrift. She watches a lot of TV. She managed to buy a TV on sale before she lost her job. She has had to stop smoking (not a serious problem) and eating out so that she can keep up her car and TV payments. She canceled her subscription to a cosmetics club. She has accumulated a lot of bizarre eye shadows and creams that she doesn't use. When she goes out to a job interview, she paints her face and feels silly. Job-hunting is like going to church—a pointless ritual of dressing up. At the factory, she had to wear a blue smock over a dark skirt. Pants weren't allowed. "I wish I could get on at the Villa Romano," she tells Mrs. Bush. "The uniform is nice, and I could wear pants."

Coy used to go to Kentucky Lake alone sometimes, for the whole weekend, to meditate and restore himself. She once thought his desire to be alone was peculiar, but now she appreciates it. Being alone is incredibly easy. Her mind sails off into unexpected trances. Sometimes she pretends she is an invalid recovering from a coma, and she rediscovers everything around her—simple things, like the noise the rotary antenna makes, a sound she never heard when the TV volume was loud. Or she pretends she is in a wheelchair, viewing the world from one certain level. She likes to see things suddenly, from new angles. Once when Coy lived there, she stepped up on a crate to dust the top of a shelf, and Coy suddenly appeared and caught her in an embrace. On the crate, she was exactly his height. The dusty shelf was at eye level. For a day or two, she went around noticing the spaces that would be in his line of vision—the top of the refrigerator, the top of an old cardboard wardrobe her father had given her, curtain rods, moldings.

Today, when Jane leaves the apartment to pick up her unemployment check, Mrs. Bush is outside, watering her petunias. She pulls a letter from her pocket and waves it at Jane.

"My boy's in California," she says. "They're going to let him have a furlough, but he likes it so much out there he won't come home."

"I don't blame him," says Jane. "It's too far, and California must be a lot more fun than here."

"They started him out on heavy-duty equipment, but that didn't suit him and they've switched him to electronics. They take a hundred dollars out of his pay every month, and then when he gets out they'll double it and give him a bonus so he can go to school."

Mrs. Bush fires water at a border of hollyhocks. Jane steps over the coiled hose and casually thinks of evil serpents. She says, "My brother couldn't get in the Army because he had high arches, so he became a Holy Roller preacher instead. He used to cuss like the devil, but now he's preaching up a storm." Jane looks Mrs. Bush straight in the eyes. She's not old but looks old. If she died, maybe Jane could get her job.

"My cousin was a Holy Roller," says Mrs. Bush. "He got sanctified and then got hit by a truck the next day."

Nervously, Mrs. Bush tears off the edging of paper where she has ripped open the letter from her son. She balls the bit of paper and drops it into a pot of hen and chickens.

Jane's mother died when she was fifteen, and her father, Vernon Motherall, has never learned to cook for himself. "What's in this?" he asks suspiciously that weekend, when she takes him a tuna casserole.

"Macaroni. Tuna fish. Mushroom soup."

"I don't like mushrooms. Mushrooms is poison."

"This isn't poison. It's Campbell's." Jane has brought him this same kind of casserole dozens of times, and he always argues against mushrooms. He's convinced that someday a mushroom is going to get him.

Vernon rents the bottom half of a dilapidated clapboard house. He has two dump trucks in the backyard. He hauls rock and sand

and asphalt—"whatever needs hauling," his ad in the yellow pages says. His dingy office is filled with greasy papers on spikes and piles of *Field and Stream* magazines. In a ray of sunlight, the dust whirls and sparkles. Jane sweeps her hand through it.

"I wish I had some money," she says. "I'd buy you one of those things that takes the negative ions out of the air."

"What good's that do?" Vernon is swigging a Pabst, though it's still morning.

"It knocks the dust out of the air."

"What for?" The way Jane's father speaks is more like an extended grunt than conversation. He sits in a large stuffed chair that seems to be part of his own big lumpy body.

"I don't know. I think the dust just falls down instead of circulating. If you had one of those, your sinuses wouldn't be so bad."

"They ain't been bothering me none lately."

"Those ionizers make you feel good, too. They do something to your mood."

"I've got all I need for my mood," he says, lifting his bottle of beer.

"You drink too much."

"Don't look at my beer belly."

"I will if I want to," Jane says, playfully thumping his belt buckle. "You get loaded and go out and have wrecks. You're going to get yourself killed."

Vernon grins at her mockingly. They always have this conversation, and he never takes her seriously.

"Here, eat this," Jane says, plopping a scoop of casserole on a melamine plate that has discolorations on it.

Vernon plucks another beer from the refrigerator and sits down at the card table in his dirty kitchen. He eats without comment, then mops his plate with a bread heel. When he finishes, he says, "I went to hear Joe preach at his new church the other Sunday. How did I turn out a boy like that? He's bound and determined to make a fool out of himself. His wife runs out on him, and he turns around and starts preaching Holy Roller. Did you know he talks in tongues now? What will he think of next?"

"Well, Joe goes at anything like killing snakes," says Jane. "It's all or nothing."

Vernon laughs. "His text for the day was the Twenty-third Psalm, and he comes to the part where the Lord maketh me lie down in green pastures and restoreth my soul? And he reads it 'he *storeth* my soul,' and starts preaching on the Lord's store-houses." Vernon doubles over laughing. "He thinks the Lord stores souls—like corn in a grain elevator!"

"I wonder what ever happened to all those grain-elevator explosions we used to hear about," Jane says, giggling.

"If the Lord stores some of those pitiful souls Joe's dragged in, his storehouse is liable to explode!" Vernon laughs, and beer sprays out of his mouth.

"Have some more tuna casserole," Jane says affectionately. When it comes to her brother, who was always in trouble, she and her father are in cahoots.

"You should have a good man to cook for. Not Coy Wilson. He's too prissy, and he took advantage of you, living with you with no intention of marrying."

"You're still feeling guilty 'cause you ran out on me and Joe and Mother that time," says Jane, shifting the subject.

"The trouble is, too many women are working and the men can't get jobs," her father says. "Women should stay home."

"Don't start in," Jane says in a warning voice. "I've got enough trouble."

"You could move back home with me," Vernon says plain-tively. "Parents always used to take care of their kids till they married."

"I guess that's why Coy ran home to his mama."

"You can come home to your old daddy anytime," Vernon says, moving back to his easy chair. The vinyl upholstery makes obscene noises when he lands.

"It would never work," Jane says. "We don't like the same TV shows anymore."

Waiting in the unemployment line the next afternoon is tedious, and all the faces have deadpan expressions, but Jane is feeling elated, almost euphoric, though for no substantial reason. In the car, driving past a local radio transmitter, she suddenly realized that she had no idea how sound got from the transmitter to the radio. She felt so ignorant. The idea of sound waves seemed farfetched. She went to the library and asked for a book about radio. The librarian showed her a pamphlet about Nathan Stubblefield.

"He invented radio," the woman said. "They say it was Marconi, but Stubblefield was really the first, and he was from right around here. He lived five miles from my house."

"I always heard radio was invented in Kentucky," Jane said.

"He just never got credit for it." The woman reminded Jane of a bouncy game-show contestant. "Kentucky never gets enough credit, if you ask me. We've got so much here to be proud of. Kentucky even has a Golden Pond, like in the movie."

Reading the pamphlet in the unemployment line, Jane feels strangely connected to something historically important. It is a miracle that sound can travel long distances through the air and then appear instantaneously, like a genie from a bottle, and that a man from Kentucky was the first to make it happen. Who can she tell? Who would care? This is the sort of thing that wouldn't register on her father, and Coy would think she was crazy. Her brother, though, would recognize the feeling. It occurs to Jane that he probably hears voices from heaven every day, just as though he were tuned in to heaven's airways. She wonders if he can really talk in tongues. Her brother is a radio! Jane feels like dancing. In her mind, the unemployment line suddenly turns into a chorus line, a movie scene. For a moment, she's afraid she's going nuts. The line inches forward.

After collecting her check, she cashes it at the bank's drive-in window, talking to the teller through a speaker, then goes to Jerry's Drive-In and orders a Coke through another speaker. A voice confirms her order, and in the background behind the voice, Jane hears a radio playing—Rock-95, the same station she is hearing on her car radio.

Coy calls up during a "Mary Tyler Moore" rerun that week, one Jane hasn't seen before. Jane is eating canned ravioli. The clarity of his voice startles her. He could be in the same room.

"I got a job! Floorwalking at Wal-Mart."

"Oh, I'm glad." Jane spears a pillow of ravioli and listens while Coy describes his hours and his duties and the amount of take-home pay he gets—less than he made at the plant before his layoff, but with more security. The job sounds incredibly boring.

"When I get on my feet, maybe we can reconsider some things," he says.

"If you're floorwalking, you're already on your feet," she says. "That's a joke," she says, when he doesn't respond. "I don't want to get back together if money's the issue."

"I thought we went through all that."

"I've been thinking, and I can't let you support me."

"Well, I've got a job now, and you don't."

"You wouldn't let *me* support *you*," Jane says. "Why should I let you support me?"

"If we got back together, you could go to school part-time."

"I have to find a job first. I'd go to school now if I could go and still draw unemployment, but they won't let you draw and go to school too. Let's change the subject. How's your stomach?"

Coy tells Jane that on the news he saw pictures of starving children in Africa, and managed to watch without getting queasy. Jane always told him he was too sensitive to misfortunes that had nothing to do with him.

An awkward silence follows. Finally, Jane says, "My brother's got a Holy Roller church. He's preaching."

"That sounds about like him," Coy says, without surprise.

"I think I'll go Sunday. I need some religion. Do you want to go?"

"Hell, no. I don't want to invite a migraine."

"I thought your nerves were getting better."

"They are, but they're not that good yet."

After Coy hangs up, Jane feels lonely, wishing Coy were there, touching her lightly with promising caresses, like the women on "Donahue" always wanted. Once, Rita Jenrette, whose husband was involved in a political scandal, was on Donahue's show, and during the program her husband called up. Coy's job sounds so depressing. Jane wishes he were the host of a radio call-in show. She could call him up and talk to him, pretending there was nothing personal between them. She would ask him about love. She'd ask whether he thought the magic of love worked anything at all like radio waves. Her ravioli grows cold.

Joe's church is called the Foremost Evangelical Assembly. The church is a converted house trailer, with a perpendicular extension. There is a Coke machine in the corridor. People sit around drinking Cokes and 7-Ups. No one is dressed up.

"Can you believe it!" cries Joe, clasping both of Jane's hands and jerking her forward as though about to swing her around in a game children play.

"Can you pray for me to find a job?" Jane says, grinning. "Daddy said you could talk in tongues, and I thought that might help."

"Was Daddy drinking when you saw him last?" Joe asks anxiously.

"Of course. Is the Pope Catholic?"

"I told him I could stop him from that if he'd just get his tail down here every Sunday." Joe has on a pin-striped double-knit suit with an artificial daisy in the lapel. He looks the part.

"Are you going to talk in tongues today?" Jane asks. "I want to see how you do it."

"Watch close," he says with a wink. "But I'm not allowed to give away the secret."

"Is it like being a magician?"

Her brother only grins mysteriously.

Jane sits cross-legged on the floor behind the folding chairs. People turn around and stare at her, probably wondering if she is Joe's girlfriend. The congregation loves Joe. He is a large man, and his size makes him seem powerful and authoritative, like an Army general. He has always been a goof-off, calling attention to himself, staging some kind of show. If Alexander Haig became a stand-up comedian, he would be just like Joe. He stands behind a card table with two overturned plastic milk crates stacked on it. On his right, a TV set stares at the congregation.

The service is long and peculiar and filled with individual testimonials that seem to come randomly, interrupting Joe's talk. It's not really a sermon. It's just Joe telling stories about how bad he used to be before he found Christ. He always had the gift of the gab, Vernon used to say. Joe tells a long anecdote about how his wife's infidelity made him turn to the Lord. He exaggerates parts of the story that Jane recognizes. (He *never* gave his wife a beautiful house with a custom-built kitchen and a two-car garage. It was a dumpy old house that they rented.) She almost giggles aloud when he opens the Bible and reads from "the Philippines," and she makes a mental note to tell her father. A woman takes a crying baby into the corridor and tries to make it drink some Coke. Jane wishes she had a cigarette. In this crazy setting, if Joe talked in tongues, nobody would notice it as anything odd.

When a young couple brings forth a walleyed child to be healed, Joe cries out in astonishment, "Who, me? I can't heal nobody!" He paces around in front of the TV set. "But I can guarantee that if you just let the spirit in, miracles have been known to happen." He rambles along on this point, and the little girl's head droops indifferently. "Just open up your heart and let him in!" Joe shouts. "Let the spirit in, and the Lord will shake up the alignment of them eyes." A song from *Hair*, "Let the Sunshine In," starts going through Jane's head. The child's eye shoots out across the room. While Joe is ranting, Jane gets a Coke and stands in the doorway.

"Icky-bick-eye-bo!" Joe cries suddenly. He looks embarrassed and bows his head. "Freema-di-kibbi-fidra," he says softly.

Jane has been thinking of talking in tongues as an involuntary expression—a kind of gibberish that pours forth when people are possessed by the spirit of God. But now, in amazement, she watches her brother, his hands folded and eyes closed, as though bowing his head for a moment of prayer, chanting strange words slowly and carefully, as methodically as Mrs. Bush hangs out her wash. He is speaking a singsong language made of hard, disturbing sounds. "Shecky-beck-be-floyt-I-shecky-tibby-libby. Dabcree-la-croo-la-crow.'' He seems to be trying hard not to say "abracadabra" or any other familiar words. Jane, disappointed, doubts that these words are messages from heaven. Joe seems afraid that some repressed obscenity might rush out. He used to cuss freely. Now he probably really believes he is tuned in to heaven.

"Where's Coy?" he asks her after the service. He has failed to correct the child's eyes but won't admit it.

"We don't get along so good. After he lost his job, he couldn't handle it."

"Well, get him on down here! We'll help him."

He tries to talk Jane into bringing Coy for Wednesday-night prayer meeting. "There's two kinds of men," Joe says. "Them that goes to church and them that don't. You should never get mixed up with some boy who won't take you to church."

"I know."

Joe says goodbye, with his arms around her like a lover's. Jane can smell the Tic Tacs on his breath.

"Do you want one hamburger patty or two?" Jane asks her father.

"One. No, two." Vernon looks confused. "No, make it one."

They are at the lake, in a trailer belonging to Jane's former boss, who had promised to let her use it some weekend. Jane, wanting a change of scene for her father, brought a cooler of supplies, and Vernon brought his dog, Buford. He grumbled because Jane wouldn't let him bring any beer, but he sneaked along a quart of Heaven Hill, and he is already drunk. Jane is furious.

"How can you watch 'Hogan's Heroes' on that cruddy TV?" she asks. "The reception's awful."

"I've seen this one so many times I know what's going on. See that machine gun? Watch that guy in the tower. He's going to shoot."

"That's a tower? I thought it was a giraffe."

When they sit down to eat at the picnic table outside, Buford tries to get in Jane's lap. He has the broad shoulders of a bulldog and the fine facial features of a chihuahua. He goes around in a little cloud of gnats.

"I can't eat with a dog in my lap," Jane says, pushing the dog away. "Coy wants to come back to me," she tells her father. "He's got his pride again."

"Don't let him."

"He's more of a man than you think." Jane laughs. "Joe says he can help us work things out. He wants us to come to Wednesday-night prayer meetings."

"How did I go wrong?" Vernon asks helplessly, addressing a tree. "One kid starts preaching just to stay out of jail, and the other one wants to live in sin and ruin her reputation." Vernon turns to the dog and says, "It's all my fault. Children always hurt you."

"And what about you?" Jane shouts at him. "You worry us half to death with your drinking and then expect us to be little angels."

She takes her plate indoors and turns on "M*A*S*H." The reception is so poor without a cable that the figures undulate on the screen. Hawkeye and B.J. turn into wavy lines, staggering drunks.

That night, Vernon's drunken sleep on the couch is loud and unrestrained. Jane thinks of his sleep as slumber. She always thought of Coy's sleep as catnapping. She misses Coy, but wonders if she can ever get along with any man. In all her relationships with people, she has to deal with one or another intolerable habit. Jane is not sure the hard-rock music has hardened her to pain and distraction. Her father is hopeless. He used to get drunk and throw her mother's good dishes against the wall. He lined them up on the table and broke them one by one until her mother relented and gave him the keys to the car. He had accidents. He was always apologetic afterward, and he made it up to them in lavish ways, bringing home absurd presents, such as a bushel of peaches or a pint of oysters in a little white fold-together cardboard container like the ones goldfish come in. Once, he brought goldfish, but Jane's mother had expected oysters. Her disappointment hurt him, and he went back and bought oysters. One year, he ran away to Detroit. When he came back, months later, Jane's mother forgave him. By then, she was dying of cancer, and Jane suspects that he never really forgave himself for being there too late to make it up to her.

Buford paces around the trailer fretfully. Jane can't sleep. The bed is musty and lumpy. She recalls a story her mother once told her about a woman who was trapped in a lion cage by a lion who tried to mate with her. From outside the cage, the lion's trainer yelled instructions to her—how she had to stroke the lion until he was satisfied. Pinned under the lion, the woman saved her life by obeying the man's instructions. That was more or less how her mother always told her she had to be with a husband, or a rapist. She thinks of her mother as the woman in the cage, listening to the lion tamer shouting instructions—do anything to keep from being murdered. As Jane recalls her mother telling it, the lion's eyes went all dreamy, and he rolled over on his back and went to sleep.

Jane suspects that what she really wants is a man something like the lion. She loves Coy's gentleness, but she wants him to be aggressive at times. The women on "Donahue" said they wanted that, too. Someone in the audience said women can't have it both ways.

During the weekend, Jane tries to get Vernon to go fishing, but he hasn't renewed his fishing license since the price went up. He complains about the snack cakes she brought, and he sits around drinking. Jane listens to the radio and reads a book called *Working*, about people's jobs. "It takes all kinds," she tells her father when he asks about the book. She has given up trying to entertain him, but by Sunday evening he seems mellow and talkative.

At the picnic table, Jane watches the sun setting behind the oak trees. "Look how pretty it is. The light on the water looks like a melted orange Popsicle."

Vernon grunts, acknowledging the sunset.

"I want you to enjoy yourself," Jane says calmly.

"I'm an old fool," he says, sloshing his drink. "I never amounted to anything. This country is taking away every chance the little man ever had. If it weren't for the Republicans and the Democrats, we'd be better off."

"Don't we have to have one or the other?"

"Throw 'em all out. They cancel each other out anyway."
Vernon snatches at a mosquito. "The minorities rule this country.
They've meddled with the Constitution till it's all out of shape."

The sun disappears, and the mosquitoes come out. Jane slaps
her arms. Her toes are under the dog, warming like buns in a
toaster oven. She nudges him away, and he pads across the
porch, taking his gnat cloud with him.

"Tell me something," Jane asks later, as they are eating. "What
did you do in Detroit that time when you ran off and left Mom
with Joe and me?"

Vernon shrugs and drinks from a fresh drink. "Worked at
Chrysler."

"Why did you leave us?"

"Your mother couldn't put up with me."

Jane can't see her father's face in the growing dark, so she feels
bolder. Taking a deep breath, she says, "I guess for a long time I
felt guilty after you left—not because you left but because I
wanted you to leave. Mom and Joe and me got along just fine
without you. I liked moving into that restaurant, living upstairs
with Mom, and her going downstairs to cook hamburgers for
people. I think I liked it so much not just because I could have all
the hamburgers and milk shakes I wanted but because *she* loved
it. She loved waiting on people and cooking for the public. But we
were glad when you came back and we moved back home."

Vernon nods and nods, about to say something. Jane gets up
and turns on the bug light on the porch. She says, "That's how
I've been feeling, living by myself. If I found something I liked as
much as Mom liked cooking for the public, I'd be happy."

Vernon pours some more bourbon into his Yosemite Sam jelly
glass and nods thoughtfully. He sips his drink and looks out onto
the darkening lake for so long that Jane thinks he must be working up to a spectacular confession or apology. Finally, he says,
"The Constitution is damaged all to hell." He sets his plate on the
ground for the dog to lick.

The next morning is work-pants day. On Mrs. Bush's line is a row
of dark-green work pants and matching shirts. The pants are

heavy and wrinkled. The sun comes out, and by afternoon, when Jane returns from shopping, the wrinkles are gone and the pants look fluffy. Jane reaches into the back seat of her car for her sack of groceries—soup, milk, cereal, and a Sara Lee cheesecake, marked down.

"Faired up nice, didn't it?" cries Mrs. Bush, appearing with her laundry basket. "They say another front's coming through and we'll have a storm."

"I hope so," says Jane, wishing it would be a tornado.

"I've got some news for you," Mrs. Bush says, as she drops clothespins into a plastic bucket. "A girl I work with is pregnant, and she's quitting next week."

"I thought I wanted to work at the Villa Romano more than anything, but now I'm not sure," Jane says. What would it be like, waiting tables with Mrs. Bush?

"It's a good job, and they feed you all you can eat. They've got the *best* ambrosia!"

She drops a clothespin and Jane picks it up. Jane says, "I think I'll join the Army."

Mrs. Bush laughs. "Jimmy's still in California. They would have flown him here and back, but he wouldn't come home. Is that any way for a boy to do his mama?" She tests a pant leg for dampness, and frowns. "I've got to go. Could you bring in these britches for me later?" she asks. "If I'm late to work, my boss will shoot me."

When Jane puts her groceries away, the cereal tumbles to the floor. The milk carton is leaking. She turns on Rock-95 full blast, then rips the cover off the cheesecake and starts eating from the middle. Jane feels strange, quivery. One simple idea could suddenly change everything, the same way a tornado could. Everything in her life is converging, narrowing, like a multitude of tiny lines trying to get through one pinhole. She imagines straightening out a rainbow and rolling it up in a tube. The sound waves travel on rainbows. She can't explain these notions to Coy. They don't even make sense to her. Today, he looked worried about her when she stopped in at Wal-Mart. It has been a crazy day, a stupid weekend. After picking up her unemployment check, she applied for a job at Betty's Boutique, but the opening had been filled five minutes earlier. At Wal-Mart, Coy was patrolling the pet department. In his brown plaid pants, blue shirt, and yellow tie, he looked stylish and comfortable, as though he had finally found a place where he belonged. He seemed like a man whose ambition was to get a service award so he could have his picture in the paper, shaking hands with his boss.

"I hope you're warming a place in the bed for me," he whispered to her, within earshot of customers. He touched her elbow, and his thumb poked surreptitiously at her waist. "I have to work tonight," he went on. "We're doing inventory. But we've got to talk."

"O.K.," she said, her eyes fixing on a fish tank in which some remarkably blue fish were darting around like darning-needle flies.

On her way out of the store, without thinking, she stopped and bought a travel kit for her cosmetics, with plastic cases inside for her toothbrush, lotion, and soap. She wasn't sure where she was going. Driving out of the parking lot, she thought how proudly Coy had said, "We're taking inventory," as though he were in thick with Wal-Mart executives. It didn't seem like him. She had deluded herself, expecting more of him just because he was such a sweet lover. She had thought he was an ideal man, like the new contemporary man described in the women's magazines, but he was just a floorwalker. There was no future in that. Women had been walking the floors for years. She remembered her mother walking the floor with worry, when her father was out late, drinking.

At the Army recruiting station, Jane stuffed the literature into her purse. She took one of everything. On a bulletin board, she read down a list of career-management fields, strange-sounding phrases like Air Defense Artillery, Missile Maintenance, Ballistic Missile Maintenance, Combat Engineering, Intercept Systems Maintenance, Cryptologic Operations, Topographic Engineering. The words stirred her, filled her with awe.

"Here's what I want," she said to the recruiter. "Communications and Electronics Operations."

"That's our top field," said the man, who was wearing a beautiful uniform trimmed with bright ribbons. "You join that and you'll get somewhere."

Later, in her kitchen, her mouth full of cheesecake, Jane reads the electronics brochure, pausing over the phrases "field radio," "teletype," and "radio relay equipment." Special security clearance is required for some electronics operations. She pictures herself someplace remote, in a control booth, sending signals for war, like an engineer in charge of a sports special on TV. She doesn't want to go to war, but if there is one, women should go. She imagines herself in a war, crouching in the jungle, sweating, on the lookout for something to happen. The sounds of warfare would be like the sounds of rock and roll, hard-driving and satisfying.

She sleeps so soundly that when Coy calls the next morning, the telephone rings several times. Rock-95 is already blasting away, and she wonders groggily if it is loud enough over the telephone to upset his equilibrium.

"I'm trying to remember what you used to say about waking up," she says sleepily.

"You know I could never talk till I had my coffee."

"I thought you were giving up coffee. Does your mama make you coffee?"

"Yeah."

"I knew she would." Jane sits up and turns down the radio. "Oh, now I remember what you said. You said it was like being born."

Coy had said that the relaxation of sleep left him defenseless and shattered, so that the daytime was spent restructuring himself, rebuilding defenses. Sleep was a forgetting, and in the daylight he had to gather his strength, remember who he was. For him, the music was an intrusion on a fragile life, and now it makes Jane sad that she hasn't been fair to him.

"Can I come for breakfast?" he asks.

"You took the toaster, and I can't make toast the way you like it."

"Let's go to the Dairy Barn and have some country ham and biscuits."

Jane's sheets are dirty. She was going to wash them at the laundromat and bring them home to dry—to save money and to score a point with her landlady. She says, "I'll meet you as soon as I drop off my laundry at the Washeteria. I've got something to tell you."

"I hope it's good."

"It's not what you think." On the radio, Rod Stewart is bouncing blithely away on "Young Turks." Jane feels older, too old for her and Coy to be young hearts together, free tonight, as the song directs. Jane says, "Red-eye gravy. That's what I want. Do you think they'll have red-eye gravy?"

"Of course they'll have red-eye gravy. Who ever heard of country ham without red-eye gravy?"

After hanging up, Jane lays the sheets on the living-room rug, and in the center she tosses her underwear and blouses and slacks. The colors clash. A tornado in a flower garden. After throwing in her jeans, she ties the corners of the sheets and sets the bundle by the door. As she puts on her makeup, she rehearses what she has to tell Coy. She has imagined his stunned silence. She imagines gathering everyone she knows in the same room, so she can make her announcement as if she were holding a press conference. It would be so much more official.

With her bundle of laundry, she goes bumping down the stairs. A stalk of light from a window on the landing shoots down the stairway. Jane floats through the light, with the dust motes shining all around her, penetrating silently, and then she remembers a dirty T-shirt in the bathroom. Letting the bundle slide to the bottom of the stairs, she turns back to her apartment. She has left the radio on, and for a moment on the landing she thinks that someone must be home.

Sorghum

*L*iz woke up at 3 A.M., when she recognized Danny's car rumbling into the driveway. It had a hole in the muffler. Then she heard the car turn around and speed down the street. In the distance, the tires kept squealing as Danny tore up and down the streets of the subdivision. She waited for the crash, but the car returned. Again, Danny backed out of the driveway and went zooming down the street, the tires screeching. Someone will call the police, she thought, terrified.

"What's Daddy doing?" said Melissa, a little silhouette in the dim light of the bedroom doorway. She was dragging her Cabbage Patch–style doll by an arm.

"It's all right, sugar." Liz got out of bed and bent down to hug her child.

"Kiss Maretta Louise, too," Melissa said.

Liz held on to Melissa, her free hand untangling the little girl's hair. To be fair, Liz patted Maretta Louise's hair, too.

"He's just having a little joy ride, sweetie," Liz said. "There's not any traffic, so he has the street all to himself."

"Daddy doesn't love Maretta Louise," Melissa said, whining. "He told her she was ugly."

"She's not ugly! She's precious." Liz herded Melissa back to her own bed. "I'll stay in here with you," she said. "Let's be real quiet so we won't wake Michael up."

The car roared into the driveway again, and the door slammed.

198

Danny worked the four-to-midnight shift at the tire plant, and for the past several Friday nights he had been coming in late, usually drunk. Liz worked all day at a discount store, and the only times she was with Danny during the week, they were asleep. Weekends were shocking, when they saw each other awake and older. They had something like a commuter marriage, she thought, with none of the advantages. Liz didn't love Danny in the same way anymore. When he was drunk, he made love as though he were plowing corn, and she did not enjoy it.

"I'm home!" yelled Danny, bursting into the house.

On Thursday after supper, when Michael and Melissa were playing at friends' houses down the street, Liz tuned in to Sue Ann Grooms, a psychic on the radio.

"Hello. You're on the air."

A man said, "Could you tell me if I'm going to get laid off?"

"No, you're not," said Sue Ann Grooms.

"O.K.," the man said.

"Hello, you're on the air."

A woman with a thin, halting voice said, "I lost my wedding ring. Where can I go find it?"

"I see a tall building," said Sue Ann. "With a basement."

"You must mean when I worked at the courthouse."

"I'm getting a strong picture of a large building with a basement."

"Well, I'll look there, then."

Sue Ann Grooms was local. Liz's brother had been in her class at school. Her show had been on for nearly a year, and people called up with money problems, family troubles, a lot of cancer operations. Sue Ann always had an answer on the tip of her tongue. It was amazing. She was right, too. Liz knew people who had called in.

Nervously, Liz dialed the radio station. She had to dial several times before she got through. She was put on hold, and she sat in a kitchen chair while music played in her ear. When Sue Ann Grooms said, "You're on the air," Liz jumped. Flustered, she said, "Uh—is my husband cheating on me?"

Sue Ann paused. The psychic didn't normally pause for thought. "I'm afraid the answer is yes," she said.

"Oh."

Sue Ann Grooms went into fast-forward, it seemed, on other calls. Sick babies, cancer, husbands out of work. The answers blurred together. Chills rushed over Liz. Her friend Faye, at the store, had urged Liz to go out and have adventures. Faye, who was divorced, dumped her children at her mother's on weekends and went out on dates to fancy restaurants up in Paducah. It wasn't just men Faye was after. She had an interest in the peculiar. It could be a strange old woman who raised peacocks and made her own apple butter, or a belly dancer. Faye had met a belly dancer at the Western Inn, a woman who learned the art just to please her husband, because her navel turned him on, but then she took her show on the road. She had belly-danced her way across America, Faye said.

It was still daylight, and Liz went for a drive, wishing she had a little sports car instead of a Chevette. She passed the Holiday Inn. The marquee said "WELCOME TEXACO BIGWIGS." She stopped for a fill-up at a Texaco, wondering what bigwigs would come to this little town. The conventions centered in Paducah, where they could buy liquor. A surly teenager gassed her up.

"Where are the bigwigs?" she asked.

"Huh?"

She explained about the Holiday Inn sign.

"I don't know." He shrugged and fumbled with the change. He didn't look retarded, just devoid of life. Liz shot out of the station. She felt a burning desire, for no one in particular, nothing she knew, but she expected it would make sense sooner or later. She slowed down at a triangle intersection on the highway where some teenagers were washing windshields for leukemia victims.

"Why don't we go out to eat at someplace fancy sometime?" she asked Danny that weekend. Faye had been to a restaurant at the lake where the bread was baked in flowerpots. The restaurant was decorated with antiques and stuffed wild animals.

"You're always wanting something we can't afford," Danny said, as he twisted open a bottle of beer. "You wanted a microwave, and now you've got it. The more you get, the more you want."

Liz started to remind him about the Oldsmobile he was longing for (his father swore by Oldsmobiles), but it took too much energy. He hauled her toward him in a rough embrace. "What have I done to you?" he asked when she pushed him away.

"Nothing."

"You're acting funny."

"I'm just frustrated. I want to go back to college and finish. I didn't finish, and I think I ought to finish."

"But the two years you went didn't do you any good. There's not any jobs around here that call for college."

"I just wish I could finish what I started," she said.

He grinned, cocking his beer bottle at her. "This fellow at work says his wife went to college, and she changed one hundred percent. She changed her hair and the way she cooked and everything. He keeps looking at her picture, thinking maybe he's been tricked and she's not the same person. There's a lot of that going around," he said thoughtfully.

"Well, there's more to life than just getting by," Liz snapped. Danny looked at her strangely.

Faye had told Liz about a man who made sorghum molasses. "He's a darling old man I met at a flea market, and he makes it with all the old equipment and stuff." Liz had a craving for sorghum. She hadn't had any since she was a child. On Friday after work, she drove out to the place.

The Summer farm was five miles out in the country, near a run-down old settlement with an old-fashioned general store (peeling paint, Dr Pepper sign). Cletus Summer lived in a new brick ranch house, with a shiny white dish antenna squatting possessively in the backyard. The outbuildings were gray and sagged with age. Near a shed, several visitors were watching the old man boiling down cane syrup in a vat. The heat from the fire beneath the vat burned Liz's face, and she stepped back. This old man had been making sorghum for generations, she thought. Yet she couldn't even get Danny to grill chickens.

The vat was sectioned like a rat maze, and Cletus Summer was swooshing the fluid through the maze with a spade. Now and then he scooped foam from the surface. It was green, like pond slime.

"This is the second batch," he said to the visitors. "Yesterday I throwed away a whole batch that took all day to make. It didn't taste right. It tasted green."

"It sure looks green," Liz said.

A younger man, in a red T-shirt and a cowboy hat, said, "You're supposed to have mules walking in a circle to mash the cane. But Daddy built a machine to squeeze the juice out." He laughed. "The real old-timers don't like that, do they, Daddy?" The man wore a large brass belt buckle that said "ED" in large letters superimposed on crossed Confederate rifles. "Remember the time that old farmer made some hooch out of his sorghum and the pigs got into it and got drunk?"

The men howled together. The older man said, "It was 'soo-ee' all over the place! The farmer got plowed, too, and he passed out in the pigpen." Viciously, he kicked at a log on the fire. "Damn! Them logs ain't burning. They're plumb green."

"Everything's green here," Liz said, gazing at the slippery scum. The cane leaves strewn around on the ground were bright green.

"An old-timey sorghum-making had a picnic, and the whole neighborhood helped," Ed said, gazing straight at Liz. She decided he was good-looking.

"Nowadays people ain't work brittle," the old man mumbled.

"What do you mean?" Liz asked.

"If you ain't work brittle, it means you're lazy."

Later, after she had taken the gallon of sorghum she bought to the car and had stopped to pet some cats, Liz saw the man named Ed under a tree, reading a paperback. He had a good build and a strong, craggy face. He smiled at her, a crooked smile like the label pasted on the sorghum can.

"Do you live here?" she asked. "I never saw a farmer laze around under a tree with a book before."

"No, I just came up from Memphis to help Daddy out. I've got a business there—I sell sound systems?" He closed the book on his thumb. The book was about Hitler.

"I always liked sorghum on pancakes," Liz said. "But I never knew what all went into it."

"It's an education being around Daddy. He could do everything the old way. But he doesn't have to anymore." Ed glanced over at his father, who was hunched over the vat and tasting the syrup from a wooden spoon. He still seemed dissatisfied with the taste. "Daddy's getting real bad—forgetful and stuff. It's not stopping him, though. He's got a girlfriend and he still drives to town. By the way, my name's Ed."

"That's what I figured. I'm Liz."

"What's your favorite food, Liz?" he asked.

"Ice cream. Why?"

"Just asking. Who's your favorite star?"

"Sometimes Clint Eastwood. Sometimes Paul Newman."

"You want to go out with me for ice cream and then a Paul Newman movie?"

She laughed. "My husband might not like it if he found out."

Ed said, "If ifs and buts was candy and nuts, we'd have Christmas every day."

She laughed, and he tilted his cowboy hat down over his eyes and peered out from under it flirtatiously. He said, "What's your husband got that I ain't got?" he asked.

"I don't know. I never see him," she said, wishing she hadn't mentioned she had a husband. "We don't get along."

"Well, there you go. Come on."

In Ed's red Camaro, they headed for Paducah, on back roads, past ripening tobacco fields and corn scorching in the late-summer haze. Ed was a careful driver. Liz couldn't imagine him terrorizing the neighborhood at 3 A.M. As the road twisted through abandoned towns, past run-down farms and shabby gas stations, Liz felt excited. It was all so easy. This was what Faye did every weekend.

"When I die, I don't want to be cremated," Ed said when they passed a small family cemetery.

"A lot of people are getting cremated now. I guess it's all right."

"My sister burnt her dog. The vet had to put it to sleep, and she had it cremated. She keeps it in a milk jug on the mantel. It's antique."

Liz felt goose bumps rush over her arms. She saw herself as a character in a movie, in one of those romantic boy-meets-girl scenes. She said, "There's this new movie I want to see that has Chevy Chase in it."

"I thought he was dead."

"No, he's not."

"I can't remember what stars have died," he said.

At the mall, they priced some stereo components in a Radio Shack ("a little check on the competition," Ed said), and then they had their pictures made in Wild West costumes at a booth in the center of the mall. From a rack of old clothing, Liz selected a low-cut gown and a feather boa. She giggled at herself in the mirror as she changed behind a curtain. Ed chose a severe black hat, a string tie, a worn green jacket, and wool pants with suspenders. The woman who ran the booth said, "Y'all look good. Everybody gets such a kick out of this. I guess it takes them back to a simpler time."

"If there ever *was* such a time," Ed said, nodding. As they posed for the camera, he said, "This is the seduction of Miss Jones by the itinerant preacher." Liz spotted a woman she knew across the corridor in front of a shoe store. Liz turned her head, hoping she wouldn't be recognized, while Ed filled out a form for the picture to be mailed to him in Memphis.

"Order anything you want," Ed said at a restaurant in the mall. Liz ordered Cajun chicken and a margarita. She had never had Cajun chicken. It was expensive, but she suspected Ed must have a lot of money. She began to relax and enjoy herself. She liked margaritas. She said, "My friend Faye at work went out to eat last week at a place where you choose your meat from a big platter they bring and then you grill it at your table. I told her I didn't see the point in going out to eat if you had to cook it yourself." She licked salt from the edge of her glass.

"Does your husband take you out to eat?"

"No. He works the four-to-midnight shift. And his idea of going out to eat is McDonald's."

"Does he make you happy?" Ed sipped his drink and stared at her.

"No," Liz said, embarrassed. "He gets drunk, and he's fooling around with somebody, so what I do is none of his business." She explained about the psychic.

"I had my palm read once," he said. "There's this whole town of psychics in Florida."

"Really?"

"Yeah. I was there once and had my palm read by six different palm readers."

"What did you find out?"

"My life line is squiggly. I'm supposed to have a dangerous and unfulfilled life." He held his palm out and traced his life line. Liz could see the squiggle, like those back roads to Paducah.

"Do you have any kids?" she asked.

"Not exactly. I never stayed married long enough."

Liz laughed. "It doesn't take long to make kids."

"Have you got any?"

"Yeah—two, Michael and Melissa. They're eight and six. They drive me crazy, but I wouldn't take anything for them."

After ordering more drinks, Ed said, "Once I saw this great little kid who played Little League. He was a perfect little guy— blond hair and blue eyes and smart as a whip. He had a good grip on that bat, and he could run. You know what I did? I found his mother and married her and had an instant great kid. Somebody I could take fishing and play catch with."

"What happened to him—and her?"

"Oh, he grew up and got in trouble. I left a long time before that."

"Tell me about yourself," she said eagerly. "I want to know everything."

Feeling reckless and liberated, Liz began meeting Ed on occasional Friday nights throughout the late summer and fall. It was easy to get Michael and Melissa to spend Friday evenings with her parents, who had cable. Supposedly, Liz was playing cards with Faye and the girls.

Ed called her at the store on those weekends when he came up from Memphis to help his father out. Mr. Summer had a girlfriend who looked after him during the week, but she spent weekends traveling to visit her family (her husband was in jail and her son was in a mental institution). Ed had been married twice, both times to women who worked in dress stores and always looked like fashion plates. But he insisted neither of them was as good-looking as Liz. He told her she was sexy and that he liked the way she said whatever came to mind. She met him at the mall, and they usually ate something, and then Liz left her car there and went with Ed out to the Summer farm, to a small apartment Ed had fixed up in the shed where the sorghum-making equipment was stored. The place had been his clubhouse when he was a boy. The room was nice. Ed had even installed a sound system, and sonorous music Liz couldn't identify flooded the room like a church organ as they made passionate love on a single bed by the window. Liz felt happy, but the moon shining in made her shiver with the knowledge of what she was doing, as if the moon were spying on her. But she couldn't believe it mattered. She wondered what Danny would do if he found out, whether he could take the kids from her. She didn't think so. She didn't know any woman who had lost custody of her kids, especially when the father was drunk and unfaithful. Some people thought an unfaithful woman was worse, though. They expected it of men, but women were supposed to be better. Liz didn't understand this. And she didn't know how she could possibly leave Danny and support the kids on her own. She wished she could take her kids to Memphis and live with Ed. He had told her his apartment building had a swimming pool, and he belonged to a country club. Liz didn't know whether to believe him. His reported life-style seemed farfetched, incongruous with the old farm and the sorghum shed. But in that shed on those Friday nights, she felt her whole life take off, like a car going into fifth gear. Liz never saw Ed's father, who was alone in his small brick ranch house, watching something that soared in from outer space to his satellite dish.

One Friday in the fall, Ed told Liz he wanted to take her down to Reelfoot Lake the next weekend. He straightened the quilt out and brushed dirt and debris from it. He began dressing. He said, "I want to take you to the annual game dinner me and my hunting buddies have."

"But it's too far to get back by midnight."

"You could stay there. A friend of mine has a house on the lake."

"Danny would find out." She couldn't see Ed's face in the dark. He was by the window, pulling on his boots, with one foot propped on a sorghum can.

He said, "I wouldn't care if he did, except he might come after me and blow my head off."

"He's not very big," said Liz, buttoning her blouse. "He's not as big as you are. But I'm afraid. I don't know what I'm getting into with you."

"Well, I don't know what I'm getting into with you either," Ed said, buckling his "ED" belt. "But we'll have a good time down at Reelfoot. This game dinner's something. We'll have duck and all kinds of game—possum, coon, bunny-rabbit, armadillo. . . ."

"Oh, you're teasing!" she cried. "You're such a kidder."

"But you come down with me. It's a tradition, one of those things that's supposed to mean something."

On Thursday night, Liz stayed up late to speak to Danny when he got in. She had ignored his Friday-night sprees, not wanting to pick a fight with him. As he shed his work clothes, tossing them into the laundry basket, she said, "I might not be here when you come in tomorrow night."

"Why not?"

"I'm going with Faye to this place down in Tennessee where you can go to a mall that's nothing but factory outlets." It was true that there was such a mall, and Faye had been there. "It's so far we thought we'd go down Friday night and stay with this friend of Faye's." Liz had worked out this story with Faye.

"Fine," Danny said. "If you can get a good price on some 501 jeans, I need a pair."

"O.K.," said Liz. "I'll look." She suddenly realized Danny had gained weight—maybe ten pounds.

After work, Liz left her car at the train depot in Fulton, and Ed met her there. He looked handsome in a green blazer and a tie printed with geese in flight. She was nervous about meeting his friends. "Wow, look at Miss America," he said after they had stopped at a gas station for her to change clothes. She had brought her clothes in tote bags instead of a suitcase, to avoid suspicion.

"I never get to dress up," Liz said, pleased. "But I love this dress, and I got it on sale."

By the time Reelfoot Lake came into view, the sun was setting and Liz was hungry. Ed slowed down and said, "Look at that lake. Can you imagine the earthquake that made that lake—way back yonder? They say we're due for another one."

"I hope it's not this weekend," Liz said. "That's what I always thought about going to California—it would be just my luck for it to hit when I was there. If there was an earthquake here this weekend, it would be to punish me. Maybe I should have called up Sue Ann Grooms."

Ed reached for her hand. "Don't be nervous," he said.

"Don't you get nervous when you're on the verge of something?"

"Verge of what?"

"I don't know. I just feel like something's going to happen."

"I always feel like I'm on the verge of something," said Ed.

"Well, you've done a lot, and you've got a lot to show for it."

"I can't complain. I made it off the farm, and that's something."

"Are you happy?" she asked.

"Happy?"

"Have you got what you want?"

"Nobody ever gets all they want," he said. "Everybody's always dissatisfied. The sad thing is, money ain't everything."

Liz said, "It's not everything, but it helps."

Ed turned into a narrow dirt road. "We're just about there," he said. "Joe's country house is real nice. Speaking of money, he made his off of women's hats, in Memphis." He laughed. "His store is called Le Chateau Chapeau."

"Is he rich?" cried Liz. "I've never been around people with money. I won't know how to act."

"Oh, he's not really rich," Ed assured her.

"Will they have finger bowls? They're rich if they've got finger bowls. And a lot of forks." She giggled.

Ed laughed. "You've been watching too much 'Dynasty.' "

"Yes, they *are* rich," Liz said when she saw the house. "I know what lakefront property goes for! I bet that house cost a hundred and fifty thousand dollars."

"Hey, it's O.K.," Ed said. "For one thing, you're younger and better-looking than anybody here. Just remember that. They'll all be jealous."

It was a two-story chalet-style house with large windows. Ed led Liz inside, on the basement level, where there was a wet bar. Several people in subdued, tasteful clothing were standing around, drinking and laughing. Liz had worn her loud red dress —Faye's idea. As she was introduced, Liz felt out of place and all the names instantly escaped her. When Ed had kissed her in the car, his shaving lotion was strong, like something from Christmas, and he seemed warm and familiar. But in this classy house, plunging into hunting talk with his buddies, he was a stranger. For all she knew, Ed could be a drug dealer.

"Margarita?" Ed asked, and Liz nodded.

With her drink, Liz explored the house. A woman named Nancy showed her around. Liz figured out that she was the owner's wife. "We haven't had this much company in months," Nancy said, laughing. "I'm so proud!"

"That's a pretty love seat," Liz murmured. She wondered what it cost. It was Wedgwood-blue velvet, with white wood trim. In her house, the kids would spill something on it within ten minutes.

"We bought that love seat to celebrate our tenth anniversary," Nancy said. "Ten years and still in love! We thought it was romantic." She laughed giddily and sipped something pale from a long-stemmed glass. "But we're romantic fools," she said. "When our son was born, in 1979, I wrote a whole book of poems! They just came pouring out, while I was in the hospital. We got a friend of ours who's a printer to print them up. It turned out real nice."

Liz combed her hair in a luxurious gold-and-beige bathroom large enough to dance in. She set her drink on a long marble counter. Next to a greenhouse window—with huge hanging fuchsias and airplane plants—was a Jacuzzi, sunken into the floor. Liz had never seen a hot tub before. The water was bubbling, steaming up the windows of the greenhouse. It was dark outside now, but she could dimly make out the tall cypress trees standing in the lake like gigantic wading birds. She hurried out of the bathroom, wobbling on her high heels. She suddenly had the scary thought that the guests were going to strip naked and get in that hot tub together. Otherwise, why would it be heated up? She had heard about orgies among trendy sets of people.

Liz found Ed in the den, talking to a short fat man wearing a dinner jacket made of camouflage material. The den had shelves and shelves of wooden duck decoys, lined up, all facing the same way. Liz expected them to move, the way they did at the carnival. She felt like pitching baseballs at them.

"I've been collecting these little babies for twenty years," said the man in the camouflage jacket to the guests gathered around him. For several minutes, he narrated the history of the duck decoys, pointing out which ones were antiques.

"Hey, Ed. That's a good-looking gal you've got there with you," he said suddenly. His voice sounded off-key, like an artificial voice from a mechanical box.

"I think I'll keep her," Ed said, grinning. "Joe, meet Liz. This is

Joe Callaway. This is his house. Joe and me go way back."

"Nice to meet you," Liz said. "I've been talking to your wife.
She showed me around."

In front of a gun rack, Ed said to Liz, "What's wrong? You look
funny."

"Nothing. I'm just nervous."

"You're fine," he said, patting her on the behind.

"I guess I expected a lot of mannequins in hats—not ducks.
That jacket's a scream. My kid has some jeans made out of that
material."

At the dinner table—two forks, no finger bowls—Liz sat between Ed and Joe and across from a man in a black curly wig that
sat on his head askew. A small pink plastic goose marked each
place setting, and the centerpiece of the table was an enormous
duck decoy resting on a bed of cabbage leaves, the curly kind.
The duck had artificial flowers sprouting out of holes in its back
and a smug expression. Liz noticed a woman using her fingers to
pick out the cherries in her fruit cocktail, and she realized that if
you had enough money it didn't matter how you behaved. The
thought was comforting, and it made her feel a little reckless.
Maybe if Liz used bad manners, they would just think she was
being original. The woman eating with her fingers wore a derby
hat and reminded Liz of Susan St. James on "Kate & Allie." There
were five men and five women at the table, and Liz couldn't keep
their names straight because most of them reminded her of someone else. Then she almost shrieked as she turned to face a platter
of little birds, posed exactly like tiny roast turkeys. They were
quail.

"Welcome to our critter dinner," Nancy said to Liz. "It's a
tradition. We've been doing this every duck season for ten years."

Liz had forgotten what Ed had said about the game dinner.
Several dishes circulated, and Ed served Liz, plopping something
from each one on her plate.

"We've got everything but rattlesnake here," Ed said, smiling.

"I think I've got some of that on my plate," joked a man who
had said he owned his own bush-hog rental company.

"Most of it's out of season, but we freeze it and then the women fix it up and we have everything at once," Ed explained to Liz.

"I was cooking all day on this rabbit," the woman in the hat said. "It was so tough I must have used a quart of tenderizer."

"It tastes just divine, Cindy," said Nancy. Earlier, Nancy had passed around souvenir tie tacks for the men—little silver ducks in flight. She gave the women oven mitts in the shape of fish. Liz had seen them in craft stores, and they were worth ten dollars. She stuffed hers in her purse. An irresistible bargain from a housewares outlet—fifty cents, she would tell Danny.

"What's this?" Liz asked, when a dish of something that looked like cat paws reached her.

"Possum," Joe said. "I claim credit for that."

"They say you have to trap a possum and feed it milk for ten days before you butcher it," the woman in the hat, Cindy, said. "Did you do that, Joe?"

"Hell, no. I just blasted it out of my sycamore tree out front." He whooped, a clown guffaw.

"Possum's gamy, but you acquire a taste for it," said the woman who was with the man in the wig. Her hair looked real.

The goose had a cream sauce on it; the duck was cooked with cherries and felt leathery; the quail was stuffed with liver; the rabbit seemed to be pickled. Liz stared at her plate. Ed was discussing duck calls with the bush-hog man. The women chattered about someone's custom-made drapes.

The bush-hog man's wife, who looked older than he did, said to Liz, "Don't you just hate it when somebody says they'll come out to work on something and you stay home and then they don't show up?"

"Excuse me," Liz said, rising. "I'll be right back."

Her face burned red. Everyone at the table looked at her. In the large bathroom she tried to throw up, but she had been too excited all day to eat. Her face in the mirror was younger. The wrinkles under her eyes had plumped out, as her new eye cream had promised. She looked young, innocent. If she dropped dead of a heart attack—or lead poisoning from eating buckshot—and

Danny found out where she was, what would he make of it?

She clutched a gold towel rack, trying to steady herself. She stared hard in the mirror at the person she had become for the evening, in the red dress Faye had recommended. It was like a whore dress, she thought. Danny was right about the way she always wanted something she didn't have. What did she really want? She didn't know. She didn't want to lose her kids. She didn't want to stay with Danny. She *would* like a hot tub—but she didn't need any duck decoys. She would not have paid even fifty cents for that fish mitt.

The assorted dishes at the dinner reminded her of a picture she saw once of a vase of flowers, impossible combinations: pansies, irises, daisies, zinnias, roses, a fantasy mixture of flowers throughout the seasons, from the early-spring hyacinths to the fall asters. The arrangement was beautiful, but it was something you could never see in real life. That was the way she thought of life with Ed, in a house like this—something grand that could never come true.

The greenhouse windows were steamy, and the hanging plants dripped moisture. The whirling water in the tub sounded like the ocean. Liz wished she could go to the ocean, just once in her life. That was one thing she truly wanted. She checked the lock on the door and slipped out of her shoes. She laid her purse on the counter next to the sink and carefully removed her stockings and dress. She touched her toe in the hot water. It seemed too hot to bear, but she decided she would bear it—like a punishment, or an acquired taste that would turn delicious when she was used to it.

Memphis

O n Friday, after Beverly dropped the children off at her former husband's place for the weekend, she went dancing at the Paradise Club with a man she had met at the nature extravaganza at the Land Between the Lakes. Since her divorce she had not been out much, but she enjoyed dancing, and her date was a good dancer. She hadn't expected that, because he was shy and seemed more at home with his hogs than with people.

Emerging from the rest room, Beverly suddenly ran into her ex-husband, Joe. For a confused moment she almost didn't recognize him, out of context. He was with a tall, skinny woman in jeans and a fringed cowboy shirt. Joe looked sexy, in a black T-shirt with the sleeves ripped out to show his muscles, but the woman wasn't pretty. She looked bossy and hard.

"Where are the kids?" Beverly shouted at Joe above the music.

"At Mama's. They're all right. Hey, Beverly, this is Janet."

"I'm going over there and get them right now," Beverly said, ignoring Janet.

"Don't be silly, Bev. They're having a good time. Mama fixed up a playroom for them."

"Maybe next week I'll just take them straight to her house. We'll bypass you altogether. Eliminate the middleman." Beverly was a little drunk.

"For Christ's sake."

214

"This goes on your record," she warned him. "I'm keeping a list."

Janet was touching his elbow possessively, and then the man Beverly had come with showed up with beer mugs in his fists. "Is there something I should know?" he said.

Beverly and Joe had separated the year before, just after Easter, and over the summer they tried unsuccessfully to get back together for the sake of the children. A few times after the divorce became final, Beverly spent the night with Joe, but each time she felt it was a mistake. It felt adulterous. A little thing, a quirky habit—like the way he kept the glass coffeepot simmering on the stove—could make her realize they shouldn't see each other. Coffee turned bitter when it was left simmering like that.

Joe never wanted to probe anything very deeply. He accepted things, even her request for a divorce, without asking questions. Beverly could never tell if that meant he was calm and steady or dangerously lacking in curiosity. In the last months they lived together, she had begun to feel that her mind was crammed with useless information, like a landfill, and there wasn't space deep down in her to move around in, to explore what was there. She didn't trust her intelligence anymore. She couldn't repeat the simplest thing she heard on the news and have it make sense to anyone. She would read a column in the newspaper—about something important, like taxes or the death penalty—but be unable to remember what she had read. She felt she had strong ideas and meaningful thoughts, but often when she tried to reach for one she couldn't find it. It was terrifying.

Whenever she tried to explain this feeling to Joe, he just said she expected too much of herself. He didn't expect enough of himself, though, and now she felt that the divorce hadn't affected him deeply enough to change him at all. She was disappointed. He should have gone through a major new phase, especially after what had happened to his friend Chubby Jones, one of his fishing buddies. Chubby burned to death in his pickup truck. One night soon after the divorce became final, Joe woke Beverly up with his pounding on the kitchen door. Frightened, and still not used to being alone with the children, she cracked the venetian blind, one hand on the telephone. Then she recognized the silhouette of Joe's truck in the driveway.

"I didn't want to scare you by using the key," he said when she opened the door. She was furious: he might have woken up the children.

It hadn't occurred to her that he still had a key. Joe was shaking, and when he came inside he flopped down at the kitchen table, automatically choosing his usual place facing the door. In the eerie glow from the fluorescent light above the kitchen sink, he told her about Chubby. Nervously spinning the lazy Susan, Joe groped for words, mostly repeating in disbelief the awful facts. Beverly had never seen him in such a state of shock. His news seemed to cancel out their divorce, as though it were only a trivial fit they had had.

"We were at the Blue Horse Tavern," he said. "Chubby was going on about some shit at work and he had it in his head he was going to quit and go off and live like a hermit and let Donna and the kids do without. You couldn't argue with him when he got like that—a little too friendly with Jack Daniel's. When he went out to his truck we followed him. We were going to follow him home to see he didn't have a wreck, but then he passed out right there in his truck, and so we left him there in the parking lot to sleep it off." Joe buried his head in his hands and started to cry. "We thought we were doing the best thing," he said.

Beverly stood behind him and draped her arms over his shoulders, holding him while he cried.

Chubby's cigarette must have dropped on the floor, Joe explained as she rubbed his neck and shoulders. The truck had caught fire some time after the bar closed. A passing driver reported the fire, but the rescue squad arrived too late.

"I went over there," Joe said. "That's where I just came from. It was all dark, and the parking lot was empty, except for his truck, right where we left it. It was all black and hollow. It looked like something from Northern Ireland."

He kept twirling the lazy Susan, watching the grape jelly, the sugar bowl, the honey bear, the salt and pepper shakers go by.

"Come on," Beverly said after a while. She led him to the bedroom. "You need some sleep."

After that, Joe didn't say much about his friend. He seemed to get over Chubby's death, as a child would forget some disappointment. It was sad, he said. Beverly felt so many people were like Joe—half conscious, being pulled along by thoughtless impulses and notions, as if their lives were no more than a load of freight hurtling along on the interstate. Even her mother was like that. After Beverly's father died, her mother became devoted to "The PTL Club" on television. Beverly knew her father would have argued her out of such an obsession when he was alive. Her mother had two loves now: "The PTL Club" and Kenny Rogers. She kept a scrapbook on Kenny Rogers and she owned all his albums, including the ones that had come out on CD. She still believed fervently in Jim and Tammy Bakker, even after all the fuss. They reminded her of Christmas elves, she told Beverly recently.

"Christmas elves!" Beverly repeated in disgust. "They're the biggest phonies I ever saw."

"Do you think you're better than everybody else, Beverly?" her mother said, offended. "That's what ruined your marriage. I can't get over how you've mistreated poor Joe. You're always judging everybody."

That hurt, but there was some truth in it. She was like her father, who had been a plainspoken man. He didn't like for the facts to be dressed up. He could spot fakes as easily as he noticed jimsonweed in the cornfield. Her mother's remark made her start thinking about her father in a new way. He died ten years ago, when Beverly was pregnant with Shayla, her oldest child. She remembered his unvarying routines. He got up at sunup, ate the same breakfast day in and day out, never went anywhere. In the spring, he set out tobacco plants, and as they matured he suckered them, then stripped them, cured them, and hauled them to auction. She remembered him burning the tobacco beds—the pungent smell, the threat of wind. She used to think his life was dull, but now she had started thinking about those routines as beliefs. She compared them to the routines in her life with Joe: her CNN news fix, telephoning customers at work and entering orders on the computer, the couple of six-packs she and Joe used to drink every evening, Shayla's tap lessons, Joe's basketball night, family night at the sports club. Then she remembered her father running the combine over his wheat fields, wheeling that giant machine around expertly, much the same way Joe handled a motorcycle.

When Tammy, the youngest, was born, Joe was not around. He had gone out to Pennyrile Forest with Jimmy Stone to play war games. Two teams of guys spent three days stalking each other with pretend bullets, trying to make believe they were in the jungle. In rush-hour traffic, Beverly drove herself to the hospital, and the pains caused her to pull over onto the shoulder several times. Joe had taken the childbirth lessons with her and was supposed to be there, participating, helping her with the breathing rhythms. A man would find it easier to go to war than to be around a woman in labor, she told her roommate in the hospital. When Tammy was finally born, Beverly felt that anger had propelled the baby out of her.

But when Joe showed up at the hospital, grinning a moon-pie grin, he gazed into her eyes, running one of her curls through his fingers. "I want to check out that maternal glow of yours," he said, and she felt trapped by desire, even in her condition. For her birthday once, he had given her a satin teddy and "fantasy slippers" with pink marabou feathers, whatever those were. He told the children that the feathers came from the marabou bird, a cross between a caribou and a marigold.

On Friday afternoon after work the week following the Paradise Club incident, Beverly picked up Shayla from her tap lesson and Kerry and Tammy from day care. She drove them to Joe's house, eight blocks from where she lived.

From the back seat Shayla said, "I don't want to go to the dentist tomorrow. When Daddy has to wait for me, he disappears for about *two hours*. He can't stand to wait."

Glancing in the rearview mirror at Shayla, Beverly said, "You tell your daddy to set himself down and read a magazine if he knows what's good for him."

"Daddy said you were trying to get rid of us," Kerry said.

"That's not true! Don't you let him talk mean about me. He can't get away with that."

"He said he'd take us to the lake," Kerry said. Kerry was six, and snaggletoothed. His teeth were coming in crooked—more good news for the dentist.

Joe's motorcycle and three-wheeler were hogging the driveway, so Beverly pulled up to the curb. His house was nice—a brick ranch he rented from his parents, who lived across town. The kids liked having two houses—they had more rooms, more toys.

"Give me some sugar," Beverly said to Tammy, as she unbuckled the child's seat belt. Tammy smeared her moist little face against Beverly's. "Y'all be good now," Beverly said. She hated leaving them.

The kids raced up the sidewalk, their backpacks bobbing against their legs. She saw Joe open the door and greet them. Then he waved at her to come inside. "Come on in and have a beer!" he called loudly. He held his beer can up like the Statue of Liberty's torch. He had on a cowboy hat with a large feather plastered on the side of the crown. His tan had deepened. She felt her stomach do a flip and her mind fuzz over like mold on fruit. I'm an idiot, she told herself.

She shut off the engine and pocketed the keys. Joe's fat black cat accompanied her up the sidewalk. "You need to put that cat on a diet," Beverly said to Joe when he opened the door for her. "He looks like a little hippo in black pajamas."

"He goes to the no-frills mouse market and loads up," Joe said, grinning. "I can't stop him."

The kids were already in the kitchen, investigating the refrigerator—one of those with beverage dispensers on the outside. Joe kept the dispensers filled with surprises—chocolate milk or Juicy Juice.

"Daddy, can I microwave a burrito?" asked Shayla.

"No, not now. We'll go to the mall after-while, so you don't want to ruin your supper now."

"Oh, boy. That means Chi-Chi's."

The kids disappeared into the family room in the basement, carrying Cokes and bags of cookies and potato chips. Joe opened a beer for Beverly. She was sitting on the couch smoking a cigarette and staring blankly at his pocket-knife collection in a case on the coffee table when Joe came forward and stood over her. Something was wrong.

"I'm being transferred," he said, handing her the beer. "I'm moving to Columbia, South Carolina."

She sat very still, her cigarette poised in midair like a freeze-frame scene on the VCR. A purple stain shaped like a flower was on the arm of the couch. His rug was the nubby kind made of tiny loops, and one patch had unraveled. She could hear the blip-blip-crash of video games downstairs.

"What?" she said.

"I'm being transferred."

"I heard you. I'm just having trouble getting it from my ears to my mind." She was stunned. She had never imagined Joe anywhere except right here in town.

"The plant's got an opening there, and I'll make a whole lot more."

"But you don't have to go. They can't make you go."

"It's an opportunity. I can't turn it down."

"But it's too far away."

He rested his hand lightly on her shoulder. "I'll want to have the kids on vacations—and all summer."

"Well, tough! You expect me to send them on an airplane all that way?"

"You'll have to make some adjustments," he said calmly, taking his hand away and sitting down beside her on the couch.

"I couldn't stay away from them that long," she said. "And Columbia, South Carolina? It's not interesting. They'll hate it. Nothing's there."

"You don't know that."

"What would you do with them? You can never think of what

to do with them when you've got them, so you stuff them with junk or dump them at your mother's." Beverly felt confused, unable to call upon the right argument. Her words came out wrong, more accusing than she meant.

He was saying, "Why don't you move there, too? What would keep you here?"

"Don't make me laugh." Her beer can was sweating, making cold circles on her bare leg.

He scrunched his empty can into a wad, as if he had made a decision. "We could buy a house and get back together," he said. "I didn't like seeing you on that dance floor the other night with that guy. I didn't like you seeing me with Janet. I didn't like being there with Janet. I suddenly wondered why we had to be there in those circumstances, when we could have been home with the kids."

"It would be the same old thing," Beverly said impatiently. "My God, Joe, think of what you'd do with three kids for three whole months."

"I think I know how to handle them. It's you I never could handle." He threw the can across the room straight into the kitchen wastebasket. "We've got a history together," he said. "That's the positive way to look at it." Playfully he cocked his hat and gave her a wacky, ironic look—his imitation of Jim-Boy McCoy, a used-furniture dealer in a local commercial.

"You take the cake," she said, with a little burst of laughter. But she couldn't see herself moving to Columbia, South Carolina, of all places. It would be too hot, and the people would talk in drippy, soft drawls. The kids would hate it.

After she left Joe's, she went to Tan Your Hide, the tanning salon and fitness shop that Jolene Walker managed. She worked late on Fridays. Beverly and Jolene had been friends since junior high, when they entered calves in the fair together.

"I need a quick hit before I go home," Beverly said to Jolene.

"Use number two—number one's acting funny, and I'm scared to use it. I think the light's about to blow."

In the changing room, Jolene listened sympathetically to Beverly's news about Joe. "Columbia, South Carolina!" Jolene cried. "What will I do with myself if you go off?"

"A few years ago I'd have jumped at the chance to move someplace like South Carolina, but it wouldn't be right to go now unless I love him," Beverly said. As she pulled on her bathing suit, she said, "Damn! I couldn't bear to be away from the kids for a whole summer!"

"Maybe he can't either," said Jolene, skating the dressing-room curtain along its track. "Listen, do you want to ride to Memphis with me tomorrow? I've got to pick up some merchandise coming in from California—a new line of sweatsuits. It's cheaper to go pick it up at the airport than have it flown up here by commuter."

"Yeah, sure. I don't know what else to do with my weekends. Without the kids, my weekends are like black holes." She laughed. "Big empty places you get sucked into." She made a comic sucking noise that made Jolene smile.

"We could go hear some of that good Memphis blues on Beale Street," Jolene suggested.

"Let me think about it while I work on my tan. I want to get in here and do some meditating."

"Are you still into that? That reminds me of my ex-husband and that born-again shit he used to throw at me."

"It's not the same thing," Beverly said, getting into the sunshine coffin, as she called it. "Beam me up," she said. She liked to meditate while she tanned. It was private, and she felt she was accomplishing something at the same time. In meditation, the jumbled thoughts in her mind were supposed to settle down, like the drifting snowflakes in a paperweight.

Jolene adjusted the machine and clicked the dial. "Ready for takeoff?"

"As ready as I'll ever be," said Beverly, her eyes hidden under big cotton pads. She was ruining her eyes at work, staring at a video display terminal all day. Under the sunlamp, she imagined her skin broiling as she slowly moved through space like that space station in *2001* that revolved like a rotisserie.

Scenes floated before her eyes. Helping shell purple-hull peas one hot afternoon when she was about seventeen; her mother shelling peas methodically, with the sound of Beverly's father in the bedroom coughing and spitting into a newspaper-lined cigar box. Her stomach swelled out with Kerry, and a night then when Joe didn't come back from a motorcycle trip and she was so scared she could feel the fear deep inside, right into the baby's heartbeat. Her father riding a horse along a fencerow. In the future, she thought, people would get in a contraption something like the sunshine coffin and go time traveling, unbounded by time and space or custody arrangements.

One winter afternoon two years ago: a time with Joe and the kids. Tammy was still nursing, and Kerry had just lost a tooth. Shayla was reading a Nancy Drew paperback, which was advanced for her age, but Shayla was smart. They were on the living-room floor together, on a quilt, having a picnic and watching *Chitty Chitty Bang Bang*. Beverly felt happy. That day, Kerry learned a new word—"soldier." She teased him. "You're my little soldier," she said. Sometimes she thought she could make moments like that happen again, but when she tried, it felt forced. They would be at the supper table, and she'd give the children hot dogs or tacos—something they liked—and she would say, "This is such fun!" and they would look at her funny.

Joe used to say to anyone new they met, "I've got a blue collar and a red neck and a white ass. I'm the most patriotic son of a bitch on two legs!" She and Joe were happy when they started out together. After work, they would sit on the patio with the stereo turned up loud and drink beer and pitch horseshoes while the steak grilled. On weekends, they used to take an ice chest over to the lake and have cookouts with friends and go fishing. When Joe got a motorcycle, they rode together every weekend. She loved the feeling, her feet clenching the foot pegs and her hands gripping the seat strap for dear life. She loved the wind burning her face, her hair flying out from under the helmet, her chin boring into Joe's back as he tore around curves. Their friends all worked at the new plants, making more money than they ever had before. Everyone they knew had a yard strewn with vehicles:

motorcycles, three-wheelers, sporty cars, pickups. One year, people started buying horses. It was just a thing people were into suddenly, so that they could ride in the annual harvest parade in Fenway. Joe and Beverly never got around to having a horse, though. It seemed too much trouble after the kids came along. Most of the couples they knew then drank a lot and argued and had fights, but they had a good time. Now marriages were splitting up. Beverly could name five divorces or separations in her crowd. It seemed no one knew why this was happening. Everybody blamed it on statistics: half of all marriages nowadays ended in divorce. It was a fact, like traffic jams—just one of those things you had to put up with in modern life. But Beverly thought money was to blame: greed made people purely stupid. She admired Jolene for the simple, clear way she divorced Steve and made her own way without his help. Steve had gone on a motorcycle trip alone, and when he came back he was a changed man. He had joined a bunch of born-again bikers he met at a campground in Wyoming, and afterward he tried to convert everybody he knew. Jolene refused to take the Lord as her personal savior. "It's amazing how much spite Steve has in him," Jolene told Beverly after she moved out. "I don't even care anymore."

It made Beverly angry not to know why she didn't want Joe to go to South Carolina. Did he just want her to come to South Carolina for convenience, for the sake of the children? Sometimes she felt they were both stalled at a crossroads, each thinking the other had the right-of-way. But now his foot was on the gas.

Jolene was saying, "Get out of there before you cook!"

Beverly removed the cotton pads from her eyes and squinted at the bright light.

Jolene said, "Look at this place on my arm. It looks just like one of those skin cancers in my medical guide." She pointed to an almost invisible spot in the crook of her arm. Jolene owned a photographer's magnifying glass a former boyfriend had given her, and she often looked at her moles with it. Under the glass, tiny moles looked hideous and black, with red edges.

Beverly, who was impatient with Jolene's hypochondria, said,

"I wouldn't worry about it unless I could see it with my bare naked eyes."

"I think I should stop tanning," Jolene said.

The sky along the western horizon was a flat yellow ribbon with the tree line pasted against it. After the farmland ran out, Beverly and Jolene passed small white houses in disrepair, junky little clusters of businesses, a K mart, then a Wal-Mart. As Jolene drove along, Beverly thought about Joe's vehicles. It had never occurred to her before that he had all those wheels and hardly went anywhere except places around home. But now he was actually leaving.

She was full of nervous energy. She kept twisting the radio dial, trying to find a good driving song. She wished the radio would play "Radar Love," a great driving song. All she could get was country stations and gospel stations. After a commercial for a gigantic flea market, with dealers coming from thirty states, the announcer said, "Elvis would be there—if he could." Jolene hit the horn. "Elvis, we're on our way, baby!"

"There's this record store I want to go to if we have time," said Jolene. "It's got all these old rock songs—everything you could name, going way back to the very beginning."

"Would they have 'Your Feet's Too Big,' by Fats Waller? Joe used to sing that."

"Honey, they've got *everything*. Why, I bet they've got a tape of Fats Waller humming to himself in the outhouse." They laughed, and Jolene said, "You're still stuck on Joe."

"I can't let all three kids go to South Carolina on one airplane! If it crashed, I'd lose all three of them at once."

"Oh, don't think that way!"

Beverly sighed. "I can't get used to not having a child pulling on my leg every minute. But I guess I should get out and have a good time."

"Now you're talking."

"Maybe if he moves to South Carolina, we can make a clean break. Besides, I better not fight him, or he might kidnap them."

"Do you really think that?" said Jolene, astonished.

"I don't know. You hear about cases like that." Beverly changed the radio station again.

"I can't stand to see you tear yourself up this way," said Jolene, giving Beverly's arm an affectionate pat.

Beverly laughed. "Hey, look at that bumper sticker—'A WOMAN'S PLACE IS IN THE MALL.' "

"All *right*!" said Jolene.

They drove into Memphis on Route 51, past self-service gas stations in corrugated-tin buildings with country hams hanging in the windows. Beverly noticed a memorial garden between two cornfields, with an immense white statue of Jesus rising up from the center like the Great White Shark surfacing. They passed a display of black-velvet paintings beside a van, a ceramic-grassware place, a fireworks stand, motels, package stores, auto-body shops, car dealers that sold trampolines and satellite dishes. A stretch of faded old wooden buildings—grim and gray and ramshackle—followed, then factories, scrap-metal places, junk-yards, ancient grills and poolrooms, small houses so old the wood looked rotten. Then came the housing projects. It was all so familiar. Beverly remembered countless trips to Memphis when her father was in the hospital here, dying of cancer. The Memphis specialists prolonged his misery, and Beverly's mother said afterward, "We should have set him out in the corncrib and let him go naturally, the way he wanted to go."

Beverly and Jolene ate at a Cajun restaurant that night, and later they walked down Beale Street, which had been spruced up and wasn't as scary as it used to be, Beverly thought. The side-walks were crowded with tourists and policemen. At a blues club, she and Jolene giggled like young girls out looking for love. Beverly had been afraid Memphis would make her sad, but after three strawberry Daiquiris she was feeling good. Jolene had a headache and was drinking ginger ale, which turned out to be Sprite with a splash of Coke—what bartenders do when they're out of ginger ale, Beverly told her. She didn't know how she knew that. Probably Joe had told her once. He used to tend bar.

Forget Joe, she thought. She needed to loosen up a little. The kids had been saying she was like either Kate or Allie on that TV show—whichever was the uptight one; she couldn't remember.

The band was great—two white guys and two black guys. Between numbers, they joked with the waitress, a middle-aged woman with spiked red hair and shoulder pads that fit cockeyed. The white lead singer clowned around with a cardboard stand-up figure of Marilyn Monroe in her white dress from *The Seven Year Itch*. He spun her about the dance floor, sneaking his hand onto Marilyn's crotch where her dress had flown up. He played her like a guitar. A pretty black woman in a dark leather skirt and polka-dotted jacket danced with a slim young black guy with a brush haircut. Beverly wondered how he got his hair to stick up like that. Earlier, when she and Jolene stopped at a Walgreen's for shampoo, Beverly had noticed a whole department of hair-care products for blacks. There was a row of large jugs of hair conditioner, like the jugs motor oil and bleach came in.

Jolene switched from fake ginger ale to Fuzzy Navels, which she had been drinking earlier at the Cajun restaurant. She blamed her headache on Cajun frog legs but said she felt better now. "I'm having a blast," she said, drumming her slender fingers on the table in time with the band.

"I'm having a blast, too," Beverly said, just as an enormous man with tattoos of outer-space monsters on his arms asked Jolene to dance.

"No way!" Jolene said, cringing. On his forearm was an astounding picture of a creature that reminded Beverly of one of Kerry's dinosaur toys.

"That guy's really off the moon," Jolene said as the man left.

During the break, the waitress passed by with a plastic bucket, collecting tips for the band. Beverly thought of an old song, "Bucket's Got a Hole in It." Her grandmother's kitchen slop bucket with its step pedal. Going to hell in a bucket. Kick the bucket. She felt giddy.

"That boy's here every night," the waitress said, with a turn of her head toward the tattooed guy, who had approached another pair of women. "I feel so sorry for him. His brother killed himself and his mother's in jail for drugs. He never could hold a job. He's trouble waiting for a ride."

"Does the band know 'Your Feet's Too Big'?" Beverly asked the waitress, who was stuffing requests into her pocket.

"Is that a song, or are you talking about my big hoofs?" the woman said, with a wide, teasing grin.

On the way back to their motel on Elvis Presley Boulevard, Jolene got on a one-way street and ended up in downtown Memphis, where the tall buildings were. Beverly would hate to work so high up in the air. Her cousin had a job down here in life insurance and said she never knew what the weather was. Beverly wondered if South Carolina had any skyscrapers.

"There's the famous Peabody Hotel," Jolene was saying. "The hotel with the ducks."

"Ducks?"

"At that hotel it's ducks galore," explained Jolene. "The towels and stationery and stuff. I know a girl who stayed there, and she said a bunch of ducks come down every morning on the elevator and go splash in the fountain. It's a tourist attraction."

"The kids would like that. That's what I should be doing down here—taking the kids someplace, not getting smashed like this." Beverly felt disembodied, her voice coming from the glove compartment.

"Everything is *should* with you, Beverly!" Jolene said, making a right on red.

Jolene didn't mean to sound preachy, Beverly thought. Fuzzy Navels did that to her. If Beverly mentioned what she was feeling about Joe, Jolene would probably say that Joe just looked good right now compared to some of the weirdos you meet out in the world.

Down the boulevard, the lights spread out extravagantly. As Beverly watched, a green neon light winked off, and the whole scene seemed to shift slightly. It was like making a correction on the VDT at work—the way the screen readjusted all the lines and spacing to accommodate the change. Far away, a red light was inching across the black sky. She thought about riding behind Joe on his Harley, flashing through the dark on a summer night, cool in the wind, with sparkling, mysterious lights flickering off the lake.

The music from the night before was still playing in Beverly's head when she got home Sunday afternoon. It was exhilarating, like something she knew well but hadn't thought of in years. It came soaring up through her with a luxurious clarity. She could still hear the henna-haired waitress saying, "Are you talking about my big hoofs?" Beverly's dad used to say, "Oh, my aching dogs!" She clicked "Radar Love" into the cassette player and turned the volume up loud. She couldn't help dancing to its hard frenzy. "Radar Love" made her think of Joe's Fuzzbuster, which he bought after he got two speeding tickets in one month. One time, he told the children his razor was a Fuzzbuster. Speeding, she whirled joyfully through the hall.

The song was only halfway through when Joe arrived with the kids—unexpectedly early. Kerry ejected the tape. Sports voices hollered out from the TV. Whenever the kids returned from their weekends, they plowed through the place, unloading their belongings and taking inventory of what they had left behind. Tammy immediately flung all her toys out of her toybox, looking for a rag doll she had been worried about. Joe said she had cried about it yesterday.

"How was the dentist?" Beverly asked Shayla.

"I don't want to talk about it," said Shayla, who was dumping dirty clothes on top of the washing machine.

"Forty bucks for one stupid filling," Joe said.

Joe had such a loud voice that he always came on too strong. Beverly remembered with embarrassment the time he called up Sears and terrorized the poor clerk over a flaw in a sump pump, when it wasn't the woman's fault. But now he lowered his voice to a quiet, confidential tone and said to Beverly in the kitchen, "Yesterday at the lake Shayla said she wished you were there with us, and I tried to explain to her how you had to have some time for yourself, how you said you had to have your own space and find yourself—you know, all that crap on TV. She seemed to get a little depressed, and I thought maybe I'd said the wrong thing, but a little later she said she'd been thinking, and she knew what you meant."

"She's smart," Beverly said. Her cheeks were burning. She popped ice cubes out of a tray and began pouring Coke into a glass of ice.

"She gets it honest—she's got smart parents," he said with a grin.

Beverly drank the Coke while it was still foaming. Bubbles burst on her nose. "It's not crap on TV," she said angrily. "How can you say that?"

He looked hurt. She observed the dimple on his chin, the corresponding kink of his hairline above his ear, the way his hat shaded his eyes and deepened their fire. Even if he lived to be a hundred, Joe would still have those seductive eyes. Kerry wandered into the kitchen, dragging a green dinosaur by a hind foot. "We didn't have any corny cakes," he whined. He meant cornflakes.

"Why didn't Daddy get you some?"

After Kerry drifted away, Joe said, "I'm going to South Carolina in a couple of weeks. Check it out and try to find a place to live."

Beverly opened the freezer and took chicken thighs out to thaw, then began clearing dishes to keep from bursting into tears.

"Columbia's real progressive," he said. "Lots of businesses are relocating there. It's a place on the way up."

The foam had settled on her Coke, and she poured some more. She began loading the dishwasher. One of her new nonstick pans already had a scratch.

"How was Memphis?" Joe asked, his hand on the kitchen doorknob.

"Fine," she said. "Jolene had too many Fuzzy Navels."

"That figures."

Shayla rushed in then and said, "Daddy, you got to fix that thing in my closet. The door won't close."

"That track at the top? Not again! I don't have time to work on it right now."

"He doesn't live here," Beverly said to Shayla.

"Well, my closet's broke, and who's going to fix it?" Shayla threw up her hands and stomped out of the kitchen.

Joe said, "You know, in the future, if we're going to keep this up, we're going to have to learn to carry on a better conversation, because this stinks." He adjusted his hat, setting it firmly on his head. "You're so full of wants you don't know what you want," he said.

Through the glass section of the door she could see him walking to his truck with his hands in his pockets. She had seen him march out the door exactly that way so many times before—whenever he didn't want to hear what was coming next, or when he thought he had had the last word. She hurried out to speak to him, but he was already pulling away, gunning his engine loudly. She watched him disappear, his tail-lights winking briefly at a stop sign. She felt ashamed.

Beverly paused beside the young pin-oak tree at the corner of the driveway. When Joe planted it, there were hardly any trees in the subdivision. All the houses were built within the last ten years, and the trees were still spindly. The house just to her left was Mrs. Grim's. She was a widow and kept cats. On the other side, a German police dog in a backyard pen spent his time barking across Beverly's yard at Mrs. Grim's cats. The man who owned the dog operated a video store, and his wife mysteriously spent several weeks a year out of town. When she was away her husband stayed up all night watching TV, like a child freed from rules. Beverly could see his light on when she got up in the night with the kids. She had never really noticed that the bricks of all three houses were a mottled red and gray, like uniformly splattered paint. There was a row of vertical bricks supporting each window. She stood at the foot of the driveway feeling slightly amazed that she should be stopped in her tracks at this particular time and place.

It ought to be so easy to work out what she really wanted.

Beverly's parents had stayed married like two dogs locked together in passion, except it wasn't passion. But she and Joe didn't
have to do that. Times had changed. Joe could up and move to
South Carolina. Beverly and Jolene could hop down to Memphis
just for a fun weekend. Who knew what might happen or what
anybody would decide to do on any given weekend or at any
stage of life?

  She brought in yesterday's mail—a car magazine for Joe, a
credit-card bill he was supposed to pay, some junk mail. She laid
the items for Joe on a kitchen shelf next to the videotape she had
borrowed from him and forgotten to return.

Wish

Sam tried to hold his eyes open. The preacher, a fat-faced boy with a college degree, had a curious way of pronouncing his *r*'s. The sermon was about pollution of the soul and started with a news item about an oil spill. Sam drifted into a dream about a flock of chickens scratching up a bed of petunias. His sister Damson, beside him, knifed him in the ribs with her bony elbow. Snoring, she said with her eyes.

Every Sunday after church, Sam and Damson visited their other sister, Hortense, and her husband, Cecil. Ordinarily, Sam drove his own car, but today Damson gave him a ride because his car was low on gas. Damson lived in town, but Hort and Cecil lived out in the country, not far from the old homeplace, which had been sold twenty years before, when Pap died. As they drove past the old place now, Sam saw Damson shudder. She had stopped saying "Trash" under her breath when they passed by and saw the junk cars that had accumulated around the old house. The yard was bare dirt now, and the large elm in front had split. Many times Sam and his sisters had wished the new interstate had gone through the homeplace instead. Sam knew he should have bought out his sisters and kept it.

"How are you, Sam?" Hort asked when he and Damson arrived. Damson's husband, Porter, had stayed home today with a bad back.

"About dead." Sam grinned and knuckled his chest, pretending heart trouble and exaggerating the arthritis in his hands.

"Not again!" Hort said, teasing him. "You just like to growl, Sam. You've been that way all your life."

"You ain't even knowed me that long! Why, I remember the night you was born. You come in mad at the world, with your stinger out, and you've been like that ever since."

Hort patted his arm. "Your barn door's open, Sam," she said as they went into the living room.

He zipped up his fly unself-consciously. At his age, he didn't care.

Hort steered Damson off into the kitchen, murmuring something about a blue dish, and Sam sat down with Cecil to discuss crops and the weather. It was their habit to review the week's weather, then their health, then local news—in that order. Cecil was a small, amiable man who didn't like to argue.

A little later, at the dinner table, Cecil jokingly asked Sam, "Are you sending any money to Jimmy Swaggart?"

"Hell, no! I ain't sending a penny to that bastard."

"Sam never gave them preachers nothing," Hort said defensively as she sent a bowl of potatoes au gratin Sam's way. "That was Nova."

Nova, Sam's wife, had been dead eight and a half years. Nova was always buying chances on Heaven, Sam thought. There was something squirrelly in her, like the habit she had of saving out extra seed from the garden or putting up more preserves than they could use.

Hort said, "I still think Nova wanted to build on that ground she heired so she could have a house in her own name."

Damson nodded vigorously. "She didn't want you to have your name on the new house, Sam. She wanted it in her name."

"Didn't make no sense, did it?" Sam said, reflecting a moment on Nova. He could see her plainly, holding up a piece of fried chicken like a signal for attention. The impression was so vivid he almost asked her to pass the peas.

Hort said, "You already had a nice house with shade trees and a tobacco patch, and it was close to your kinfolks, but she just *had* to move toward town."

"She told me if she had to get to the hospital the ambulance would get there quicker," said Damson, taking a second biscuit. "Hort, these biscuits ain't as good as you usually make."

"I didn't use self-rising," said Hort.

"It wouldn't make much difference, with that new highway," said Cecil, speaking of the ambulance.

On the day they moved to the new house, Sam stayed in bed with the covers pulled up around him and refused to budge. He was still there at four o'clock in the evening, after his cousins had moved out all the furniture. Nova ignored him until they came for the bed. She laid his clothes on the bed and rattled the car keys in his face. She had never learned to drive. That was nearly fifteen years ago. Only a few years after that, Nova died and left him in that brick box she called a dream home. There wasn't a tree in the yard when they built the house. Now there were two flowering crab apples and a flimsy little oak.

After dinner, Hort and Cecil brought out new pictures of their great-grandchildren. The children had changed, and Sam couldn't keep straight which ones belonged to Linda and which ones belonged to Donald. He felt full. He made himself comfortable among the crocheted pillows on Hort's high-backed couch. For ten minutes, Hort talked on the telephone to Linda, in Louisiana, and when she hung up she reported that Linda had a new job at a finance company. Drowsily, Sam listened to the voices rise and fall. Their language was so familiar; his kinfolks never told stories or reminisced when they sat around on a Sunday. Instead, they discussed character. "He's the stingiest man alive." "She was nice to talk to on the street but *H* to work with." "He never would listen when you tried to tell him anything." "She'd do anything for you."

Now, as Sam stared at a picture of a child with a Depression-style bowl haircut, Damson was saying, "Old Will Stone always referred to himself as 'me.' '*Me* did this. *Me* wants that.'"

Hort said, "The Stones were always trying to get you to do something for them. Get around one of them and they'd think of something they wanted you to do." The Stones were their mother's people.

"I never would let 'em tell me what to do," Damson said with a laugh. "I'd say, 'I can't! I've got the nervous trembles.'"

Damson was little then, and her aunt Rue always complained of nervous trembles. Once, Damson had tried to get out of picking English peas by claiming she had nervous trembles, too. Sam remembered that. He laughed—a hoot so sudden they thought he hadn't been listening and was laughing about something private.

Hort fixed a plate of fried chicken, potatoes, field peas, and stewed apples for Sam to take home. He set it on the back seat of Damson's car, along with fourteen eggs and a sack of biscuits. Damson spurted out of the driveway backward, scaring the hound dog back to his hole under a lilac bush.

"Hort and Cecil's having a time keeping up this place," Sam said, noticing the weed-clogged pen where they used to keep hogs.

Damson said, "Hort's house always smelled so good, but today it smelled bad. It smelled like fried fish."

"I never noticed it," said Sam, yawning.

"Ain't you sleeping good, Sam?"

"Yeah, but when my stomach sours I get to yawning."

"You ain't getting old on us, are you?"

"No, I ain't old. Old is in your head."

Damson invited herself into Sam's house, saying she wanted to help him put the food away. His sisters wouldn't leave him alone. They checked on his housekeeping, searched for ruined food, made sure his commode was flushed. They had fits when he took in a stray dog one day, and they would have taken her to the pound if she hadn't got hit on the road first.

Damson stored the food in the kitchen and snooped in his refrigerator. Sam was itching to get into his bluejeans and watch something on Ted Turner's channel that he had meant to watch.

He couldn't remember now what it was, but he knew it came on at four o'clock. Damson came into the living room and began to peer at all his pictures, exclaiming over each great-grandchild. All Sam's kids and grandkids were scattered around. His son worked in the tire industry in Akron, Ohio, and his oldest granddaughter operated a frozen-yogurt store in Florida. He didn't know why anybody would eat yogurt in any form. His grandson Bobby had arrived from Arizona last year with an Italian woman who spoke in a sharp accent. Sam had to hold himself stiff to keep from laughing. He wouldn't let her see him laugh, but her accent tickled him. Now Bobby had written that she'd gone back to Italy.

Damson paused over an old family portrait—Pap and Mammy and all six children, along with Uncle Clay and Uncle Thomas and their wives, Rosie and Zootie, and Aunt Rue. Sam's three brothers were dead now. Damson, a young girl in the picture, wore a lace collar, and Hort was in blond curls and a pinafore. Pap sat in the center on a chair with his legs set far apart, as if to anchor himself to hold the burden of this wild family. He looked mean and willful, as though he were about to whip somebody.

Suddenly Damson blurted out, "Pap ruined my life."

Sam was surprised. Damson hadn't said exactly that before, but he knew what she was talking about. There had always been a sadness about her, as though she had had the hope knocked out of her years ago.

She said, "He ruined my life—keeping me away from Lyle."

"That was near sixty years ago, Damson. That don't still bother you now, does it?"

She held the picture close to her breast and said, "You know how you hear on the television nowadays about little children getting beat up or treated nasty and it makes such a mark on them? Nowadays they know about that, but they didn't back then. They never knowed how something when you're young can hurt you so long."

"None of that happened to you."

"Not that, but it was just as bad."

"Lyle wouldn't have been good to you," said Sam.

"But I loved him, and Pap wouldn't let me see him."

"Lyle was a drunk and Pap didn't trust him no further than he could throw him."

"And then I married Porter, for pure spite," she went on. "You know good and well I never cared a thing about him."

"How come you've stayed married to him all these years then? Why don't you do like the kids do nowadays—like Bobby out in Arizona? Him and that Italian. They've done quit!"

"But she's a foreigner. I ain't surprised," said Damson, blowing her nose with a handkerchief from her pocketbook. She sat down on Sam's divan. He had towels spread on the upholstery to protect it, a habit of Nova's he couldn't get rid of. That woman was so practical she had even orchestrated her deathbed. She had picked out her burial clothes, arranged for his breakfast. He remembered holding up hangers of dresses from her closet for her to choose from.

"Damson," he said, "if you could do it over, you'd do it different, but it might not be no better. You're making Lyle out to be more than he would have been."

"He wouldn't have shot hisself," she said calmly.

"It was an accident."

She shook her head. "No, I think different."

Damson had always claimed he killed himself over her. That night, Lyle had come over to the homeplace near dark. Sam and his brothers had helped Pap put in a long day suckering tobacco. Sam was already courting Nova, and Damson was just out of high school. The neighborhood boys came over on Sundays after church like a pack of dogs after a bitch. Damson had an eye for Lyle because he was so daresome, more reckless than the rest. That Saturday night when Lyle came by for her, he had been into some moonshine, and he was frisky, like a young bull. Pap wouldn't let her go with him. Sam heard Damson in the attic, crying, and Lyle was outside, singing at the top of his lungs, calling her. "Damson! My fruit pie!" Pap stepped out onto the porch then, and Lyle slipped off into the darkness.

Damson set the family picture back on the shelf and said, "He was different from all the other boys. He knew a lot, and he'd been to Texas once with his daddy—for his daddy's asthma. He had a way about him."

"I remember when Lyle come back late that night," Sam said. "I heard him on the porch. I knowed it must be him. He was loud and acted like he was going to bust in the house after you."

"I heard him," she said. "From my pallet up there at the top. It was so hot I had a bucket of water and a washrag and I'd wet my face and stand in that little window and reach for a breeze. I heard him come, and I heard him thrashing around down there on the porch. There was a loose board you always had to watch out for."

"I remember that!" Sam said. He hadn't thought of that warped plank in years.

"He fell over it," Damson said. "But then he got up and backed down the steps. I could hear him out in the yard. Then—" She clasped her arms around herself and bowed her head. "Then he yelled out, 'Damson!' I can still hear that."

A while later, they had heard the gunshot. Sam always remembered hearing a hollow thump and a sudden sound like cussing, then the explosion. He and his brother Bob rushed out in the dark, and then Pap brought a coal-oil lantern. They found Lyle sprawled behind the barn, with the shotgun kicked several feet away. There was a milk can turned over, and they figured that Lyle had stumbled over it when he went behind the barn. Sam had never forgotten Damson on the living-room floor, bawling. She lay there all the next day, screaming and beating her heavy work shoes against the floor, and people had to step around her. The women fussed over her, but none of the men could say anything.

Sam wanted to say something now. He glared at that big family in the picture. The day the photographer came, Sam's mother made everyone dress up, and they had to stand there as still as stumps for about an hour in that August heat. He remembered the kink in Damson's hair, the way she had fixed it so pretty for Lyle. A blurred chicken was cutting across the corner of the picture, and an old bird dog named Obadiah was stretched out in front, holding a pose better than the fidgety people. In the front row, next to her mother, Damson's bright, upturned face sparkled with a smile. Everyone had admired the way she could hold a smile for the camera.

Pointing to her face in the picture, he said, "Here you are, Damson—a young girl in love."

Frowning, she said, "I just wish life had been different."

He grabbed Damson's shoulders and stared into her eyes. To this day, she didn't even wear glasses and was still pretty, still herself in there, in that puffed-out old face. He said, "You wish! Well, wish in one hand and shit in the other one and see which one fills up the quickest!"

He got her. She laughed so hard she had to catch her tears with her handkerchief. "Sam, you old hound. Saying such as that— and on a Sunday."

She rose to go. He thought he'd said the right thing, because she seemed lighter on her feet now. "You've got enough eggs and bacon to last you all week," she said. "And I'm going to bring you some of that popcorn cake my neighbor makes. You'd never guess it had popcorn in it."

She had her keys in her hand, her pocketbook on her arm. She was wearing a pretty color of pink, the shade of baby pigs. She said, "I know why you've lived so long, Sam. You just see what you want to see. You're like Pap, just as hard and plain."

"That ain't the whole truth," he said, feeling a mist of tears come.

That night he couldn't get to sleep. He went to bed at eight-thirty, after a nature special on the television—grizzly bears. He lay in bed and replayed his life with Nova. The times he wanted to leave home. The time he went to a lawyer to inquire about a divorce. (It turned out to cost too much, and anyway he knew his folks would never forgive him.) The time she hauled him out of bed for the move to this house. He had loved their old place, a wood-frame house with a porch and a swing, looking out over tobacco fields and a strip of woods. He always had a dog then, a special dog, sitting on the porch with him. Here he had no porch, just some concrete steps, where he would sit sometimes and watch the traffic. At night, drunk drivers zoomed along, occasionally plowing into somebody's mailbox.

She had died at three-thirty in the morning, and toward the end she didn't want anything—no food, no talk, no news, nothing soft. No kittens to hold, no memories. He stayed up with her in case she needed him, but she went without needing him at all. And now he didn't need her. In the dim light of the street lamp, he surveyed the small room where he had chosen to sleep—the single bed, the bare walls, his jeans hanging up on a nail, his shoes on a shelf, the old washstand that had belonged to his grandmother, the little rag rug beside the bed. He was happy. His birthday was two months from today. He would be eighty-four. He thought of that bird dog, Obadiah, who had been with him on his way through the woods the night he set out to meet someone—the night he first made love to a girl. Her name was Nettie, and at first she had been reluctant to lie down with him, but he had brought a quilt, and he spread it out in the open pasture. The hay had been cut that week, and the grass was damp and sweet-smelling. He could still feel the clean, soft, cool cotton of that quilt, the stubble poking through and the patterns of the quilting pressing into his back. Nettie lay there beside him, her breath blowing on his shoulder as they studied the stars far above the field—little pinpoint holes punched through the night sky like the needle holes around the tiny stitches in the quilting. Nettie. Nettie Slade. Her dress had self-covered buttons, hard like seed corn.